C0-ATQ-352

CASTLE NOWHERE:

LAKE-COUNTRY SKETCHES.

BY

CONSTANCE FENIMORE WOOLSON.

AMS PRESS

NEW YORK

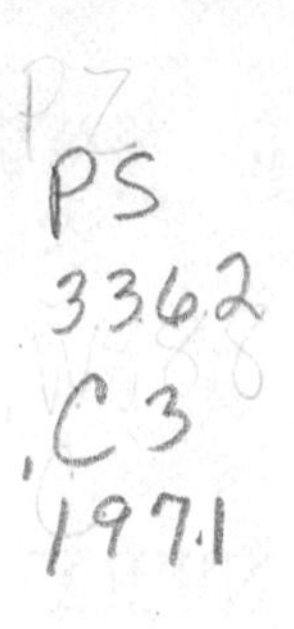

Reprinted from the edition of 1875, Boston
First AMS EDITION published 1971
Manufactured in the United States of America

International Standard Book Number: 0-404-07035-3

Library of Congress Number: 79-137308

AMS PRESS INC.
NEW YORK, N.Y. 10003

CONTENTS.

Three of these stories originally appeared in the *Atlantic Monthly*, two in *Scribner's Monthly*, and one each in *Harper's Magazine, The Galaxy*, and *Appleton's Journal.*

CASTLE NOWHERE.

NOT many years ago the shore bordering the head of Lake Michigan, the northern curve of that silver sea, was a wilderness unexplored. It is a wilderness still, showing even now on the school-maps nothing save an empty waste of colored paper, generally a pale, cold yellow suitable to the climate, all the way from Point St. Ignace to the iron ports on the Little Bay de Noquet, or Badderknock in lake phraseology, a hundred miles of nothing, according to the map-makers, who, knowing nothing of the region, set it down accordingly, withholding even those long-legged letters, "Chip-pe-was," "Ric-ca-rees," that stretch accommodatingly across so much townless territory farther west. This northern curve is and always has been off the route to anywhere; and mortals, even Indians, prefer as a general rule, when once started, to go somewhere. The earliest Jesuit explorers and the captains of yesterday's schooners had this in common, that they could not, being human, resist a cross-cut; and thus, whether bark canoes of two centuries ago or the high, narrow propellers of to-day, one and all, coming and going, they veer to the southeast or west, and sail gayly out of sight, leaving this northern curve of ours unvisited and alone. A wilderness still, but not unexplored; for that railroad of the future which is to make of British America a garden of roses, and turn the wild trappers of the Hudson's Bay Company into gently smiling congressmen, has it not sent its missionaries thither, to the astonishment and joy of the beasts that dwell therein? According to tradition, these men surveyed the territory, and then crossed over (those of them at least whom the beasts had spared) to the lower peninsula, where, the pleasing variety of swamps being added to the labyrinth of pines and sand-hills, they soon lost themselves, and to this day have never found what they lost. As the gleam of a camp-fire is occasionally seen, and now and then a distant shout heard by the hunter passing along the outskirts, it is supposed that they are in there somewhere, surveying still.

Not long ago, however, no white man's foot had penetrated within our curve. Across the great river and over the deadly plains, down to the burning clime of Mexico and up to the arctic darkness, journeyed our countrymen, gold to gather and strange countries to see; but this little pocket of land and water passed they by without a glance, inasmuch as no iron mountains rose among its pines, no copper lay hidden in its sand ridges, no harbors dented its shores. Thus it remained an unknown region, and enjoyed life accordingly. But the white man's foot, well booted, was on the way, and one fine afternoon came tramping through. "I wish I was a tree," said to himself this white man, one Jarvis Waring by name. "See that young pine, how lustily it grows, feeling its life to the very tip of each green needle! How it thrills in the sun's rays, how strongly, how completely it carries out the intention of its existence! *It* never has a headache, it — Bah! what a miserable, half-way thing is man, who should be a demigod, and is — a creature for the very trees to pity!" And then he built his camp-fire, called in his dogs, and slept the sleep of youth and health, none the less deep because of that Spirit of Discontent that had driven him forth into the wilderness; probably the Spirit of Discontent knew what it was about. Thus for days, for weeks, our white man wandered through the forest and wandered at random, for, being an exception, he preferred to go nowhere; he had his compass, but never used it, and, a practised hunter, eat what came in his way and planned not for the morrow. "Now am I living the life of a good, hearty, comfortable bear," he said to himself with satisfaction.

"No, you are not, Waring," replied the Spirit of Discontent, "for you know you have your compass in your pocket and can direct yourself back to the camps on

Lake Superior or to the Sault for supplies, which is more than the most accomplished bear can do."

"O come, what do you know about bears?" answered Waring; "very likely they too have their depots of supplies, — in caves perhaps — "

"No caves here."

"In hollow trees, then."

"You are thinking of the stories about bears and wild honey," said the pertinacious Spirit.

"Shut up, I am going to sleep," replied the man, rolling himself in his blanket; and then the Spirit, having accomplished his object, smiled blandly and withdrew.

Wandering thus, all reckoning lost both of time and place, our white man came out one evening unexpectedly upon a shore; before him was water stretching away grayly in the fog-veiled moonlight; and so successful had been his determined entangling of himself in the webs of the wilderness, that he really knew not whether it was Superior, Huron, or Michigan that confronted him, for all three bordered the eastern end of the upper peninsula. Not that he wished to know; precisely the contrary. Glorifying himself in his ignorance, he built a fire on the sands, and leaning back against the miniature cliffs that guard the even beaches of the inland seas, he sat looking out over the water, smoking a comfortable pipe of peace, and listening, meanwhile, to the regular wash of the waves. Some people are born with rhythm in their souls, and some not; to Jarvis Waring everything seemed to keep time, from the songs of the birds to the chance words of a friend; and during all this pilgrimage through the wilderness, when not actively engaged in quarrelling with the Spirit, he was repeating bits of verses and humming fragments of songs that kept time with his footsteps, or rather they were repeating and humming themselves along through his brain, while he sat apart and listened. At this moment the fragment that came and went apropos of nothing was Shakespeare's sonnet,

> "When to the sessions of sweet silent thought,
> I summon up remembrance of things past."

Now the small waves came in but slowly, and the sonnet, in keeping time with their regular wash, dragged its syllables so dolorously that at last the man woke to the realization that something was annoying him.

> "When to — the ses — sions of — sweet si — lent thought,"

chanted the sonnet and the waves together.

"O double it, double it, can't you?" said the man, impatiently; "this way: —

> 'When to the ses — sions of sweet si — lent thought, te-tum, — te-tum, te-tum.'"

But no; the waves and the lines persisted in their own idea, and the listener finally became conscious of a third element against him, another sound which kept time with the obstinate two and encouraged them in their obstinacy, — the dip of light oars somewhere out in the gray mist.

> "When to — the ses — sions of — sweet si — lent thought,
> I sum — mon up — remem — brance of — things past,"

chanted the sonnet and the waves and the oars together, and went duly on, sighing the lack of many things they sought, away down to that "dear friend," who in some unexplained way made all their "sorrows end." Even then, while peering through the fog and wondering where and what was this spirit boat that one could hear but not see, Waring found time to make his usual objections. "This summoning up remembrance of things past, sighing the lack, weeping afresh, and so forth, is all very well," he remarked to himself, "we all do it. But that friend who sweeps in at the death with his opportune dose of comfort is a poetical myth whom I, for one, have never yet met."

"That is because you do not deserve such a friend," answered the Spirit, briskly reappearing on the scene. "A man who flies into the wilderness to escape — "

"Spirit, are you acquainted with a Biblical personage named David?" interrupted Waring, executing a flank movement.

The Spirit acknowledged the acquaintance, but cautiously, as not knowing what was coming next.

"Did he or did he not have anything to say about

flying to wildernesses and mountain-tops? Did he or did he not express wishes to sail thither in person?"

"David had a voluminous way of making remarks," replied the Spirit, "and I do not pretend to stand up for them all. But one thing is certain; whatever he may have wished, in a musical way, regarding wildernesses and mountain-tops, when it came to the fact he did not go. And why? Because he — "

"Had no wings," said Waring, closing the discussion with a mighty yawn. "I say, Spirit, take yourself off. Something is coming ashore, and were it old Nick in person I should be glad to see him and shake his clawed hand."

As he spoke, out of the fog and into the glare of the fire shot a phantom skiff, beaching itself straight and swift at his feet, and so suddenly that he had to withdraw them like a flash to avoid the crunch of the sharp bows across the sand. "Always let the other man speak first," he thought; "this boomerang of a boat has a shape in it, I see."

The shape rose, and, leaning on its oar, gazed at the camp and its owner in silence. It seemed to be an old man, thin and bent, with bare arms, and a yellow handkerchief bound around its head, drawn down almost to the eyebrows, which, singularly bushy and prominent, shaded the deep-set eyes and hid their expression.

"But, supposing he won't, don't stifle yourself," continued Waring; then aloud, "Well, old gentleman, where do you come from?"

"Nowhere."

"And where are you going?"

"Back there."

"Could n't you take me with you? I have been trying all my life to go nowhere, but never could learn the way; do what I would, I always found myself going in the opposite direction, namely, somewhere."

To this the shape replied nothing, but gazed on.

"Do the nobodies reside in Nowhere, I wonder," pursued the smoker; "because if they do, I am afraid I shall meet all my friends and relatives. What a pity the somebodies could not reside there! But perhaps they do; cynics would say so."

But at this stage the shape waved its oar impatiently and demanded, "Who are you?"

"Well, I do not exactly know. Once I supposed I was Jarvis Waring, but the wilderness has routed that prejudice. We can be anybody we please; it is only a question of force of will; and my latest character has been William Shakespeare. I have been trying to find out whether I wrote my own plays. Stay to supper and take the other side; it is long since I have had an argument with flesh and blood. And you are that, — are n't you?"

But the shape frowned until it seemed all eyebrow. "Young man," it said, "how came you here? By water?"

"No; by land."

"Alongshore?"

"No; through the woods."

"Nobody ever comes through the woods."

"Agreed; but I am somebody."

"Do you mean that you have come across from Lake Superior on foot?"

"I landed on the shore of Lake Superior a month or two ago, and struck inland the same day; where I am now I neither know nor want to know."

"Very well," said the shape,—"very well." But it scowled more gently. "You have no boat?"

"No."

"Do you start on to-morrow?"

"Probably; by that time the waves and 'the sessions of sweet silent thought' will have driven me distracted between them."

"I will stay to supper, I think," said the shape, unbending still further, and stepping out of the skiff.

"Deeds before words then," replied Waring, starting back towards a tree where his game-bag and knapsack were hanging. When he returned the skiff had disappeared; but the shape was warming its moccasined feet at the fire in a very human sort of way. They cooked and eat with the appetites of the wilderness, and grew sociable after a fashion. The shape's name was Fog, Amos Fog, or old Fog, a fisherman and a hunter among the islands farther to the south; he had come inshore to see what that fire meant, no person had camped there in fifteen long years.

"You have been here all that time, then?"

"Off and on, off and on; I live a wandering life," replied old Fog; and then, with the large curiosity that solitude begets, he turned the conversation back towards the other and his story. The other, not unwilling to tell his adventures, began readily; and the old man listened, smoking meanwhile a second pipe produced from the compact stores in the knapsack. In the web of encounters and escapes, he placed his little questions now and then; no, Waring had no plan for exploring the region, no intention of settling there, was merely idling away a summer in the wilderness and would then go back to civilization never to return, at least, not that way; might go west across the plains, but that would be farther south. They talked on, one much, the other little; after a time, Waring, whose heart had been warmed by his flask, began to extol his ways and means.

"Live? I live like a prince," he said. "See these tin cases; they contain concentrated stores of various kinds. I carry a little tea, you see, and even a few lumps of white sugar as a special treat now and then on a wet night."

"Did you buy that sugar at the Sault?" said the old man, eagerly.

"O no; I brought it up from below. For literature I have this small edition of Shakespeare's sonnets, the cream of the whole world's poetry; and when I am tired of looking at the trees and the sky, I look at this, Titian's lovely daughter with her upheld salver of fruit. Is she not beautiful as a dream?"

"I don't know much about dreams," replied old Fog, scanning the small picture with curious eyes; "but is n't she a trifle heavy in build? They dress like that nowadays, I suppose,—flowered gowns and gold chains around the waist?"

"Why, man, that picture was painted more than three centuries ago."

"Was it now? Women don't alter much, do they?" said old Fog, simply. "Then they don't dress like that nowadays?"

"I don't know how they dress, and don't care," said the younger man, repacking his treasures.

Old Fog concluded to camp with his new friend that night and be off at dawn. "You see it is late," he said, "and your fire 's all made and everything comfortable. I 've a long row before me to-morrow: I 'm on my way to the Beavers."

"Ah! very intelligent animals, I am told. Friends of yours?"

"Why, they 're islands, boy; Big and Little Beaver! What do you know, if you don't know the Beavers?"

"Man," replied Waring. "I flatter myself I know the human animal well; he is a miserable beast."

"Is he?" said old Fog, wonderingly; "who 'd have thought it!" Then, giving up the problem as something beyond his reach,—"Don't trouble yourself if you hear me stirring in the night," he said; "I am often mighty restless." And rolling himself in his blanket, he soon became, at least as regards the camp-fire and sociability, a nonentity.

"Simple-minded old fellow," thought Waring, lighting a fresh pipe; "has lived around here all his life, apparently. Think of that,—to have lived around here all one's life! I, to be sure, am here now; but then, have I not been—" And here followed a revery of remembrances, that glittering network of gayety and folly which only young hearts can weave, the network around whose border is written in a thousand hues, "Rejoice, young man, in thy youth, for it cometh not again."

> "Alas, what sighs from our boding hearts
> The infinite skies have borne away!"

sings a poet of our time; and the same thought lies in many hearts unexpressed, and sighed itself away in this heart of our Jarvis Waring that still foggy evening on the beach.

The middle of the night, the long watch before dawn; ten chances to one against his awakening! A shape is moving towards the bags hanging on the distant tree. How the sand crunches, — but he sleeps on. It reaches the bags, this shape, and hastily rifles them; then it steals back and crosses the sand again, its moccasined feet making no sound. But, as it happened, that one chance (which so few of us ever see!) appeared on the scene at this moment and guided those feet directly towards a large, thin, old shell masked with newly blown sand; it broke with a crack; Waring woke, and gave chase. The old man was unarmed, he had noticed that; and then such a simple-minded, harmless old fellow! But simple-minded, harmless old fellows do not run like mad if one happens to wake; so the younger pursued. He was strong, he was fleet; but the shape was fleeter, and the space between them grew wider. Suddenly the shape turned and darted into the water, running out until only its head was visible above the surface, a dark spot in the foggy moonlight. Waring pursued, and saw meanwhile another dark spot beyond, an empty skiff which came rapidly inshoreward until it met the head, which forthwith took to itself a body, clambered in, lifted the oars, and was gone in an instant. "Well," said Waring, still pursuing down the gradual slope of the beach, "will a phantom bark come at my call, I wonder?

At any rate I will go out as far as he did, and see." But no; the perfidious beach at this instant shelved off suddenly and left him afloat in deep water. Fortunately he was a skilled swimmer, and soon regained the shore, wet and angry. His dogs were whimpering at a distance, both securely fastened to trees, and the light of the fire had died down; evidently the old Fog was not, after all, so simple as some other people!

"I might as well see what the old rogue has taken," thought Waring; "all the tobacco and whiskey, I'll be bound." But nothing had been touched save the lump-sugar, the little book, and the picture of Titian's daughter! Upon this what do you suppose Waring did? He built a boat.

When it was done, and it took some days and was nothing but a dug-out after all (the Spirit said that), he sailed out into the unknown; which being interpreted means that he paddled southward. From the conformation of the shore, he judged that he was in a deep curve, protected in a measure from the force of wind and wave. "I'll find that ancient mariner," he said to himself, "if I have to circumnavigate the entire lake. My book of sonnets, indeed, and my Titian picture! Would nothing else content him? This voyage I undertake from a pure inborn sense of justice — "

"Now, Waring, you know it is nothing of the kind," said the Spirit who had sailed also. "You know you are tired of the woods and dread going back that way, and you know you may hit a steamer off the islands; besides, you are curious about this old man who steals Shakespeare and sugar, leaving tobacco and whiskey untouched."

"Spirit," replied the man at the paddle, "you fairly corrupt me with your mendacity. Be off and unlimber yourself in the fog; I see it coming in."

He did see it indeed; in it rolled upon him in columns, a soft silvery cloud enveloping everything, the sunshine, the shore, and the water, so that he paddled at random, and knew not whither he went, or rather saw not, since knowing was long since out of the question. "This is pleasant," he said to himself when the morning had turned to afternoon and the afternoon to night, "and it is certainly new. A stratus of tepid cloud a thousand miles long and a thousand miles deep, and a man in a dug-out paddling through! Sisyphus was nothing to this." But he made himself comfortable in a philosophic way, and went to the only place left to him, — to sleep.

At dawn the sunshine colored the fog golden, but that was all; it was still fog, and lay upon the dark water thicker and softer than ever. Waring eat some dried meat, and considered the possibilities; he had reckoned without the fog, and now his lookout was uncomfortably misty. The provisions would not last more than a week; and though he might catch fish, how could he cook them? He had counted on a shore somewhere; any land, however desolate, would give him a fire; but this fog was muffling, and unless he stumbled ashore by chance he might go on paddling in a circle forever. "*Bien,*" he said, summing up, "my part at any rate is to go on; *I,* at least, can do my duty."

"Especially as there is nothing else to do," observed the Spirit.

Having once decided, the man kept at his work with finical precision. At a given moment he eat a lunch, and very tasteless it was too, and then to work again; the little craft went steadily on before the stroke of the strong arms, its wake unseen, its course unguided. Suddenly at sunset the fog folded its gray draperies, spread its wings, and floated off to the southwest, where that night it rested at Death's Door and sent two schooners to the bottom; but it left behind it a released dug-out, floating before a log fortress which had appeared by magic, rising out of the water with not an inch of ground to spare, if indeed there was any ground; for might it not be a species of fresh-water boat, anchored there for clearer weather?

"Ten more strokes and I should have run into it," thought Waring as he floated noiselessly up to this watery residence; holding on by a jutting beam, he reconnoitred the premises. The building was of logs, square, and standing on spiles, its north side, under which he lay, showed a row of little windows all curtained in white, and from one of them peeped the top of a rose-bush; there was but one story, and the roof was flat. Nothing came to any of these windows, nothing stirred, and the man in the dug-out, being curious as well as hungry, decided to explore, and touching the wall at intervals pushed his craft noiselessly around the eastern corner; but here was a blank wall of logs and nothing more. The south side was the same, with the exception of two loopholes, and the dug-out glided its quietest past these. But the west shone out radiant, a rude little balcony overhanging the water, and in it a girl in a mahogany chair, nibbling something and reading.

"My sugar and my sonnets, as I am alive!" ejaculated Waring to himself.

The girl took a fresh bite with her little white teeth, and went on reading in the sunset light.

"Cool," thought Waring.

And cool she looked truly to a man who had paddled two days in a hot sticky fog, as, clad in white, she sat still and placid on her airy perch. Her hair, of the very light fleecy gold seldom seen after babyhood, hung over her shoulders unconfined by comb or ribbon, falling around her like a veil and glittering in the horizontal sunbeams; her face, throat, and hands were white as the petals of a white camelia, her features infantile, her cast-down eyes invisible under the full-orbed lids. Waring gazed at her cynically, his boat motionless; it accorded with his theories that the only woman he had seen for months should be calmly eating and reading stolen sweets. The girl turned a page, glanced up, saw him, and sprang forward smiling; as she stood at the balcony, her beautiful hair fell below her knees.

"Jacob," she cried, gladly, "is that you at last?"

"No," replied Waring, "it is not Jacob; rather Esau. Jacob was too tricky for me. The damsel Rachel, I presume!"

"My name is Silver," said the girl, "and I see you are not Jacob at all. Who are you, then?"

"A hungry, tired man who would like to come aboard and rest awhile."

"Aboard? This is not a boat."

"What then?"

"A castle, — Castle Nowhere."

"You reside here?"

"Of course; where else should I reside? Is it not a beautiful place?" said the girl, looking around with a little air of pride.

"I could tell better if I was up there."

"Come, then."

"How?"

"Do you not see the ladder?"

"Ah, yes, — Jacob had a ladder, I remember; he comes up this way, I suppose?"

"He does not; but I wish he would."

"Undoubtedly. But you are not Leah all this time?"

"I am Silver, as I told you before; I know not what you mean with your Leah."

"But, mademoiselle, your Bible —"

"What is Bible?"

"You have never read the Bible?"

"It is a book, then. I like books," replied Silver, waving her hand comprehensively; "I have read five, and now I have a new one."

"Do you like it, — your new one?" asked Waring, glancing towards his property.

"I do not understand it all; perhaps you can explain to me?"

"I think I can," answered the young man, smiling in spite of himself; "that is, if you wish to learn."

"Is it hard?"

"That depends upon the scholar; now, some minds —" Here a hideous face looked out through one of the little windows, and then vanished. "Ah," said Waring, pausing, "one of the family?"

"That is Lorez, my dear old nurse."

The face now came out on to the balcony and showed itself as part of an old negress, bent and wrinkled with age.

"He came in a boat, Lorez," said Silver, "and yet you see he is not Jacob. But he says he is tired and hungry, so we will have supper now, without waiting for father."

The old woman smiled and nodded, stroking the girl's glittering hair meanwhile with her black hand.

"As soon as the sun has gone it will be very damp," said Silver, turning to her guest; "you will come within. But you have not told me your name."

"Jarvis," replied Waring, promptly.

"Come, then, Jarvis." And she led the way through a low door into a long narrow room with a row of little square windows on each side all covered with little square white curtains. The walls and ceiling were planked, and the workmanship of the whole rude and clumsy; but a gay carpet covered the floor, a chandelier adorned with lustres hung from a hook in the ceiling, large gilded vases and a mirror in a tarnished gilt frame adorned a shelf over the hearth, mahogany chairs stood in ranks against the wall under the little windows, and a long narrow table ran down the centre of the apartment from end to end. It all seemed strangely familiar; of what did it remind him? His eyes fell upon the table-legs; they were riveted to the floor. Then it came to him at once, — the long narrow cabin of a lake steamer.

"I wonder if it is not anchored after all," he thought.

"Just a few shavings and one little stick, Lorez,"

said Silver; "enough to give us light and drive away the damp."

Up flared the blaze and spread abroad in a moment the dear home feeling. (O hearth-fire, good genius of home, with thee a log-cabin is cheery and bright, without thee the palace a dreary waste!)

"And now, while Lorez is preparing supper, you will come and see my pets," said Silver, in her soft tone of unconscious command.

"By all means," replied Waring. "Anything in the way of mermaidens?"

"Mermaidens dwell in the water, they cannot live in houses as we can; did you not know that? I have seen them on moonlight nights, and so has Lorez; but Aunt Shadow never saw them."

"Another member of the family,—Aunt Shadow?"

"Yes," replied Silver; "but she is not here now. She went away one night when I was asleep. I do not know why it is," she added, sadly, "but if people go away from here in the night they never come back. Will it be so with you, Jarvis?"

"No; for I will take you with me," replied the young man, lightly.

"Very well; and father will go too, and Lorez," said Silver.

To this addition, Waring, like many another man in similar circumstances, made no reply. But Silver did not notice the omission. She had opened a door, and behold, they stood together in a bower of greenery and blossom, flowers growing everywhere, — on the floor, up the walls, across the ceiling, in pots, in boxes, in baskets, on shelves, in cups, in shells, climbing, crowding each other, swinging, hanging, winding around everything, — a riot of beauty with perfumes for a language. Two white gulls stood in the open window and gravely surveyed the stranger.

"They stay with me almost all the time," said the water-maiden; "every morning they fly out to sea for a while, but they always come back."

Then she flitted to and fro, kissed the opening blossoms and talked to them, tying back the more riotous vines, and gravely admonishing them.

"They are so happy here," she said; "it was dull for them on shore. I would not live on the shore! Would you?"

"Certainly not," replied Waring, with an air of having spent his entire life upon a raft. "But you did not find all these blossoms on the shores about here, did you?"

"Father found them, — he finds everything; in his boat almost every night is something for me. I hope he will come soon; he will be so glad to see you."

"Will he? I wish I was sure of that," thought Waring. Then aloud, "Has he any men with him?" he asked, carelessly.

"O no; we live here all alone now, — father, Lorez, and I."

"But you were expecting a Jacob?"

"I have been expecting Jacob for more than two years. Every night I watch for him, but he comes not. Perhaps he and Aunt Shadow will come together, — do you think they will?" said Silver, looking up into his eyes with a wistful expression.

"Certainly," replied Waring.

"Now am I glad, so glad! For father and Lorez will never say so. I think I shall like you, Jarvis." And, leaning on a box of mignonette, she considered him gravely with her little hands folded.

Waring, man of the world, — Waring, who had been under fire, — Waring the impassive, — Waring the unflinching, — turned from this scrutiny.

Supper was eaten at one end of the long table; the dishes, tablecloth, and napkins were marked with an anchor, the food simple but well cooked.

"Fish, of course, and some common supplies I can understand," said the visitor; "but how do you obtain flour like this, or sugar?"

"Father brings them," said Silver, "and keeps them locked in his storeroom. Brown sugar we have always, but white not always, and I like it so much! Don't you?"

"No; I care nothing for it," said Waring, remembering the few lumps and the little white teeth.

The old negress waited, and peered at the visitor out of her small bright eyes; every time Silver spoke to her, she broke into a radiance of smiles and nods, but said nothing.

"She lost her voice some years ago," explained the little mistress when the black had gone out for more coffee; "and now she seems to have forgotten how to form words, although she understands us."

Lorez returned, and, after refilling Waring's cup, placed something shyly beside his plate, and withdrew into the shadow. "What is it?" said the young man, examining the carefully folded parcel.

"Why, Lorez, have you given him that!" exclaimed Silver as he drew out a scarlet ribbon, old and frayed, but brilliant still. "We think it must have belonged to her young master," she continued in a low tone. "It is her most precious treasure, and long ago she used to talk about him, and about her old home in the South."

The old woman came forward after a while, smiling and nodding like an animated mummy, and taking the red ribbon threw it around the young man's neck, knotting it under the chin. Then she nodded with treble radiance and made signs of satisfaction.

"Yes, it *is* becoming," said Silver, considering the effect thoughtfully, her small head with its veil of hair bent to one side, like a flower swayed by the wind.

The flesh-pots of Egypt returned to Jarvis Waring's mind; he remembered certain articles of apparel left behind in civilization, and murmured against the wilderness. Under the pretence of examining the vases, he took an early opportunity of looking into the round mirror. "I am hideous," he said to himself, uneasily.

"Decidedly so," echoed the Spirit in a cheerful voice. But he was not; only a strong dark young man of twenty-eight, browned by exposure, clad in a gray flannel shirt and the rough attire of a hunter.

The fire on the hearth sparkled gayly. Silver had brought one of her little white gowns, half finished, and sat sewing in its light, while the old negress came and went about her household tasks.

"So you can sew?" said the visitor.

"Of course I can. Aunt Shadow taught me," answered the water-maiden, threading her needle deftly. "There is no need to do it, for I have so many dresses; but I like to sew, don't you?"

"I cannot say that I do. Have you so many dresses, then?"

"Yes; would you like to see them? Wait."

Down went the little gown trailing along the floor, and away she flew, coming back with her arms full, — silks, muslins, laces, and even jewelry. "Are they not beautiful?" she asked, ranging her splendor over the chairs.

"They are indeed," said Waring, examining the garments with curious eyes. "Where did you get them?"

"Father brought them. O, there he is now, there he is now! I hear the oars. Come, Lorez."

She ran out; the old woman hastened, carrying a brand from the hearth; and after a moment Waring followed them. "I may as well face the old rogue at once," he thought.

The moon had not risen and the night was dark; under the balcony floated a black object, and Lorez, leaning over, held out her flaming torch. The face of the old rogue came out into the light under its yellow handkerchief, but so brightened and softened by loving gladness that the gazer above hardly knew it. "Are you there, darling, well and safe?" said the old man, looking up fondly as he fastened his skiff.

"Yes, father; here I am and so glad to see you," replied the water-maiden, waiting at the top of the ladder. "We have a visitor, father dear; are you not glad, so glad to see him?"

The two men came face to face, and the elder started back. "What are you doing here?" he said, sternly.

"Looking for my property."

"Take it, and begone!"

"I will, to-morrow."

All this apart, and with the rapidity of lightning.

"His name is Jarvis, father, and we must keep him with us," said Silver.

"Yes, dear, as long as he wishes to stay; but no doubt he has home and friends waiting for him."

They went within, Silver leading the way. Old Fog's eyes gleamed and his hands were clinched. The younger man watched him warily.

"I have been showing Jarvis all my dresses, father, and he thinks them beautiful."

"They certainly are remarkable," observed Waring, coolly.

Old Fog's hands dropped, he glanced nervously towards the visitor.

"What have you brought for me to-night, father dear?"

"Nothing, child; that is, nothing of any consequence. But it is growing late; run off to your nest."

"O no, papa; you have had no supper, nor —"

"I am not hungry. Go, child, go; do not grieve me," said the old man in a low tone.

"Grieve you? Dear papa, never!" said the girl, her voice softening to tenderness in a moment. "I will run straight to my room. — Come, Lorez."

The door closed. "Now for us two," thought Waring.

But the cloud had passed from old Fog's face, and he drew up his chair confidentially. "You see how it is," he began in an apologetic tone; "that child is the darling of my life, and I could not resist taking those things for her; she has so few books, and she likes those little lumps of sugar."

"And the Titian picture?" said Waring, watching him doubtfully.

"A father's foolish pride; I knew she was lovelier, but I wanted to see the two side by side. She is lovelier, is n't she?"

"I do not think so."

"Don't you?" said old Fog in a disappointed tone. "Well, I suppose I am foolish about her; we live here all alone, you see: my sister brought her up."

"The Aunt Shadow who has gone away?"

"Yes; she was my sister, and — and she went away last year," said the old man. "Have a pipe?"

"I should think you would find it hard work to live here."

"I do; but a poor man cannot choose. I hunt, fish, and get out a few furs sometimes; I traffic with the Beaver Island people now and then. I bought all this furniture in that way; you would not think it, but they have a great many nice things down at Beaver."

"It looks like steamboat furniture."

"That is it; it is. A steamer went to pieces down there, and they saved almost all her furniture and stores; they are very good sailors, the Beavers."

"Wreckers, perhaps?"

"Well, I would not like to say that; you know we do have terrible storms on these waters. And then there is the fog; this part of Lake Michigan is foggy half the time, why, I never could guess; but twelve hours out of the twenty-four the gray mist lies on the water here and outside, shifting slowly backwards and forwards from Little Traverse to Death's Door, and up into this curve, like a waving curtain. Those silks, now, came from the steamer; trunks, you know. But I have never told Silver; she might ask where were the people to whom they belonged. You do not like the idea? Neither do I. But how could we help the drowning when we were not there, and these things were going for a song down at Beaver. The child loves pretty things; what could a poor man do? Have a glass of punch; I'll get it ready in no time." He bustled about, and then came back with the full glasses. "You won't tell her? I may have done wrong in the matter, but it would kill me to have the child lose faith in me," he said, humbly.

"Are you going to keep the girl shut up here forever?" said Waring, half touched, half disgusted; the old fellow had looked abject as he pleaded.

"That is it; no," said Fog, eagerly. "She has been but a child all this time, you see, and my sister taught her well. We did the best we could. But as soon as I have a little more, just a little more, I intend to move to one of the towns down the lake, and have a small house and everything comfortable. I have planned it all out, I shall have —"

He rambled on, garrulously detailing all his fancies and projects while the younger man sipped his punch (which was very good), listened until he was tired, fell into a doze, woke and listened awhile longer, and then, wearied out, proposed bed.

"Certainly. But, as I was saying — "

"I can hear the rest to-morrow," said Waring, rising with scant courtesy.

"I am sorry you go so soon; could n't you stay a few days?" said the old man, lighting a brand. "I am going over to-morrow to the shore where I met you. I have some traps there; you might enjoy a little hunting."

"I have had too much of that already. I must get my dogs, and then I should like to hit a steamer or vessel going below."

"Nothing easier; we 'll go over after the dogs early in the morning, and then I 'll take you right down to the islands if the wind is fair. Would you like to look around the castle, — I am going to draw up the ladders. No? This way, then; here is your room."

It was a little side-chamber with one window high up over the water; there was an iron bolt on the door, and the walls of bare logs were solid. Waring stood his gun in one corner, and laid his pistols by the side of the bed, — for there was a bed, only a rude framework like a low-down shelf, but covered with mattress and sheets none the less, — and his weary body longed for those luxuries with a longing that only the wilderness can give, — the wilderness with its beds of boughs, and no undressing. The bolt and the logs shut him in safely; he was young and strong, and there were his pistols. "Unless they burn down their old castle," he said to himself, "they cannot harm me." And then he fell to thinking of the lovely childlike girl, and his heart grew soft. "Poor old man," he said, "how he must have worked and stolen and starved to keep her safe and warm in this far-away nest of his hidden in the fogs! I won't betray the old fellow, and I'll go to-morrow. Do you hear that, Jarvis Waring? I'll go to-morrow!"

And then the Spirit, who had been listening as usual, folded himself up silently and flew away.

To go to sleep in a bed, and awake in an open boat drifting out to sea, is startling. Waring was not without experiences, startling and so forth, but this exceeded former sensations; when a bear had him, for instance, he at least understood it, but this was not a bear, but a boat. He examined the craft as well as he could in the darkness. "Evidently boats in some shape or other are the genii of this region," he said; "they come shooting ashore from nowhere, they sail in at a signal without oars, canvas, or crew, and now they have taken to kidnapping. It is foggy too, I'll warrant; they are in league with the fogs." He looked up, but could see nothing, not even a star. "What does it all mean anyway? Where am I? Who am I? Am I anybody? Or has the body gone and left me. only an any?" But no one answered. Finding himself partly dressed, with the rest of his clothes at his feet, he concluded that he was not yet a spirit; in one of his pockets was a match, he struck it and came back to reality in its flash. The boat was his own dug-out, and he himself and no other was in it: so far, so good. Everything else, however, was fog and night. He found the paddle and began work. "We shall see who will conquer," he thought, doggedly, "Fate or I!" So he paddled on an hour or more.

Then the wind arose and drove the fog helter-skelter across to Green Bay, where the gray ranks curled themselves down and lay hidden until morning. "I 'll go with the wind," thought Waring, "it must take me somewhere in time." So he changed his course and paddled on. The wind grew strong, then stronger. He could see a few stars now as the ragged dark clouds scudded across the heavens, and he hoped for the late moon. The wind grew wild, then wilder. It took all his skill to manage his clumsy boat. He no longer asked himself where he was or who; he knew,—a man in the grasp of death. The wind was a gale now, and the waves were pressed down flat by its force as it flew along. Suddenly the man at the paddle, almost despairing, espied a light, high up, steady, strong. "A lighthouse on one of the islands," he said, and steered for it with all his might. Good luck was with him; in half an hour he felt the beach under him, and landed on a shore; but the light he saw no longer. "I must be close in under it," he thought. In the train of the gale came thunder and lightning. Waring sat under a bush watching the powers of the air in conflict, he saw the fury of their darts and heard the crash of their artillery, and mused upon the wonders of creation, and the riddle of man's existence. Then a flash came, different from the others in that it brought the human element upon the scene; in its light he saw a vessel driving helplessly before the gale. Down from his spirit-heights he came at once, and all the man within him was stirred for those on board, who, whether or not they had ever perplexed themselves over the riddle of their existence, no doubt now shrank from the violent solution offered to them. But what could he do? He knew nothing of the shore, and yet there must be a harbor somewhere, for was there not the light? Another flash showed the vessel still nearer, drifting broadside on; involuntarily he ran out on the long sandy point where it seemed that soon she must strike. But sooner came a crash, and a grinding sound; there was a reef outside then, and she was on it, the rocks cutting her, and the waves pounding her down on their merciless edges. "Strange!" he thought. "The harbor must be on the other side I suppose, and yet it seems as though I came this way." Looking around, there was the light high up behind him, burning clearly and strongly, while the vessel was breaking to pieces below. "It is a lure," he said, indignantly, "a false light." In his wrath he spoke aloud; suddenly a shape came out of the darkness, cast him down, and tightened a grasp around his throat. "I know you," he muttered, strangling. One hand was free, he drew out his pistol, and fired; the shape fell back. It was old Fog. Wounded? Yes, badly.

Waring found his tinder-box, made a blaze of drift-wood, and bound up the bleeding arm and leg roughly. "Wretch," he said, "you set that light."

Old Fog nodded.

"Can anything be done for the men on board? Answer, or I 'll end your miserable life at once; I don't know why, indeed, I have tried to save it."

Old Fog shook his head. "Nothing," he murmured; "I know every inch of the reef and shore."

Another flash revealed for an instant the doomed vessel, and Waring raged at his own impotence as he strode to and fro, tears of anger and pity in his eyes. The old man watched him anxiously. "There are not more than six of them," he said; "it was only a small schooner."

"Silence!" shouted Waring; "each man of the six now suffering and drowning is worth a hundred of such as you!"

"That may be," said Fog.

Half an hour afterwards he spoke again. "They 're about gone now, the water is deadly cold up here. The wind will go down soon, and by daylight the things will be coming ashore; you 'll see to them, won't you?"

"I 'll see to nothing, murderer!"

"And if I die, what are you?"

"An avenger."

"Silver must die too then; there is but little in the house, she will soon starve. It was for her that I came out to-night."

"I will take her away; not for your sake, but for hers."

"How can you find her?"

"As soon as it is daylight I will sail over."

"Over? Over where? That is it, you do not know," said the old man, eagerly, raising himself on his unwounded arm. "You might row and sail about here for days, and I 'll warrant you 'd never find the castle; it 's hidden away more carefully than a nest in the reeds, trust me for that. The way lies through a perfect tangle of channels and islands and marshes, and the fog is sure for at least a good half of the time. The sides of the castle towards the channel show no light at all; and even when you 're once through the outlying islets, the only approach is masked by a movable bed of sedge which I contrived, and which turns you skilfully back into the marsh by another way. No; you might float around there for days, but you'd never find the castle."

"I found it once."

"That was because you came from the north shore. I did not guard that side, because no one has ever come that way; you remember how quickly I saw your light and rowed over to find out what it was. But you are miles away from there now."

The moon could not pierce the heavy clouds, and the night continued dark. At last the dawn came slowly up the east and showed an angry sea, and an old man grayly pallid on the sands near the dying fire; of the vessel nothing was to be seen.

"The things will be coming ashore, the things will be coming ashore," muttered the old man, his anxious eyes turned towards the water that lay on a level with his face; he could not raise himself now. "Do you see things coming ashore?"

Waring looked searchingly at him. "Tell me the truth," he said, "has the girl no boat?"

"No."

"Will any one go to rescue her; does any one know of the castle?"

"Not a human being on this earth."

"And that aunt,—that Jacob?"

"Did n't you guess it? They are both dead. I rowed them out by night and buried them,—my poor old sister, and the boy who had been our serving-lad. The child knows nothing of death. I told her they had gone away."

"Is there no way for her to cross to the islands or mainland?"

"No; there is a circle of deep water all around the castle, outside."

"I see nothing for it, then, but to try and save your justly forfeited life," said Waring, kneeling down with an expression of repugnance. He was something of a surgeon, and knew what he was about. His task over, he made up the fire, warmed some food, fed the old man, and helped his waning strength with the contents of his flask. "At least you placed all my property in the dug-out before you set me adrift," he said; "may I ask your motive?"

"I did not wish to harm you; only to get rid of you. You had provisions, and your chances were as good as many you had had in the woods."

"But I might have found my way back to your castle?"

"Once outside, you could never do that," replied the old man, securely.

"I could go back along-shore."

"There are miles of piny-wood swamps where the streams come down; no, you could not do it, unless you went away round to Lake Superior again, and struck across the country as you did before. That would take you a month or two, and the summer is almost over. You would not risk a Northern snow-storm, I reckon. But say, do you see things coming ashore?"

"The poor bodies will come, no doubt," said Waring, sternly.

"Not yet; and they don't often come in here, any way; they 're more likely to drift out to sea."

"Miserable creature, this is not the first time, then!"

"Only four times, — only four times in fifteen long years, and then only when she was close to starvation," pleaded the old man. "The steamer was honestly wrecked, — the Anchor, of the Buffalo line, — honestly, I do assure you; and what I gathered from her — she did not go to pieces for days — lasted me a long time, besides furnishing the castle. It was a god-send to me, that steamer. You must not judge me, boy; I work, I slave, I go hungry and cold, to keep her happy and warm. But times come when everything fails and starvation is at the door. She never knows it, none of them ever knew it, for I keep the keys and amuse them with little mysteries; but, as God is my judge, the wolf has been at the door, and is there this moment unless I have luck. Fish? There are none in shore where they can catch them. Why do I not fish for them? I do; but my darling is not accustomed to coarse fare, her delicate life must be delicately nourished. O, you do not know, you do not know! I am growing old, and my hands and eyes are not what they were. That very night when I came home and found you there, I had just lost overboard my last supplies, stored so long, husbanded so carefully! If I could walk, I would show you my cellar and storehouse back in the woods. Many things that they have held were honestly earned, by my fish and my game, and one thing and another. I get out timber and raft it down to the islands sometimes, although the work is too hard for an old man alone; and I trade my furs off regularly at the settlements on the islands and even along the mainland,—a month's work for a little flour or sugar. Ah, how I have labored! I have felt my muscles crack, I have dropped like a log from sheer weariness. Talk of tortures; which of them have I not felt, with the pains and faintness of exposure and hunger racking me from head to foot? Have I stopped for snow and ice? Have I stopped for anguish? Never; I have worked, worked, worked, with the tears of pain rolling down my cheeks, with my body gnawed by hunger. That night, in some way, the boxes slipped and fell overboard as I was shifting them; just slipped out of my grasp as if on purpose, they knowing all the time that they were my last. Home I came, empty-handed, and found you there! I would have taken your supplies, over on the north beach, that night, yes, without pity, had I not felt sure of those last boxes; but I never rob needlessly. You look at me with scorn? You are thinking of those dead men? But what are they to Silver, — the rough common fellows, — and the wolf standing at the castle door! Believe me, though, I try everything before I resort to this, and only twice out of the four times have I caught anything with my tree-hung light; once it was a vessel loaded with provisions, and once it was a schooner with grain from Chicago, which washed overboard and was worthless. O, the bitter day when I stood here in the biting wind and watched it float by out to sea! But say, has anything come ashore? She will be waking soon, and we have miles to go."

But Waring did not answer; he turned away. The old man caught at his feet. "You are not going," he cried in a shrill voice, — "you are not going? Leave me to die, — that is well; the sun will come and burn me, thirst will come and madden me, these wounds will torture me, and all is no more than I deserve. But Silver? If I die, she dies. If you forsake me, you forsake her. Listen; do you believe in your Christ, the dear Christ? Then, in his name I swear to you that you cannot reach her alone, that only I can guide you to her. O save me, for her sake! Must she suffer and linger and die? O God, have pity and soften his heart!" The voice died away in sobs, the weak slow sobs of an old man.

But Waring, stern in avenging justice, drew himself from the feeble grasp, and walked down towards the boats. He did not intend fairly to desert the miserable old creature. He hardly knew what he intended, but his impulse was to put more space between them, between himself and this wretch who gathered his evil living from dead men's bones. So he stood gazing out to sea. A faint cry roused him, and, turning, he saw that the old man had dragged himself half across the distance between them, marking the way with his blood, for the bandages were loosened by his movements. As Waring turned, he held up his hands, cried aloud, and fell as if dead on the sands. "I am a brute," said Waring. Then he went to work and brought back consciousness, rebound the wounds, lifted the body in his strong arms and bore it down the beach. A sail-boat lay in a cove, with a little skiff in tow. Waring arranged a couch in the bottom, and placed the old man in an easy position on an impromptu pillow made of his coat. Fog opened his eyes. "Anything come ashore?" he asked faintly, trying to turn his head towards the reef. Conquering his repugnance, the young man walked out on the long point. There was nothing there; but farther down the coast barrels were washing up and back in the surf, and one box had stranded in shallow water. "Am I, too, a wrecker?" he asked himself, as with much toil and trouble he secured the booty and examined it. Yes, the barrels contained provisions.

Old Fog, revived by the sight, lay propped at the stern, giving directions. Waring found himself a child obeying the orders of a wiser head. The load on board, the little skiff carrying its share behind, the young man set sail and away they flew over the angry water; old Fog watching the sky, the sail, and the rudder, guiding their course with a word now and then, but silent otherwise.

"Shall we see the castle soon?" asked Waring, after several hours had passed.

"We may be there by night, if the wind does n't shift."

"Have we so far to go, then? Why, I came across in the half of a night."

"Add a day to the half and you have it. I let you down at dawn and towed you out until noon; then I spied that sail beating up, and I knew there would be a storm by night, and—and things were desperate with me. So I cast you off and came over to set the light. It was a chance I did not count on, that your dug-out should float this way; I calculated that she would beach you safely on an island farther to the south."

"And all this time, when you were letting me down— By the way, how did you do it?"

"Lifted a plank in the floor."

"When you were letting me down, and towing me out, and calculating chances, what was I, may I ask?"

"O, just a body asleep, that was all; your punch was drugged, and well done too! Of course I could not have you at the castle; that was plain."

They flew on a while longer, and then veered short to the left. "This boat sails well," said Waring, "and that is your skiff behind I see. Did you whistle for it that night?"

"I let it out by a long cord while you went after the game-bag, and the shore-end I fastened to a little stake just under the edge of the water on that long slope of beach. I snatched it up as I ran out, and kept hauling in until I met it. You fell off that ledge, did n't you? I calculated on that. You see I had found out all I wanted to know; the only thing I feared was some plan for settling along that shore, or exploring it for something. It is my weak side; if you had climbed up one of those tall trees you might have caught sight of the castle,—that is, if there was no fog."

"Will the fog come up now?"

"Hardly; the storm has been too heavy. I suppose you know what day it is?" continued the old man, peering up at his companion from under his shaggy eyebrows.

"No; I have lost all reckonings of time and place."

"Purposely?"

"Yes."

"You are worse than I am, then; I keep a reckoning, although I do not show it. To-day is Sunday, but Silver does not know it; all days are alike to her. Silver has never heard of the Bible," he added, slowly.

"Yes, she has, for I told her."

"You told her!" cried old Fog, wringing his hands.

"Be quiet, or you will disturb those bandages again. I only asked her if she had read the book, and she said no; that was all. But supposing it had not been all, what then? Would it harm her to know of the Bible?"

"It would harm her to lose faith in me."

"Then why have you not told her yourself?"

"I left her to grow up as the flowers grow," said old Fog, writhing on his couch. "Is she not pure and good? Ah, a thousand times more than any church or school could make her!"

"And yet you have taught her to read?"

"I knew not what might happen. I could not expose her defenceless in a hard world. Religion is fancy, but education is like an armor. I cannot tell what may happen."

"True. You may die, you know; you are an old man."

The old man turned away his face.

They sailed on, eating once or twice; afternoon came, and then an archipelago closed in around them;

the sail was down, and the oars out. Around and through, across and back, in and out they wound, now rowing, now poling, and now and then the sail hoisted to scud across a space of open water. Old Fog's face had grown gray again, and the lines had deepened across his haggard cheek and set mouth; his strength was failing. At last they came to a turn, broad and smooth like a canal. "Now I will hoist the sail again," said Waring.

But old Fog shook his head. "That turn leads directly back into the marsh," he said. "Take your oar and push against the sedge in front."

The young man obeyed, and lo! it moved slowly aside and disclosed a narrow passage westward; through this they poled their way along to open water, then set the sail, rounded a point, and came suddenly upon the castle. "Well, I am glad we are here," said Waring.

Fog had fallen back. "Promise," he whispered with gray lips,—"promise that you will not betray me to the child." And his glazing eyes fixed themselves on Waring's face with the mute appeal of a dying animal in the hands of its captor.

"I promise," said Waring.

But the old man did not die; he wavered, lingered, then slowly rallied,—very slowly. The weeks had grown into a month and two before he could manage his boat again. In the mean time Waring hunted and fished for the household, and even sailed over to the reef with Fog on a bed in the bottom of the boat, coming back loaded with the spoil; not once only, not twice did he go; and at last he knew the way, even through the fog, and came and went alone, bringing home the very planks and beams of the ill-fated schooner. "They will make a bright fire in the evenings," he said. The dogs lived on the north shore, went hunting when their master came over, and the rest of the time possessed their souls in patience. And what possessed Waring, do you ask? His name for it was "necessity." "Of course I cannot leave them to starve," he said to himself.

Silver came and went about the castle, at first wilfully, then submissively, then shyly. She had folded away all her finery in wondering silence, for Waring's face had shown disapproval, and now she wore always her simple white gown. "Can you not put up your hair?" he had asked one day; and from that moment the little head appeared crowned with braids. She worked among her flowers and fed her gulls as usual, but she no longer talked to them or told them stories. In the evenings they all sat around the hearth, and sometimes the little maiden sang; Waring had taught her new songs. She knew the sonnets now, and chanted them around the castle to tunes of her own; Shakespeare would not have known his stately measures, dancing along to her rippling melodies.

The black face of Orange shone and simmered with glee; she nodded perpetually, and crooned and laughed to herself over her tasks by the hour together, — a low chuckling laugh of exceeding content.

And did Waring ever stop to think? I know not. If he did, he forgot the thoughts when Silver came and sat by him in the evening with the light of the hearth-fire shining over her. He scarcely saw her at other times, except on her balcony, or at her flower-window as he came and went in his boat below; but in the evenings she sat beside him in her low chair, and laid sometimes her rose-leaf palm in his rough brown hand, or her pretty head against his arm. Old Fog sat by always; but he said little, and his face was shaded by his hand.

The early autumn gales swept over the lakes, leaving wreck and disaster behind; but the crew of the castle stayed safely at home and listened to the tempest cosily, while the flowers bloomed on, and the gulls brought all their relations and colonized the balcony and window-sills, fed daily by the fair hand of Silver. And Waring went not.

Then the frosts came, and turned the forests into splendor; they rowed over and brought out branches, and Silver decked the long room with scarlet and gold. And Waring went not.

The dreary November rains began, the leaves fell, and the dark water surged heavily; but a store of wood was piled on the flat roof, and the fire on the hearth blazed high. And still Waring went not.

At last the first ice appeared, thin flakes forming around the log foundations of the castle; then old Fog spoke. "I am quite well now, quite strong again; you must go to-day, or you will find yourself frozen in here. As it is, you may hit a late vessel off the islands that will carry you below. I will sail over with you, and bring back the boat."

"But you are not strong enough yet," said Waring, bending over his work, a shelf he was carving for Silver; "I cannot go and leave you here alone."

"It is either go now, or stay all winter. You do not, I presume, intend to make Silver your wife,— Silver, the daughter of Fog the wrecker."

Waring's hands stopped; never before had the old man's voice taken that tone, never before had he even alluded to the girl as anything more than a child. On the contrary, he had been silent, he had been humble, he had been openly grateful to the strong young man who had taken his place on sea and shore, and kept the castle full and warm. "What new thing is this?" thought Waring, and asked the same.

"Is it new?" said Fog. "I thought it old, very old. I mean no mystery, I speak plainly. You helped me in my great strait, and I thank you; perhaps it will be counted unto you for good in the reckoning up of your life. But I am strong again, and the ice is forming.

You can have no intention of making Silver your wife?"

Waring looked up, their eyes met. "No," he replied slowly, as though the words were being dragged out of him by the magnetism of the old man's gaze, "I certainly have no such intention."

Nothing more was said; soon Waring rose and went out. But Silver spied him from her flower-room, and came down to the sail-boat where it lay at the foot of the ladder. "You are not going out this cold day," she said, standing by his side as he busied himself over the rigging. She was wrapped in a fur mantle, with a fur cap on her head, and her rough little shoes were fur-trimmed. Waring made no reply. "But I shall not allow it," continued the maiden, gayly. "Am I not queen of this castle? You yourself have said it many a time. You cannot go, Jarvis; I want you here." And with her soft hands she blinded him playfully.

"Silver, Silver," called old Fog's voice above, "come within; I want you."

After that the two men were very crafty in their preparations.

The boat ready, Waring went the rounds for the last time. He brought down wood for several days and stacked it, he looked again at all the provisions and reckoned them over; then he rowed to the north shore, visited his traps, called out the dogs from the little house he had made for them, and bade them good by. "I shall leave you for old Fog," he said; "be good dogs, and bring in all you can for the castle."

The dogs wagged their tails, and waited politely on the beach until he was out of sight; but they did not seem to believe his story, and went back to their house tranquilly without a howl. The day passed as usual. Once the two men happened to meet in the passage-way. "Silver seems restless, we must wait till darkness," said Fog in a low tone.

"Very well," replied Waring.

At midnight they were off, rowing over the black water in the sail-boat, hoping for a fair wind at dawn, as the boat was heavy. They journeyed but slowly through the winding channel, leaving the sedge-gate open; no danger now from intruders; the great giant, Winter, had swallowed all lesser foes. It was cold, very cold, and they stopped awhile at dawn on the edge of the marsh, the last shore, to make a fire and heat some food before setting sail for the islands.

"Good God!" cried Waring.

A boat was coming after them, a little skiff they both knew, and in it, paddling, in her white dress, sat Silver, her fur mantle at her feet where it had fallen unnoticed. They sprang to meet her, knee-deep in the icy water; but Waring was first, and lifted her slight form in his arms.

"I have found you, Jarvis," she murmured, laying

her head down upon his shoulder; then the eyes closed, and the hand she had tried to clasp around his neck fell lifeless. Close to the fire, wrapped in furs, Waring held her in his arms, while the old man bent over her, chafing her hands and little icy feet, and calling her name in an agony.

"Let her but come back to life, and I will say not one word, not one word more," he cried with tears. "Who am I that I should torture her? You shall go back with us, and I will trust it all to God, — all to God."

"But what if I will not go back, what if I will not accept your trust?" said Waring, turning his head away from the face pillowed on his breast.

"I do not trust you, I trust God; he will guard her."

"I believe he will," said the young man, half to himself. And then they bore her home, not knowing whether her spirit was still with them, or already gone to that better home awaiting it in the next country.

That night the thick ice came, and the last vessels fled southward. But in the lonely little castle there was joy; for the girl was saved, barely, with fever, with delirium, with long prostration, but saved!

When weeks had passed, and she was in her low chair again, propped with cushions, pallid as a snow-drop, weak and languid, but still *there*, she told her story, simply and without comprehension of its meaning.

"I could not rest that night," she said, "I know not why; so I dressed softly and slipped past Orange asleep on her mattress by my door, and found you both gone, — you, father, and you, Jarvis. You never go out at night, and it was very cold; and Jarvis had taken his bag and his knapsack, and all the little things I know so well. His gun was gone from the wall, his clothes from his empty room, and that picture of the girl holding up the fruit was not on his table. From that I knew that something had happened; for it is dear to Jarvis, that picture of the girl," said Silver with a little quiver in her voice. With a quick gesture Waring drew the picture from his pocket and threw it into the fire; it blazed, and was gone in a moment. "Then I went after you," said Silver with a little look of gratitude. "I know the passage through the south channels, and something told me you had gone that way. It was very cold."

That was all, no reasoning, no excuse, no embarrassment; the flight of the little sea-bird straight to its mate.

Life flowed on again in the old channel, Fog quiet, Silver happy, and Waring in a sort of dream. Winter was full upon them, and the castle beleaguered with his white armies both below and above, on the water and in the air. The two men went ashore on the ice now, and trapped and hunted daily, the dogs following. Fagots were cut and rough roads made through the forest. One would have supposed they were planning for a lifelong residence, the young man and the old, as they came and went together, now on the snow-crust, now plunging through breast-deep into the light dry mass. One day Waring said, "Let me see your reckoning. Do you know that to-morrow will be Christmas?"

"Silver knows nothing of Christmas," said Fog, roughly.

"Then she shall know," replied Waring.

Away he went to the woods and brought back evergreen. In the night he decked the cabin-like room, and with infinite pains constructed a little Christmas-tree and hung it with everything he could collect or contrive.

"It is but a poor thing, after all," he said, gloomily, as he stood alone surveying his work. It was indeed a shabby little tree, only redeemed from ugliness by a white cross poised on the green summit; this cross glittered and shone in the firelight, — it was cut from solid ice.

"Perhaps I can help you," said old Fog's voice behind. "I did not show you this, for fear it would anger you, but — but there must have been a child on board after all." He held a little box of toys, carefully packed as if by a mother's hand, — common toys, for she was only the captain's wife, and the schooner a small one; the little waif had floated ashore by itself, and Fog had seen and hidden it.

Waring said nothing, and the two men began to tie on the toys in silence. But after a while they warmed to their work and grew eager to make it beautiful; the old red ribbon that Orange had given was considered a precious treasure-trove, and, cut in fragments, it gayly held the little wooden toys in place on the green boughs.

Fog, grown emulous, rifled the cupboards and found small cakes freshly baked by the practised hand of the old cook; these he hung exultingly on the higher boughs. And now the little tree was full, and stood bravely in its place at the far end of the long room, while the white cross looked down on the toys of the drowned child and the ribbon of the slave, and seemed to sanctify them for their new use.

Great was the surprise of Silver the next morning, and many the questions she asked. Out in the world, they told her, it was so; trees like that were decked for children.

"Am I a child?" said Silver, thoughtfully; "what do you think, papa?"

"What do *you* think?" said Waring, turning the question.

"I hardly know; sometimes I think I am, and sometimes not; but it is of no consequence what I am as long as I have you,—you and papa. Tell me more about the little tree, Jarvis. What does it mean? What is that white shining toy on the top? Is there a story about it?"

"Yes, there is a story; but—but it is not I who should tell it to you," replied the young man, after a moment's hesitation.

"Why not? Whom have I in all the world to tell me, save you?" said fondly the sweet child-voice.

They did not take away the little Christmas-tree, but left it on its pedestal at the far end of the long room through the winter; and as the cross melted slowly, a new one took its place, and shone aloft in the firelight. But its story was not told.

February came, and with it a February thaw; the ice stirred a little, and the breeze coming over the floes was singularly mild. The arctic winds and the airs from the Gulf Stream had met and mingled, and the gray fog appeared again, waving to and fro. "Spring has come," said Silver; "there is the dear fog." And she opened the window of the flower-room, and let out a little bird.

"It will find no resting-place for the sole of its foot, for the snow is over the face of the whole earth," said Waring. "Our ark has kept us cosily through bitter weather, has it not, little one?" (He had adopted a way of calling her so.)

"Ark," said Silver; "what is that?"

"Well," answered Waring, looking down into her blue eyes as they stood together at the little window, "it was a watery residence like this; and if Japheth,—he was always my favorite of the three—had

had you there, my opinion is that he would never have come down at all, but would have resided permanently on Ararat."

Silver looked up into his face with a smile, not understanding what he said, nor asking to understand; it was enough for her that he was there. And as she gazed her violet eyes grew so deep, so soft, that the man for once (give him credit, it was the first time) took her into his arms. "Silver," he whispered, bending over her, "do you love me?"

"Yes," she answered in her simple, unconscious way, "you know I do, Jarvis."

No color deepened in her fair face under his ardent gaze; and, after a moment, he released her, almost roughly. The next day he told old Fog that he was going.

"Where?"

"Somewhere, this time. I've had enough of Nowhere."

"Why do you go?"

"Do you want the plain truth, old man? Here it is, then: I am growing too fond of that girl,—a little more and I shall not be able to leave her."

"Then stay; she loves you."

"A child's love."

"She will develop—"

"Not into my wife if I know myself," said Waring, curtly.

Old Fog sat silent a moment. "Is she not lovely and good?" he said in a low voice.

"She is; but she is your daughter as well."

"She is not."

"She is not! What then?

"I—I do not know; I found her, a baby, by the wayside."

"A foundling! So much the better, that is even a step lower," said the younger man, laughing roughly. And the other crept away as though he had been struck.

Waring set about his preparations. This time Silver did not suspect his purpose. She had passed out of the quick, intuitive watchfulness of childhood. During these days she had taken up the habit of sitting by herself in the flower-room, ostensibly with her book or sewing; but when they glanced in through the open door, her hands were lying idle on her lap and her eyes fixed dreamily on some opening blossom. Hours she sat thus, without stirring.

Waring's plan was a wild one; no boat could sail through the ice, no foot could cross the wide rifts made by the thaw, and weeks of the bitterest weather still lay between them and the spring. "Along-shore," he said.

"And die of cold and hunger," answered Fog.

"Old man, why are you not afraid of me?" said Waring, pausing in his work with a lowering glance.

"Am I not stronger than you, and the master, if I so choose, of your castle of logs?"

"But you will not so choose."

"Do not trust me too far!"

"I do not trust you,—but God."

"For a wrecker and a murderer, you have, I must say, a remarkably serene conscience," sneered Waring.

Again the old man shrank, and crept silently away.

But when in the early dawn a dark figure stood on the ice adjusting its knapsack, a second figure stole down the ladder. "Will you go, then," it said, "go and leave the child?"

"She is no child," answered the younger man, sternly; "and you know it."

"To me she is."

"I care not what she is to you; but she shall *not* be more to me."

"More to you?"

"No more than any other pretty piece of waxwork," replied Waring, striding away into the gray mist.

Silver came to breakfast radiant, her small head covered from forehead to throat with the winding braids of gold, her eyes bright, her cheeks faintly tinged with the icy water of her bath. "Where is Jarvis?" she asked.

"Gone hunting," replied old Fog.

"For all day?"

"Yes; and perhaps for all night. The weather is quite mild, you know."

"Yes, papa. But I hope it will soon be cold again; he cannot stay out long then," said the girl, gazing out over the ice with wistful eyes.

The danger was over for that day; but the next morning there it was again, and with it the bitter cold.

"He must come home soon now," said Silver, confidently, melting the frost on one of the little windows so that she could see out and watch for his coming. But he came not. As night fell the cold grew intense; deadly, clear, and still, with the stars shining brilliantly in the steel-blue of the sky. Silver wandered from window to window, wrapped in her fur mantle; a hundred times, a thousand times she had scanned the ice-fields and the snow, the lake and the shore. When the night closed down, she crept close to the old man who sat by the fire in silence, pretending to mend his nets, but furtively watching her every movement. "Papa," she whispered, "where is he, — where is he?" And her tears fell on his hands.

"Silver," he said, bending over her tenderly, "do I not love you? Am I not enough for you? Think, dear, how long we have lived here, and how happy we have been. He was only a stranger. Come, let us forget him, and go back to the old days."

"What! Has he gone, then? Has Jarvis gone?"

Springing to her feet she confronted him with clinched hands and dilated eyes. Of all the words she had heard but one; he had gone! The poor old man tried to draw her down again into the shelter of his arms, but she seemed turned to stone, her slender form was rigid. "Where is he? Where is Jarvis? What have you done with him, — you, you!"

The quick unconscious accusation struck to his heart. "Child," he said in a broken voice, "I tried to keep him. I would have given him my place in your love, in your life, but he would not. He has gone, he cares not for you; he is a hard, evil man."

"He is not! But even if he were, I love him," said the girl, defiantly.

Then she threw up her arms towards heaven (alas! it was no heaven to her, poor child) as if in appeal. "Is there no one to help me?" she cried aloud.

"What can we do, dear?" said the old man, standing beside her and smoothing her hair gently. "He would not stay, — I could not keep him!"

"*I* could have kept him."

"You would not ask him to stay, if he wished to go?"

"Yes, I would; he must stay, for my sake."

"But if he had loved you, dear, he would not have gone."

"Did he say he did not love me?" demanded Silver, with gleaming eyes.

Old Fog hesitated.

"Did he say he did not love me? Did Jarvis say that?" she repeated, seizing his arm with grasp of fire.

"Yes; he said that."

But the lie meant to rouse her pride, killed it; as if struck by a visible hand, she swayed and fell to the floor.

The miserable old man watched her all the night. She was delirious, and raved of Waring through the long hours. At daylight he left her with Orange, who, not understanding these white men's riddles, and sorely perplexed by Waring's desertion, yet cherished her darling with dumb untiring devotion, and watched her every breath.

Following the solitary trail over the snow-covered ice and thence along-shore towards the east journeyed old Fog all day in the teeth of the wind, dragging a sledge loaded with furs, provisions, and dry wood; the sharp blast cut him like a knife, and the dry snow-pellets stung as they touched his face, and clung to his thin beard coated with ice. It was the worst day of the winter, an evil, desolate, piercing day; no human creature should dare such weather. Yet the old man journeyed patiently on until nightfall, and would have gone farther had not darkness concealed the track; his fear was that new snow might fall deeply enough to hide it, and then there was no more hope of following. But nothing could be done at night, so he made his camp, a lodge under a drift with the snow for walls and roof, and a hot fire that barely melted the edges of its icy hearth. As the blaze flared out into the darkness, he heard a cry, and followed; it was faint, but apparently not distant, and after some search he found the spot; there lay Jarvis Waring, helpless and nearly frozen. "I thought you farther on," he said, as he lifted the heavy, inert body.

"I fell and injured my knee yesterday; since then I have been freezing slowly," replied Waring in a muffled voice. "I have been crawling backwards and forwards all day to keep myself alive, but had just given it up when I saw your light."

All night the old hands worked over him, and they hated the body they touched; almost fiercely they fed and nourished it, warmed its blood, and brought back life. In the dawning Waring was himself again; weak, helpless, but in his right mind. He said as much, and added, with a touch of his old humor, "There is a wrong mind you know, old gentleman."

The other made no reply; his task done, he sat by the fire waiting. He had gone after this fellow, driven by fate; he had saved him, driven by fate. Now what had fate next in store? He warmed his wrinkled hands mechanically and waited, while the thought came to him with bitterness that his darling's life lay at the mercy of this man who had nothing better to do, on coming back from the very jaws of death, than make jests. But old Fog was mistaken; the man had something better to do, and did it. Perhaps he noted the expression of the face before him; perhaps he did not, but was thinking, young-man fashion, only of himself; at any rate this is what he said: "I was a fool to go. Help me back, old man; it is too strong for me, — I give it up."

"Back, — back where?" said the other, apathetically.

Waring raised his head from his pillow of furs. "Why do you ask, when you know already? Back to Silver, of course; have you lost your mind?"

His harshness came from within; in reality it was meant for himself; the avowal had cost him something as it passed his lips in the form of words; it had not seemed so when in the suffering, and the cold, and the approach of death, he had seen his own soul face to face and realized the truth.

So the two went back to the castle, the saved lying on the sledge, the savior drawing it; the wind was behind them now, and blew them along. And when the old man, weary and numb with cold, reached the ladder at last, helped Waring, lame and irritable, up to the little snow-covered balcony, and led the way to Silver's room, — when Silver, hearing the step, raised herself in the arms of the old slave and looked eagerly, not at him, no, but at the man behind, — did he shrink? He did not; but led the reluctant, vanquished, defiant, half-angry, half-shamed lover forward, and gave his darling into the arms that seemed again almost unwilling, so strong was the old opposing determination that lay bound by love's bonds.

Silver regained her life as if by magic; not so Waring, who lay suffering and irritable on the lounge in the long room, while the girl tended him with a joy that shone out in every word, every tone, every motion. She saw not his little tyrannies, his exacting demands, his surly tempers; or rather she saw and loved them as women do when men lie ill and helpless in their hands. And old Fog sat apart, or came and went unnoticed; hours of the cold days he wandered through the forests, visiting the traps mechanically, and making tasks for himself to fill up the time; hours of the cold evenings he paced the snow-covered roof alone. He could not bear to see them, but left the post to Orange, whose black face shone with joy and satisfaction over Waring's return.

But after a time fate swung around (as she generally does if impatient humanity would but give her a chance). Waring's health grew, and so did his love. He had been like a strong man armed, keeping his palace; but a stronger than he was come, and, the combat over, he went as far the other way, and adored the very sandals of the conqueror. The gates were open, and all the floods were out.

And Silver? As he advanced, she withdrew. (It is always so in love, up to a certain point; and beyond that point lies, alas! the broad monotonous country of commonplace.)

This impetuous, ardent lover was not the Jarvis she had known, the Jarvis who had been her master, and a despotic one at that. Frightened, shy, bewildered, she fled away from all her dearest joys, and stayed by herself in the flower-room with the bar across the door, only emerging timidly at meal-times and stealing into the long room like a little wraith; a rosy wraith now, for at last she had learned to blush. Waring was angry at this desertion, but only the more in love; for the face had lost its infantile calm, the violet eyes veiled themselves under his gaze, and the unconscious child-mouth began to try to control and conceal its changing expressions, and only succeeded in betraying them more helplessly than ever. Poor little solitary maiden-heart!

Spring was near now; soft airs came over the ice daily, and stirred the water beneath; then the old man spoke. He knew what was coming, he saw it all, and a sword was piercing his heart; but bravely he played his part. "The ice will move out soon, in a month or less you can sail safely," he said, breaking the silence one night when they two sat by the fire, Waring moody and restless, for Silver had openly repulsed him, and fled away early in the evening. "She is trifling with me," he thought, "or else she does not know what love is. By heavens,

I will teach her though —" As far as this his mind had journeyed when Fog spoke. "In a month you can sail safely, and I suppose you will go for good this time?"

"Yes."

Fog waited. Waring kicked a fallen log into place, lit his pipe, then let it go out, moved his chair forward, then pushed it back impatiently, and finally spoke. "Of course I shall take Silver; I intend to make Silver my wife."

"At last?"

"At last. No wonder you are glad —"

"Glad!" said old Fog,—"glad!" But the words were whispered, and the young man went on unheeding.

"Of course it is a great thing for you to have the child off your hands and placed in a home so high above your expectations. Love is a strange power. I do not deny that I have fought against it, but—but—why should I conceal? I love Silver with all my soul, she seems to have grown into my very being."

It was frankly and strongly uttered; the good side of Jarvis Waring came uppermost for the moment.

Old Fog leaned forward and grasped his hand. "I know you do," he said. "I know something of men, and I have watched you closely, Waring. It is for this love that I forgive — I mean that I am glad and thankful for it, very thankful."

"And you have reason to be," said the younger man, withdrawing into his pride again. "As my wife, Silver will have a home, a circle of friends, which — But you could not understand; let it pass. And now, tell me all you know of her."

The tone was a command, and the speaker leaned back in his chair with the air of an owner as he relighted his pipe. But Fog did not shrink. "Will you have the whole story?" he asked humbly.

"As well now as ever, I suppose, but be as brief as possible," said the young man in a lordly manner. Had he not just conferred an enormous favor, an alliance which might be called the gift of a prince, on this dull old backwoodsman?

"Forty years ago or thereabouts," began Fog in a low voice, "a crime was committed in New York City. I shall not tell you what it was, there is no need; enough that the whole East was stirred, and a heavy reward was offered for the man who did the deed. I am that man."

Waring pushed back his chair, a horror came over him, his hand sought for his pistol; but the voice went on unmoved. "Shall I excuse the deed to you, boy? No, I will not. It was done and I did it; that is enough, the damning fact that confronts and silences all talk of motive or cause. This much only will I say; to the passion of the act deliberate intention was not added, and there was no gain for the doer; only loss, the black eternal loss of everything in heaven above, on the earth beneath, or in the waters that are under the earth, for hell itself seemed to spew me out. At least so I thought as I fled away, the mark of Cain upon my brow; the horror was so strong upon me, that I could not kill myself, I feared to join the dead. I went to and fro on the earth, and walked up and down in it; I fled to the uttermost parts of the sea, and yet came back again, moved by a strange impulse to be near the scene of my crime. After years had passed, and with them the memory of the deed from the minds of others, though not from mine, I crept to the old house where my one sister was living alone, and made myself known to her. She left her home, a forlorn place, but still a home, and followed me with a sort of dumb affection,—poor old woman. She was my senior by fifteen years, and I had been her pride; and so she went with me from the old instinct, which still remained, although the pride was dead, crushed by slow horror. We kept together after that, two poor hunted creatures instead of one; we were always fleeing, always imagining that eyes knew us, that fingers pointed us out. I called her Shadow, and together we took the name of Fog, a common enough name, but to us meaning that we were nothing, creatures of the mist, wandering to and fro by night, but in the morning gone. At last one day the cloud over my mind seemed to lighten a little, and the thought came to me that no punishment can endure forever, without impugning the justice of our great Creator. A crime is committed, perhaps in a moment; the ensuing suffering, the results, linger on earth, it may be for some years; but the end of it surely comes sooner or later, and it is as though it had never been. Then, for that crime, shall a soul suffer forever, — not a thousand years, a thousand ages if you like, but forever? Out upon the monstrous idea! Let a man do evil every moment of his life, and let his life be the full threescore years and ten; shall there not come a period in the endless cycles of eternity when even his punishment shall end? What kind of a God is he whom your theologians have held up to us, — a God who creates us at his pleasure, without asking whether or not we wish to be created, who endows us with certain wild passions and capacities for evil, turns us loose into a world of suffering, and then, for our misdeeds there, our whole lives being less than one instant's time in his sight, punishes us forever! Never-ending tortures throughout the countless ages of eternity for the little crimes of threescore years and ten! Heathendom shows no god so monstrous as this. O great Creator, O Father of our souls, of all the ills done on the face of thy earth, this lie against thy justice and thy goodness, is it not the greatest? The thought came to me, as I said, that no punishment could endure forever, that somewhere in the future I, even I, should meet pardon and rest. That day I found by the wayside a little child, scarcely more than a baby; it had wandered out of the poorhouse, where its mother had died the week before, a stranger passing through the village. No one knew anything about her nor cared to know, for she was almost in rags, fair and delicate once they told me, but wasted with illness and too far gone to talk. Then a second thought came to me, — expiation. I would take this forlorn little creature and bring her up as my own child, tenderly, carefully, — a life for a life. My poor old sister took to the child wonderfully, it seemed to brighten her desolation into something that was almost happiness; we wandered awhile longer, and then came westward through the lakes, but it was several years before we were fairly settled here. Shadow took care of the baby and made her little dresses; then, when the time came to teach her to sew and read, she said more help was needed, and went alone to the towns below to find a fit servant, coming back in her silent way with old Orange, another stray lost out of its place in the world, and suffering from want in the cold Northern city. You must not think that Silver is totally ignorant; Shadow had the education of her day, poor thing, for ours was a good old family as old families go in this new country of ours, where three generations of well-to-do people constitute aristocracy. But religion, so called, I have not taught her. Is she any the worse for its want?"

"I will teach her," said Waring, passing over the question (which was a puzzling one), for the new idea, the strange interest he felt in the task before him, the fair pure mind where his hand, and his alone, would be the first to write the story of good and evil.

"That I should become attached to the child was natural," continued old Fog; "but God gave it to me to love her with so great a love that my days have flown; for her to sail out over the stormy water, for her to hunt through the icy woods, for her to dare a thousand deaths, to labor, to save, to suffer,—these have been my pleasures through all the years. When I came home, there she was to meet me, her sweet voice calling me father, the only father she could ever know. When my poor old sister died, I took her away in my boat by night and buried her in deep water; and so I did with the boy we had here for a year or two, saved from a wreck. My darling knows nothing of death; I could not tell her."

"And those wrecks," said Waring; "how do you make them balance with your scheme of expiation?"

The old man sat silent a moment; then he brought

his hand down violently on the table by his side. "I will not have them brought up in that way, I tell you I will not! Have I not explained that I was desperate?" he said in an excited voice. "What are one or two miserable crews to the delicate life of my beautiful child? And the men had their chances, too, in spite of my lure. Does not every storm threaten them with deathly force? Wait until you are tempted, before you judge me, boy. But shall I tell you the whole? Listen, then. Those wrecks were the greatest sacrifices, the most bitter tasks of my hard life, the nearest approach I have yet made to the expiation. Do you suppose I wished to drown the men? Do you suppose I did not know the greatness of the crime? Ah, I knew it only too well, and yet I sailed out and did the deed! It was for her,—to keep her from suffering; so I sacrificed myself unflinchingly. I would murder a thousand men in cold blood, and bear the thousand additional punishments without a murmur throughout a thousand ages of eternity, to keep my darling safe and warm. Do you not see that the whole was a self-immolation, the greatest, the most complete I could make? I vowed to keep my darling tenderly. I have kept my vow; see that you keep yours."

The voice ceased, the story was told, and the teller gone. The curtain over the past was never lifted again; but often, in after years, Waring thought of this strange life and its stranger philosophy. He could not judge them. Can we?

The next day the talk turned upon Silver. "I know you love her," said the old man, "but how much?"

"Does it need the asking?" answered Waring with a short laugh; "am I not giving up my name, my life, into her hands?"

"You could not give them into hands more pure."

"I know it; I am content. And yet, I sacrifice something," replied the young man, thinking of his home, his family, his friends.

Old Fog looked at him. "Do you hesitate?" he said, breaking the pause.

"Of course I do not; why do you ask?" replied Waring, irritably. "But some things may be pardoned, I think, in a case like mine."

"I pardon them."

"I can teach her, of course, and a year or so among cultivated people will work wonders; I think I shall take her abroad, first. How soon did you say we could go?"

"The ice is moving. There will be vessels through the straits in two or three weeks," replied Fog. His voice shook. Waring looked up; the old man was weeping. "Forgive me," he said, brokenly, "but the little girl is very dear to me."

The younger man was touched. "She shall be as dear to me as she has been to you," he said; "do not fear. My love is proved by the very struggle I have made against it. I venture to say no man ever fought harder against himself than I have in this old castle of yours. I kept that Titian picture as a counter-charm. It resembles a woman who, at a word, will give me herself and her fortune, — a woman high in the cultivated circles of cities both here and abroad, beautiful, accomplished, a queen in her little sphere. But all was useless. That long night in the snow, when I crawled backwards and forwards to keep myself from freezing, it came to me with power that the whole of earth and all its gifts compared not with this love. Old man, she will be happy with me."

"I know it."

"Did you foresee this end?" asked Waring after a while, watching, as he spoke, the expression of the face before him. He could not rid himself of the belief that the old man had laid his plans deftly.

"I could only hope for it: I saw that she loved you."

"Well, well," said the younger man, magnanimously, "it was natural, after all. Your expiation has ended better than you hoped; for the little orphan child you have reared has found a home and friends, and you yourself need work no more. Choose your abode here or anywhere else in the West, and I will see that you are comfortable."

"I will stay on here."

"As you please. Silver will not forget you; she

will write often. I think I will go first up the Rhine and then into Switzerland," continued Waring, going back to himself and his plans with the matter-of-course egotism of youth and love. And old Fog listened.

What need to picture the love-scene that followed? The next morning a strong hand knocked at the door of the flower-room, and the shy little maiden within had her first lesson in love, or rather in its expression, while all the blossoms listened and the birds looked on approvingly. To do him justice, Waring was an humble suitor when alone with her; she was so fair, so pure, so utterly ignorant of the world and of life, that he felt himself unworthy, and bowed his head. But the mood passed, and Silver liked him better when the old self-assertion and quick tone of command came uppermost again. She knew not good from evil, she could not comprehend or analyze the feeling in her heart; but she loved this stranger, this master, with the whole of her being. Jarvis Waring knew good from evil (more of the latter knew he than of the former), he comprehended and analyzed fully the feeling that possessed him; but, man of the world as he was, he loved this little water-maiden, this fair pagan, this strange isolated girl, with the whole force of his nature. "Silver," he said to her, seriously enough, "do you know how much I love you? I am afraid to think what life would seem without you."

"Why think of it, then, since I am here?" replied Silver. "Do you know, Jarvis, I think if I had not loved you so much, you would not have loved me, and then — it would have been — that is, I mean — it would have been different — " She paused; unused to reasoning or to anything like argument, her own words seemed to bewilder her.

Waring laughed, but soon grew serious again. "Silver," he said, taking her into his arms, "are you sure that you can love me as I crave?" (For he seemed at times tormented by the doubt as to whether she was anything more than a beautiful child.) He held her closely and would not let her go, compelling her to meet his ardent eyes. A change came over the girl, a sudden red flashed up into her temples and down into her white throat. She drew herself impetuously away from her lover's arms and fled from the room. "I am not sure but that she is a water-sprite, after all," grumbled Waring, as he followed her. But it was a pleasure now to grumble and pretend to doubt, since from that moment he was sure.

The next morning Fog seemed unusually cheerful.

"No wonder," thought Waring. But the character of benefactor pleased him, and he appeared in it constantly.

"We must have the old castle more comfortable; I will try to send up furniture from below," he remarked, while pacing to and fro in the evening.

"Is n't it comfortable now?" said Silver. "I am sure I always thought this room beautiful."

"What, this clumsy imitation of a second-class Western steamer? Child, it is hideous!"

"Is it?" said Silver, looking around in innocent surprise, while old Fog listened in silence. Hours of patient labor and risks not a few over the stormy lake were associated with each one of the articles Waring so cavalierly condemned.

Then it was, "How you do look, old gentleman! I must really send you up some new clothes.—Silver, how have you been able to endure such shabby rags so long? All the years before I came, did it never force itself upon you?"

"I do not know,—I never noticed; it was always just papa, you know," replied Silver, her blue eyes resting on the old man's clothes with a new and perplexed attention.

But Fog bore himself cheerily. "He is right, Silver," he said, "I am shabby indeed. But when you go out into the world, you will soon forget it."

"Yes," said Silver, tranquilly.

The days flew by and the ice moved out. This is the phrase that is always used along the lakes. The ice "moves out" of every harbor from Ogdensburg to Duluth. You can see the great white floes drift away into the horizon, and the question comes, Where do they go? Do they not meet out there the counter floes from the Canada side, and then do they all join hands and sink at a given signal to the bottom? Certainly, there is nothing melting in the mood of the raw spring winds and clouded skies.

"What are your plans?" asked old Fog, abruptly, one morning when the gulls had flown out to sea, and the fog came stealing up from the south.

"For what?"

"For the marriage."

"Aha!" thought Waring, with a smile of covert amusement, "he is in a hurry to secure the prize, is he? The sharp old fellow!" Aloud he said, "I thought we would all three sail over to Mackinac; and there we could be married, Silver and I, by the fort chaplain, and take the first Buffalo steamer; you could return here at your leisure."

"Would it not be a better plan to bring a clergyman here, and then you two could sail without me? I am not as strong as I was; I feel that I cannot bear— I mean that you had better go without me."

"As you please; I thought it would be a change for you, that was all."

"It would only prolong— No, I think, if you are willing, we will have the marriage here, and then you can sail immediately."

"Very well; but I did not suppose you would be in such haste to part with Silver," said Waring, unable to resist showing his comprehension of what he considered the manœuvres of the old man. Then, waiving further discussion, — "And where shall we find a clergyman?" he asked.

"There is one over on Beaver."

"He must be a singular sort of a divine to be living there!"

"He is; a strayed spirit, as it were, but a genuine clergyman of the Presbyterian church, none the less. I never knew exactly what he represented there, but I think he came out originally as a sort of missionary."

"To the Mormons," said Waring, laughing; for he had heard old Fog tell many a story of the Latter-Day Saints, who had on Beaver Island at that time their most eastern settlement.

"No; to the Indians, — sent out by some of those New England societies, you know. When he reached the islands, he found the Indians mostly gone, and those who remained were all Roman Catholics. But he settled down, farmed a little, hunted a little, fished a little, and held a service all by himself occasionally in an old log-house, just often enough to draw his salary and to write up in his semiannual reports. He is n't a bad sort of a man in his way."

"And how does he get on with the Mormons?"

"Excellently. He lets them talk, and sells them fish, and shuts his eyes to everything else."

"What is his name?"

"Well, over there they call him the Preacher, principally because he does not preach, I suppose. It is a way they have over on Beaver to call people names; they call me Believer."

"Believer?"

"Yes, because I believe nothing; at least so *they* think."

A few days later, out they sailed over the freed water, around the point, through the sedge-gate growing green again, across the channelled marsh, and out towards the Beavers,—Fog and Waring, armed as if for a foray.

"Why?" asked Waring.

"It 's safer; the Mormons are a queer lot," was the reply.

When they came in sight of the islands, the younger man scanned them curiously. Some years later an expedition composed of exasperated crews of lake schooners, exasperated fishermen, exasperated mainland settlers, sailed westward through the straits bound for these islands, armed to the teeth and determined upon vengeance and slaughter. False lights, stolen nets, and stolen wives were their grievances; and no aid coming from the general government, then as now sorely perplexed over the Mormon problem, they took justice into their own hands and sailed bravely out, with the stars and stripes floating from the mast of their flag-ship,—an old scow impressed for military service. But this was later; and when Fog and Waring came scudding into the harbor, the wild little village existed in all its pristine outlawry, a city of refuge for the flotsam vagabondage of the lower lakes.

"Perhaps he will not come with us," suggested Waring.

"I have thought of that, but it need not delay us long," replied Fog; "we can kidnap him."

"Kidnap him?"

"Yes; he is but a small chap," said the old man, tranquilly.

They fastened their boat to the long log-dock, and started ashore. The houses of the settlement straggled irregularly along the beach and inland towards the fields where fine crops were raised by the Saints, who had made here, as is their custom everywhere, a garden in the wilderness; the only defence was simple but strong,—an earthwork on one of the white sand-hills back of the village, over whose rampart peeped two small cannon, commanding the harbor. Once on shore, however, a foe found only a living, moving rampart of flesh and blood, as reckless a set of villains as New World history can produce. But this rampart came together only in times of danger; ordinary visitors, coming by twos and threes, they welcomed or murdered as they saw fit, or according to the probable contents of their pockets, each man for himself and his family. Some of these patriarchal gentlemen glared from their windows at Fog and Waring as they passed along; but the worn clothes not promising much, they simply invited them to dinner; they liked to hear the news, when there was nothing else going on. Old Fog excused himself. They had business, he said, with the Preacher; was he at home?

He was; had anything been sent to him from the East,—any clothes, now, for the Indians?

Old Fog had heard something of a box at Mackinac, waiting for a schooner to bring it over. He was glad it was on the way, it would be of so much use to the Indians,—they wore so many clothes.

The patriarchs grinned, and allowed the two to pass on. Waring had gazed within, meanwhile, and discovered the plural wives, more or less good-looking, generally less; they did not seem unhappy, however, not so much so as many a single one he had met in more luxurious homes, and he said to himself, "Women of the lower class are much better and happier when well curbed." It did not occur to him that possibly the evil tempers of men of the lower class are made more endurable by a system of co-operation; one reed bends, breaks, and dies, but ten reeds together can endure.

The Preacher was at home on the outskirts,—a little man, round and rosy, with black eyes and a cheery voice. He was attired entirely in blanket-cloth, baggy trousers and a long blouse, so that he looked not unlike a Turkish Santa Claus, Oriental as to under, and arctic as to upper rigging. "Are you a clergyman?" said Waring, inspecting him with curious eyes.

"If you doubt it, look at this," said the little man; and he brought out a clerical suit of limp black cloth, and a ministerial hat much the worse for wear. These articles he suspended from a nail, so that they looked as if a very poor lean divine had hung himself there. Then he sat down, and took his turn at staring. "I do not bury the dead," he remarked after a moment, as if convinced that the two shabby hunters before him could have no other errand.

Waring was about to explain, but old Fog stopped him with a glance. "You are to come with us, sir," he said courteously; "you will be well treated, well paid, and returned in a few days."

"Come with you! Where?"

"Never mind where; will you come?"

"No," said the little blanket-man, stoutly.

In an instant Fog had tripped him up, seized a sheet and blanket from the bed, bound his hands and feet with one, and wrapped him in the other. "Now, then," he said shouldering the load, "open the door."

"But the Mormons," objected Waring.

"O, they like a joke, they will only laugh! But if, by any chance, they should show fight, fire at once," replied the old man, leading the way. Waring followed, his mind anything but easy; it seemed to him like running the gantlet. He held his pistols ready, and glanced furtively around as they skirted the town and turned down towards the beach. "If any noise is made," Fog had remarked, "I shall know what to do."

Whereupon the captive swallowed down his wrath and a good deal of woollen fuzz, and kept silence. He was no coward, this little Preacher. He held his own manfully on the Beavers; but no one had ever carried him off in a blanket before. So he silently considered the situation.

When near the boat they came upon more patriarchs. "Put a bold face on it," murmured old Fog. "Whom do you suppose we have here?" he began, as they approached. "Nothing less than your little Preacher; we want to borrow him for a few days."

The patriarchs stared.

"Don't you believe it?—Speak up, Preacher; are you being carried off?"

No answer.

"You had better speak," said Fog, jocosely, at the same time giving his captive a warning touch with his elbow.

The Preacher had revolved the situation rapidly, and perceived that in any contest his round body would inevitably suffer from friend and foe alike. He was not even sure but that he would be used as a missile, a sort of ponderous pillow swung by one end.

So he replied briskly, "Yes, I am being carried as you see, dear brethren; I don't care about walking to-day."

The patriarchs laughed, and followed on to the boat, laughing still more when Fog gayly tossed in his load of blanket, and they could hear the little man growl as he came down. "I say, though, when are you going to bring him back, Believer?" said one.

"In a few days," replied Fog, setting sail.

Away they flew; and, when out of harbor, the captive was released, and Waring told him what was required.

"Why did n't you say so before?" said the little blanket-man; "nothing I like better than a wedding, and a drop of punch afterwards."

His task over, Fog relapsed into silence; but Waring, curious, asked many a question about the island and its inhabitants. The Preacher responded freely in all things, save when the talk glided too near himself. The Mormons were not so bad, he thought; they had their faults, of course, but you must take them on the right side.

"Have they a right side?" asked Waring.

"At least they have n't a rasping, mean, cold, starving, bony, freezing, busy-bodying side," was the reply, delivered energetically; whereat Waring concluded the little man had had his own page of history back somewhere among the decorous New England hills.

Before they came to the marsh they blindfolded their guest, and did not remove the bandage until he was safely within the long room of the castle. Silver met them, radiant in the firelight.

"Heaven grant you its blessing, maiden," said the Preacher, becoming Biblical at once. He meant it, however, for he sat gazing at her long with moistened eyes, forgetful even of the good cheer on the table; a gleam from his far-back youth came to him, a snow-drop that bloomed and died in bleak New Hampshire long, long before.

The wedding was in the early morning. Old Fog had hurried it, hurried everything; he seemed driven by a spirit of unrest, and wandered from place to place, from room to room, his eyes fixed in a vacant way upon the familiar objects. At the last moment he appeared with a prayer-book, its lettering old, its cover tarnished. "Have you any objection to using the Episcopal service?" he asked in a low tone. "I—I have heard the Episcopal service."

"None in the world," replied the affable little Preacher.

But he too grew sober and even earnest as Silver appeared, clad in white, her dress and hair wreathed with the trailing arbutus, the first flower of spring, plucked from under the vanishing snows. So beautiful her face, so heavenly its expression, that Waring, as he took her hand, felt his eyes grow dim, and he vowed to himself to cherish her with tenderest love forever.

"We are gathered together here in the sight of God," began the Preacher solemnly; and old Fog, standing behind, shrank into the shadow, and bowed his head upon his hands. But when the demand came, "Who giveth this woman to be married to this man?" he stepped forward, and gave away his child without a tear, nay, with even a smile on his brave old face.

"To love, cherish, and to obey," repeated Silver in her clear sweet voice.

And then Waring placed upon her finger the little ring he himself had carved out of wood. "It shall never be changed," he said, "but coated over with heavy gold, just as it is."

Old Orange, radiant with happiness, stood near, and served as a foil for the bridal white.

It was over; but they were not to start until noon.

Fog put the Preacher almost forcibly into the boat and sailed away with him, blindfolded and lamenting.

"The wedding feast," he cried, "and the punch! You are a fine host, old gentleman."

"Everything is here, packed in those baskets. I have even given you two fine dogs. And there is your fee. I shall take you in sight of the Beavers, and then put you into the skiff and leave you to row over alone. The weather is fine, you can reach there to-morrow."

Remonstrance died away before the bag of money; old Fog had given his all for his darling's marriage-fee. "I shall have no further use for it," he thought, mechanically.

So the little blanket-man paddled away in his skiff with his share of the wedding-feast beside him; the two dogs went with him, and became good Mormons.

Old Fog returned in the sail-boat through the channels, and fastened the sedge-gate open for the outgoing craft. Silver, timid and happy, stood on the balcony as he approached the castle.

"It is time to start," said the impatient bridegroom. "How long you have been, Fog!"

The old man made no answer, but busied himself arranging the boat; the voyage to Mackinac would last two or three days, and he had provided every possible comfort for their little camps on shore.

"Come," said Waring, from below.

Then the father went up to say good by. Silver flung her arms around his neck and burst into tears. "Father, father," she sobbed, "must I leave you? O father, father!"

He soothed her gently; but something in the expression of his calm, pallid face touched the deeper feelings of the wakening woman, and she clung to him desperately, realizing, perhaps, at this last moment, how great was his love for her, how great his desolation. Waring had joined them on the balcony. He bore with her awhile and tried to calm her grief, but the girl turned from him and clung to the old man; it was as though she saw at last how she had robbed him. "I cannot leave him thus," she sobbed; "O father, father!"

Then Waring struck at the root of the difficulty. (Forgive him; he was hurt to the core.) "But he is not your father," he said, "he has no claim upon you. I am your husband now, Silver, and you must come with me; do you not wish to come with me, darling?" he added, his voice sinking into fondness.

"Not my father!" said the girl. Her arms fell, and she stood as if petrified.

"No, dear; he is right. I am not your father," said old Fog, gently. A spasm passed over his features, he kissed her hastily, and gave her into her husband's arms. In another moment they were afloat, in two the sail filled and the boat glided away. The old man stood on the castle roof, smiling and waving his hand; below, Orange fluttered her red handkerchief from the balcony, and blessed her darling with African mummeries. The point was soon rounded, the boat gone.

That night, when the soft spring moonlight lay over the water, a sail came gliding back to the castle, and a shape flew up the ladder; it was the bride of the morning.

"O father, father, I could not leave you so, I made him bring me back, if only for a few days! O father, father! for you are my father, the only father I can ever know, — and so kind and good!"

In the gloom she knelt by his bedside, and her arms were around his neck. Waring came in afterwards, silent and annoyed, yet not unkind. He stirred the dying brands into a flame.

"What is this?" he said, starting, as the light fell across the pillow.

"It is nothing," replied Fog, and his voice sounded far away; "I am an old man, children, and all is well."

They watched him through the dawning, through the lovely day, through the sunset, Waring repentant, Silver absorbed in his every breath; she lavished upon him now all the wealth of love her unconscious years had gathered. Orange seemed to agree with her master that all was well. She came and went, but not sadly, and crooned to herself some strange African tune that rose and fell more like a chant of triumph than a dirge. She was doing her part, according to her light, to ease the going of the soul out of this world.

Grayer grew the worn face, fainter the voice, colder the shrivelled old hands in the girl's fond clasp.

"O Jarvis, Jarvis, what is this?" she murmured, fearfully.

Waring came to her side and put his strong arm around her. " My little wife," he said, " this is Death. But do not fear."

And then he told her the story of the Cross; and, as it came to her a revelation, so, in the telling, it became to him, for the first time, a belief.

Old Fog told them to bury him out in deep water, as he had buried the others; and then he lay placid, a great happiness shining in his eyes.

"It is well," he said, "and God is very good to me. Life would have been hard without you, darling. Something seemed to give way when you said good by; but now that I am called, it is sweet to know that you are happy, and sweeter still to think that you came back to me at the last. Be kind to her, Waring. I know you love her; but guard her tenderly, — she is but frail. I die content, my child, quite content; do not grieve for me."

Then, as the light faded from his eyes, he folded his hands. "Is it expiated, O God? Is it expiated?" he murmured.

There was no answer for him on earth.

They buried him as he had directed, and then they sailed away, taking the old black with them. The castle was left alone; the flowers bloomed on through the summer, and the rooms held the old furniture bravely through the long winter. But gradually the walls fell in, and the water entered. The fogs still steal across the lake, and wave their gray draperies up into the northern curve; but the sedge-gate is gone, and the castle is indeed Nowhere.

Very interesting

PETER THE PARSON.

IN November, 1850, a little mining settlement stood forlornly on the shore of Lake Superior. A log-dock ran out into the dark water; a roughly built furnace threw a glare against the dark sky; several stamping-mills kept up their monotonous tramping day and night; and evil-minded saloons beset the steps on all sides. Back into the pine forest ran the white-sand road leading to the mine, and on the right were clustered the houses, which were scarcely better than shanties, although adorned with sidling porches and sham-windowed fronts. Winter begins early in these high latitudes. Navigation was still open, for a scow with patched sails was coming slowly up the bay; but the air was cold, and the light snow of the preceding night clung unmelted on the north side of the trees. The pine forest had been burned away to make room for the village; blackened stumps rose everywhere in the weedy streets, and, on the outskirts of the clearing, grew into tall skeletons, bleached white without, but black and charred within,—a desolate framing for a desolate picture. Everything was bare, jagged, and unfinished; each poor house showed hasty makeshifts,—no doors latched, no windows fitted. Pigs were the principal pedestrians. At four o'clock this cold November afternoon, the saloons, with their pine fires and red curtains, were by far the most cheerful spots in the landscape, and their ruddy invitations to perdition were not counterbalanced by a single opposing gleam, until the Rev. Herman Peters prepared his chapel for vespers.

Herman Warriner Peters was a slender little man, whose blue eyes, fair hair, and unbearded face misled the observer into the idea of extreme youth. There was a boyishness in his air, or, rather, lack of air, and a nervous timidity in his manner, which stamped him as a person of no importance,—one of those men who, not of sufficient consequence to be disliked, are simply ignored by a well-bred world, which pardons anything rather than insignificance. And if ignored by a well-bred world, what by an ill-bred? Society at Algonquin was worse than ill-bred, inasmuch as it had never been bred at all. Like all mining settlements, it esteemed physical strength the highest good, and next to that an undaunted demeanor and flowing vocabulary, designated admiringly as "powerful sassy." Accordingly it made unlimited fun of the Rev. Herman Warriner Peters, and derived much enjoyment from calling him "Peter," pretending to think it was his real name, and solemnly persisting in the mistake in spite of all the painstaking corrections of the unsuspecting little man.

The Rev. Herman wrapped himself in his thin old cloak and twisted a comforter around his little throat, as the clock warned him of the hour. He was not leaving much comfort behind him; the room was dreary and bare, without carpet, fire, or easy-chair. A cot-bed, which sagged hopelessly, a wash-bowl set on a dry-goods box, flanked by a piece of bar-soap and a crash towel, a few pegs on the cracked wall, one wooden chair and his own little trunk, completed the furniture. The Rev. Herman boarded with Mrs. Malone, and ate her streaked biscuit and fried meat without complaint. The woman could rise to yeast and a gridiron when the surveyors visited Algonquin, or when the directors of the iron company came up in the summer; but the streaked biscuit and fried steak were "good enough for the little parson, bless him!"

There were some things in the room, however, other than furniture, namely, a shelf full of religious books, a large and appalling picture of the crucifixion, and a cross six feet in height, roughly made of pine saplings, and fixed to the floor in a wooden block. There was also a small colored picture, with the words "Santa Margarita" inscribed beneath. The picture stood on a bracket fashioned of shingles, and below it hung a poor little vase filled with the last colored leaves.

"Ye only want the Howly Vargin now, to be all right, yer riverence," said Mrs. Malone, who was, in name at least, a Roman Catholic.

"All honor and affection are, no doubt, due to the Holy Mary," answered the Rev. Herman, nervously; "but the Anglican Church does not — at present — allow her claim to — to adoration." And he sighed.

"Why don't yer jest come right out now, and be a rale Catholic?" said Mrs. Malone, with a touch of sympathy. "You 're next door to it, and it 's aisy to see yer ain't happy in yer mind. If yer was a rale praste, now, with the coat and all, 'stead of being a make-believe, the boys ud respect yer more, and would n't notice yer soize so much. Or yer might go back to the cities (for I don't deny they do loike a big fist up here), and loikely enough yer could find aisy work there that ud suit yer."

"I like hard work, Mrs. Malone," said the little parson.

"But you 're not fit for it, sir. You 'll niver get on here if yer stay till judgment day. Why, yer ain't got ten people, all told, belongin' to yer chapel, and you 're here a year already!"

The Rev. Herman sighed again, but made no answer. He sighed now as he left his cold room and stepped out into the cold street. The wind blew as he made his way along between the stumps, carefully going round the pigs, who had selected the best places for their siestas. He held down his comforter with one bare hand; the other clutched the end of a row of books, which filled his thin arm from the shoulder down. He limped as he walked. An ankle had been cruelly injured some months previously; the wound had healed, but he was left permanently and awkwardly lame. At the time, the dastardly injury had roused a deep bitterness in the parson's heart, for grace and activity had been his one poor little bodily gift, his one small pride. The activity had returned, not the grace. But he had learned to limp bravely along, and the bitterness had passed away.

Lights shone comfortably from the Pine-Cone Saloon as he passed.

"Hallo! Here's Peter the Parson," sang out a miner, standing at the door; and forth streamed all the loungers to look at him.

"Say, Peter, come in and have a drop to warm yer," said one.

"Look at his poor little ribs, will yer?" said another, as his cloak blew out like a sail.

"Let him alone! He's going to have his preaching all to himself, as usual," said a third. "Them books is all the congregation *he* can get, poor little chap!"

The parson's sensitive ears heard every word. He quickened his steps, and, with his usual nervous awkwardness, stumbled and fell, dropping all the books, amid the jeering applause of the bystanders. Silently he rose and began collecting his load, the wind every now and then blowing his cloak over his head as he stooped, and his difficulties increased by the occasional gift of a potato full in the breast, and a flood of witty commentaries from the laughing group at the saloon door. As he picked up the last volume and turned away, a missile, deftly aimed, took off his hat, and sent it over a fence into a neighboring field. The parson hesitated; but as a small boy had already given chase, not to bring it back, but to send it further away, he abandoned the hat,—his only one,—and walked on among the stumps bareheaded, his thin hair blown about by the raw wind, and his blue eyes reddened with cold and grief.

The Episcopal Church of St. John and St. James was a rough little building, with recess-chancel, ill-set Gothic windows, and a half-finished tower. It owed its existence to the zeal of a director's wife, who herself embroidered its altar-cloth and book-marks, and sent thither the artificial flowers and candles which she dared not suggest at home; the poor Indians, at least, should not be deprived of them! The director's wife died, but left by will a pittance of two hundred dollars per annum towards the rector's salary. In her fancy she saw Algonquin a thriving town, whose inhabitants believed in the Anglican succession, and sent their children to Sunday school. In reality, Algonquin remained a lawless mining settlement, whose inhabitants believed in nothing, and whose children hardly knew what Sunday meant, unless it was more whiskey than usual. The two hundred dollars and the chapel, however, remained fixed facts; and the Eastern directors, therefore, ordered a picturesque church to be delineated on their circulars, and themselves constituted a non-resident vestry. One or two young missionaries had already tried the field, failed, and gone away; but the present incumbent, who had equally tried and equally failed, remained.

On this occasion he unlocked the door and entered the little sanctuary. It was cold and dark, but he made no fire, for there was neither stove nor hearth. Lighting two candles,—one for the congregation and one for himself,—he distributed the books among the benches and the chancel, and dusted carefully the little altar, with its faded embroideries and flowers. Then he retired into the shed which served as a vestry-room, and in a few minutes issued forth, clad in his robes of office, and knelt at the chancel rail. There was no bell to summon the congregation, and no congregation to summon; but still he began in his clear voice, "Dearly beloved brethren," and continued on unwavering through the Confession, the Absolution, and the Psalms, leaving a silence for the corresponding responses, and devoutly beginning the first lesson. In the midst of "Zephaniah" there was a slight noise at the door and a step sounded over the rough floor. The solitary reader did not raise his eyes; and, the lesson over, he bravely lifted up his mild tenor in the chant, "It is a good thing to give thanks unto the Lord, and to sing praises unto thy name, O Most Highest." A girl's voice took up the air; the mild tenor dropped into its own part, and the two continued the service in a duet, spoken and sung, to its close. Then the minister retired, with his candle, to the shed, and, hanging up his surplice, patiently waited, pacing to and fro in the cold. Patiently waited; and for what? For the going away of the only friend he had in Algonquin.

The congregation lingered; its shawl must be refastened; indeed, it must be entirely refolded. Its hat must be retied, and the ribbons carefully smoothed. Still there was no sound from the vestry-room. It collected all the prayer-books, and piled them near the candle, making a separate journey for each little volume. Still no one. At last, with lingering step and backward glance, slowly it departed and carried its disappointed face homeward. Then Peter the Parson issued forth, lifted the careful pile of books with tender hand, and, extinguishing the lights, went out bareheaded into the darkness. The vesper service of St. John and St. James was over.

After a hot, unwholesome supper the minister returned to his room and tried to read; but the candle flickered, the cold seemed to blur the book, and he found himself gazing at the words without taking in their sense. Then he began to read aloud, slowly walking up and down, and carrying the candle to light the page; but through all the learned sentences there still crept to the surface the miserable consciousness of bodily cold. "And mental, too, Heaven help me!" he thought. "But I cannot afford a fire at this season, and, indeed, it ought not to be necessary. This delicacy must be subdued; I will go out and walk." Putting on his cloak and comforter, (O, deceitful name!) he remembered that he had no hat. Would his slender store of money allow a new one? Unlocking his trunk, he drew out a thin purse hidden away among his few carefully folded clothes, — the poor trunk was but half full, — and counted its contents. The sum was pitifully small, and it must yet last many weeks. But a hat was necessary, whereas a fire was a mere luxury. "I must harden myself," thought the little parson, sternly, as he caught himself shuddering with the cold; "this evil tendency to self-indulgence must and shall be crushed."

He went down towards the dock where stood the one store of Algonquin, — stealing along in the darkness to hide his uncovered condition. Buying a hat, the poorest one there, from the Jew proprietor, he lingered a moment near the stove to warm his chilled hands. Mr. Marx, rendered good-natured by the bold cheat he had perpetrated, affably began a conversation.

"Sorry to see yer still limp bad. But it ain't so hard as it would be if yer was a larger man. Yer see there ain't much of yer to limp; that 's one comfort. Hope business is good at yer chapel, and that Mrs. Malone gives yer enough to eat; yer don't look like it, though. The winter has sot in early, and times is hard." And did the parson know that "Brother Saul has come in from the mine, and is a holding forth in the school-house this very minit?"

No; the parson did not know it. But he put on his new hat, whose moth-holes had been skilfully blackened over with ink, and turned towards the door.

"It 's nothing to me, of course," continued Mr. Marx, with a liberal wave of his dirty hand; "all your religions are alike to me, I 'm free to say. But I wonder yer and Saul don't work together, parson. Yer might do a heap of good if yer was to pull at the same oar, now."

The words echoed in the parson's ears as he walked down to the beach, the only promenade in Algonquin free from stumps. Could he do a "heap of good," by working with that ignorant, coarse, roaring brother, whose blatant pride, dirty shirt, and irreverent familiarity with all things sacred were alike distasteful, nay, horrible to his sensitive mind? Pondering, he paced the narrow strip of sand under the low bluff; but all his efforts did not suffice to quicken or warm his chilled blood. Nevertheless, he expanded his sunken chest and drew in long breaths of the cold night air, and beat his little hands vigorously together, and ran to and fro. "Aha!" he said to himself, "this is glorious exercise." And then he went home, colder than ever; it was his way thus to make a reality of what ought to be.

Passing through one of the so-called streets, he saw a ruddy glow in front of the school-house; it was a pine-knot fire whose flaring summons had not been unheeded. The parson stopped a moment and warmed himself, glancing meanwhile furtively within, where Brother Saul was holding forth in clarion tones to a crowded congregation; his words reached the listener's ear, and verified the old proverb. "There 's brimstone and a fiery furnace for them as doubts the truth, I tell you. Prayin' out of a book — and flowers — and candles — and night-gownds 'stead of decent coats — for it 's night-gownds they look like, though they may call them surpluses" (applause from the miners) — "won't do no good. Sech nonsense will never save souls. You 've jest got to fall down on your knees and pray hard — hard — with groaning and roaring of the spirit

— until you 're as weak as a rag. Nothing else will do; nothing, — nothing."

The parson hurried away, shrinking (though unseen) from the rough finger pointed at him. Before he was out of hearing a hymn sounded forth on the night breeze, — one of those nondescript songs that belong to the border, a favorite with the Algonquin miners, because of a swinging chorus wherein they roared out their wish to "die a-shouting," in company with all the kings and prophets of Israel, each one fraternally mentioned by name.

Reaching his room, the parson hung up his cloak and hat, and sat down quietly with folded hands. Clad in dressing-gown and slippers, in an easy-chair, before a bright fire, — a revery, thus, is the natural ending for a young man's day. But here the chair was hard and straight-backed, there was no fire, and the candle burned with a feeble blue flame; the small figure in its limp black clothes, with its little gaitered feet pressed close together on the cold floor as if for warmth, its clasped hands, its pale face and blue eyes fixed on the blank expanse of the plastered wall, was pathetic in its patient discomfort. After a while a tear fell on the clasped hands and startled their coldness with its warmth. The parson brushed the token of weakness hastily away, and rising, threw himself at the foot of the large wooden cross with his arms clasping its base. In silence for many moments he lay thus prostrate; then, extinguishing the candle, he sought his poor couch. But later in the night, when all Algonquin slept, a crash of something falling was heard in the dark room, followed by the sound of a scourge mercilessly used, and murmured Latin prayers, — the old cries of penitence that rose during night-vigils from the monasteries of the Middle Ages. And why not English words? Was there not something of affectation in the use of these mediæval phrases? Maybe so; but at least there was nothing affected in the stripes made by the scourge. The next morning all was as usual in the little room, save that the picture of Santa Margarita was torn in twain, and the bracket and vase shattered to fragments on the floor below.

At dawn the parson rose, and, after a conscientious bath in the tub of icy water brought in by his own hands the previous evening, he started out with his load of prayer-books, his face looking haggard and blue in the cold morning light. Again he entered the chapel, and having arranged the books and dusted the altar, he attired himself in his robes and began the service at half past six precisely. "From the rising of the sun even unto the going down of the same," he read, and in truth the sun was just rising. As the evening prayer was "vespers," so this was "matins," in the parson's mind. He had his "vestments" too, of various ritualistic styles, and washed them himself, ironing them out afterwards with fear and difficulty in Mrs. Malone's disorderly kitchen, poor little man! No hand turned the latch, no step came across the floor this morning; the parson had the service all to himself, and, as it was Friday, he went through the Litany, omitting nothing, and closing with a hymn. Then, gathering up his books, he went home to breakfast.

"How peaked yer do look, sir!" exclaimed ruddy Mrs. Malone, as she handed him a cup of muddy coffee. "What, no steak? Do, now; for I ain't got nothin' else. Well, if yer won't — But there 's nothin' but the biscuit, then. Why, even Father O'Brien himself 'lows meat for the sickly, Friday or no Friday."

"I am not sickly, Mrs. Malone," replied the little parson, with dignity.

A young man with the figure of an athlete sat at the lower end of the table, tearing the tough steak voraciously with his strong teeth, chewing audibly, and drinking with a gulping noise. He paused as the parson spoke, and regarded him with wonder not unmixed with contempt.

"You ain't sickly?" he repeated. "Well, if you ain't, then I 'd like to know who is, that 's all."

"Now, you jest eat your breakfast, Steve, and let the parson alone," interposed Mrs. Malone. "Sorry to see that little picture all tore, sir," she continued, turning the conversation in her blundering good-nature. "It was a moighty pretty picture, and looked uncommonly like Rosie Ray."

"It was a copy of an Italian painting, Mrs. Malone," the parson hastened to reply; "Santa Margarita."

"O, I dare say; but it looked iver so much like Rosie, for all that!"

A deep flush had crossed the parson's pale face. The athlete saw it, and muttered to himself angrily, casting surly sidelong glances up the table, and breathing hard; the previous evening he had happened to pass the Chapel of St. John and St. James as its congregation of one was going in the door.

After two hours spent in study, the parson went out to visit the poor and sick of the parish; all were poor, and one was sick, — the child of an Englishwoman, a miner's wife. The mother, with a memory of her English training, dusted a chair for the minister, and dropped a courtesy, as he seated himself by the little bed; but she seemed embarrassed, and talked volubly of anything and everything save the child. The parson listened to the unbroken stream of words while he stroked the boy's soft cheek and held the wasted little hand in his. At length he took a small bottle from his pocket, and looked around for a spoon; it was a pure and delicate cordial which he had often given to the sick child to sustain its waning strength.

"O, if you please, sir, — indeed, I don't feel sure that it does Harry any good. Thank you for offering it so free — but — but, if you 'd just as lieve — I — I 'd rather not, sir, if you please, sir."

The parson looked up in astonishment; the costly cordial had robbed him of many a fire.

"Why don't you tell the minister the truth?" called out a voice from the inner room, the harsh voice of the husband. "Why don't you say right out that Brother Saul was here last night, and prayed over the child, and give it some of his own medicine, and telled you not to touch the parson's stuff? He said it was pizen, he did."

The parson rose, cut to the heart. He had shared his few dimes with this woman, and had hoped much from her on account of her early church-training. On Sunday she had been one of the few who came to the chapel, and when, during the summer, she was smitten with fever, he had read over her the prayers from "The Visitation of the Sick"; he had baptized this child now fading away, and had loved the little fellow tenderly, taking pleasure in fashioning toys for his baby hands, and saving for him the few cakes of Mrs. Malone's table.

"I did n't mean to have Saul, — I did n't indeed, sir," said the mother, putting her apron to her eyes. "But Harry he was so bad last night, and the neighbors sort o' persuaded me into it. Brother Saul does pray so powerful strong, sir, that it seems as though it must do some good some way; and he's a very comfortable talker too, there's no denying that. Still, I did n't mean it, sir; and I hope you'll forgive me."

"There is nothing to forgive," replied the parson, gently; and, leaving his accustomed coin on the table, he went away.

Wandering at random through the pine forest, unable to overcome the dull depression at his heart, he came suddenly upon a large bull-dog; the creature, one of the ugliest of its kind, eyed him quietly, with a slow wrinkling of the sullen upper lip.

The parson visibly trembled.

"'Fraid, are ye?" called out a voice, and the athlete of the breakfast-table showed himself.

"Call off your dog, please, Mr. Long."

"He ain't doin' nothin', parson. But you're at liberty to kick him, if you like," said the man, laughing as the dog snuffed stealthily around the parson's gaiters. The parson shifted his position; the dog followed. He stepped aside; so did the dog. He turned and walked away with a determined effort at self-control; the dog went closely behind, brushing his ankles with his ugly muzzle. He hurried; so did the dog. At last, overcome with the nervous physical timidity which belonged to his constitution, he broke into a run, and fled as if for life, hearing the dog close behind and gaining with every step. The jeering laugh of the athlete followed him through the pine-tree aisles, but he heeded it not, and when at last he spied a log-house on one side he took refuge within like a hunted hare, breathless and trembling. An old woman smoking a pipe was its only occupant. "What's the matter?" she said. "O, the dog?" And, taking a stick of wood, she drove the animal from the door, and sent him fleeing back to his master. The parson sat down by the hearth to recover his composure.

"Why, you're most frightened to death, ain't yer?" said the old woman, as she brushed against him to make up the fire. "You're all of a tremble. I would n't stray so far from home if I was you, child."

Her vision was imperfect, and she took the small, cowering figure for a boy.

The minister went home.

After dinner, which he did not eat, as the greasy dishes offended his palate, he shut himself up in his room to prepare his sermon for the coming Sunday. It made no difference whether there would be any one to hear it or not, the sermon was always carefully written and carefully delivered, albeit short, according to the ritualistic usage, which esteems the service all, the sermon nothing. His theme on this occasion was "The General Councils of the Church"; and the sermon, an admirable production of its kind, would have been esteemed, no doubt, in English Oxford or in the General Theological Seminary of New

York City. He wrote earnestly and ardently, deriving a keen enjoyment from the work; the mechanical part also was exquisitely finished, the clear sentences standing out like the work of a sculptor. Then came vespers; and the congregation this time was composed of two, or, rather, three persons,— the girl, the owner of the dog, and the dog himself. The man entered during service with a noisy step, managing to throw over a bench, coughing, humming, and talking to his dog; half of the congregation was evidently determined upon mischief. But the other half rose with the air of a little queen, crossed the intervening space with an open prayer-book, gave it to the man, and, seating herself near by, fairly awed him into good behavior. Rose Ray was beautiful; and the lion lay at her feet. As for the dog, with a wave of her hand she ordered him out, and the beast humbly withdrew. It was noticeable that the parson's voice gained strength as the dog disappeared.

"I ain't going to stand by and see it, Rosie," said the man, as, the service over, he followed the girl into the street. "That puny little chap!"

"He cares nothing for me," answered the girl, quickly.

"He sha' n't have a chance to care, if I know myself. You 're free to say 'no' to me, Rosie, but you ain't free to say 'yes' to him. A regular coward! That 's what he is. Why, he ran away from my dog this very afternoon, — ran like he was scared to death!"

"You set the dog on him, Steve."

"Well, what if I did? He need n't have run; any other man would have sent the beast flying."

"Now, Steve, do promise me that you won't tease him any more," said the girl, laying her hand upon the man's arm as he walked by her side. His face softened.

"If he had any spirit he'd be ashamed to have a girl beggin' for him not to be teased. But never mind that; I'll let him alone fast enough, Rosie, if you will too."

"If I will," repeated the girl, drawing back, as he drew closer to her side; "what can you mean?"

"O, come now! You know very well you're always after him, — a goin' to his chapel where no one else goes hardly, — a listenin' to his preachin', — and a havin' your picture hung up in his room."

It was a random shaft, sent carelessly, more to finish the sentence with a strong point than from any real belief in the athlete's mind.

"What!"

"Leastways so Mrs. Malone said. I took breakfast there this morning."

The girl was thrown off her guard, her whole face flushed with joy; she could not for the moment hide her agitation. "My picture!" she murmured, and clasped her hands. The light from the Pine-Cone crossed her face, and revealed the whole secret. Steven Long saw it, and fell into a rage. After all, then, she did love the puny parson!

"Let him look out for himself, that 's all," he muttered with a fierce gesture, as he turned towards the saloon door. (He felt a sudden thirst for vengeance, and for whiskey.) "I 'll be even with him, and I won't be long about it neither. You 'll never have the little parson alive, Rose Ray! He 'll be found missin' some fine mornin', and nobody will be to blame but you either." He disappeared, and the girl stood watching the spot where his dark, angry face had been. After a time she went slowly homeward, troubled at heart; there was neither law nor order at Algonquin, and not without good cause did she fear.

The next morning, as the parson was coming from his solitary matin service through thick-falling snow, this girl met him, slipped a note into his hand, and disappeared like a vision. The parson went homeward, carrying the folded paper under his cloak pressed close to his heart. "I am only keeping it dry," he murmured to himself. This was the note:—

"Respected Sir, — I must see you, you air in danger. Please come to the Grotter this afternoon at three and I remain yours respectful,

"Rose Ray."

The Rev. Herman Warriner Peters read these words over and over; then he went to breakfast, but ate nothing, and, coming back to his room, he remained the whole morning motionless in his chair. At first the red flamed in his cheek, but gradually it faded, and gave place to a pinched pallor; he bowed his head upon his hands, communed with his own heart, and was still. As the dinner-bell rang he knelt down on the cold hearth, made a little funeral pyre of the note torn into fragments, watched it slowly consume, and then, carefully collecting the ashes, he laid them at the base of the large cross.

At two o'clock he set out for the Grotto, a cave two miles from the village along the shore, used by the fishermen as a camp during the summer. The snow had continued falling, and now lay deep on the even ground; the pines were loaded with it, and everything was white save the waters of the bay, heaving sullenly, dark, and leaden, as though they knew the icy fetters were nearly ready for them. The parson walked rapidly along in his awkward, halting gait; overshoes he had none, and his cloak was but a sorry substitute for the blankets and skins worn by the miners. But he did not feel cold when he opened the door of the little cabin which had been built out in front of the cave, and found himself face to face with the beautiful girl who had summoned him there. She had lighted a fire of pine knots on the hearth, and set the fishermen's rough furniture in order; she had cushioned a chair-back with her shawl, and heated a flat stone for a foot-warmer.

"Take this seat, sir," she said, leading him thither.

The parson sank into the chair and placed his old soaked gaiters on the warm stone; but he said not one word.

"I thought perhaps you'd be tired after your long walk, sir," continued the girl, "and so I took the liberty of bringing something with me." As she spoke she drew into view a basket, and took from it delicate bread, chicken, cakes, preserved strawberries, and a little tin coffee-pot which, set on the coals, straightway emitted a delicious fragrance; nothing was forgotten, — cream, sugar, nor even snowy napkins.

The parson spoke not a word.

But the girl talked for both, as with flushed cheeks and starry eyes she prepared the tempting meal, using many pretty arts and graceful motions, using in short every power she possessed to charm the silent guest. The table was spread, the viands arranged, the coffee poured into the cup; but still the parson spoke not, and his blue eyes were almost stern as he glanced at the tempting array. He touched nothing.

"I thought you would have liked it all," said the girl at last, when she saw her little offerings despised. "I brought them all out myself — and I was so glad thinking you'd like them — and now —" Her voice broke, and the tears flowed from her pretty soft eyes. A great tenderness came over the parson's face.

"Do not weep," he said, quickly. "See, I am eating. See, I am enjoying everything. It is all good, nay, delicious." And in his haste he partook of each dish, and lifted the coffee-cup to his lips. The girl's face grew joyous again, and the parson struggled bravely against his own enjoyment; in truth, what with the warm fire, the easy-chair, the delicate food, the fragrant coffee, and the eager, beautiful face before him, a sense of happiness came over him in long surges, and for the moment his soul drifted with the warm tide.

"You *do* like it, don't you?" said the girl with delight, as he slowly drank the fragrant coffee, his starved lips lingering over the delicious brown drops. Something in her voice jarred on the trained nerves and roused them to action again.

"Yes, I do like it, — only too well," he answered; but the tone of his voice had altered. He pushed back his chair, rose, and began pacing to and fro in the shadow beyond the glow of the fire.

"Thou glutton body!" he murmured. "But thou shalt go empty for this." Then, after a pause, he said in a quiet, even tone, "You had something to tell me, Miss Ray."

The girl's face had altered; but rallying, she told her story earnestly, — of Stevén Long, his fierce temper, his utter lawlessness, and his threats.

"And why should Steven Long threaten me?" said the parson. "But you need not answer," he continued in an agitated voice. "Say to Steven Long, — say to him," he repeated in louder tones, "that I shall never marry. I have consecrated my life to my holy calling."

There was a long silence; the words fell with crushing weight on both listener and speaker. We do not realize even our own determinations, sometimes, until we have told them to another. The girl rallied first; for she still hoped.

"Mr. Peters," she said, taking all her courage in her hands and coming towards him, "is it wrong to marry?"

"For me — it is."

"Why?"

"Because I am a priest."

"Are you a Catholic, then?"

"I am a Catholic, although not in the sense you mean. Mine is the true Catholic faith which the Anglican Church has kept pure from the errors of Rome, and mine it is to make my life accord with the high office I hold."

"Is it part of your high office to be cold — and hungry — and wretched?"

"I am not wretched."

"You are; now, and at all times. You are killing yourself."

"No; else I had died long, long ago."

"Well, then, of what use is your poor life as you now live it, either to yourself or any one else? Do you succeed among the miners? How many have you brought into the church?"

"Not one."

"And yourself? Have you succeeded, so far, in making yourself a saint?"

"God knows I have not," replied the parson, covering his face with his hands as the questions probed his sore, sad heart. "I have failed in my work, I have failed in myself, I am of all men most miserable! — most miserable!"

The girl sprang forward and caught his arm, her eyes full of love's pity. "You know you love me," she murmured; "why fight against it? For I — I love you!"

What did the parson do?

He fell upon his knees, but not to her, and uttered a Latin prayer, short but fervid.

"All the kingdoms of the world and the glory of them," he murmured, "would not be to me so much as this!" Then he rose.

"Child," he said, "you know not what you do." And, opening the door, he went away into the snowy forest. But the girl's weeping voice called after him, "Herman, Herman." He turned; she had sunk upon the threshold. He came back and lifted her for a moment in his arms.

"Be comforted, Rosamond," he said, tenderly. "It is but a fancy; you will soon forget me. You do not really love me, — such a one as I," he continued, bringing forward, poor heart! his own greatest sorrow with unpitying hand. "But thank you, dear, for the gentle fancy." He stood a moment, silent; then touched her dark hair with his quivering lips and disappeared.

Sunday morning the sun rose unclouded, the snow lay deep on the ground, the first ice covered the bay; winter had come. At ten o'clock the customary service began in the Chapel of St. John and St. James, and the little congregation shivered, and whispered that it must really try to raise money enough for a stove. The parson did not feel the cold, although he looked almost bloodless in his white surplice. The Englishwoman was there, repentant, — the sick child had not rallied under the new ministration; Mrs. Malone was there, from sheer good-nature; and several of the villagers and two or three miners had strolled in because they had nothing else to do, Brother Saul having returned to the mine. Rose Ray was not there. She was no saint, so she stayed at home and wept like a sinner.

The congregation, which had sat silent through the service, fell entirely asleep during the sermon on the "General Councils." Suddenly, in the midst of a sentence, there came a noise that stopped the parson and woke the sleepers. Two or three miners rushed into the chapel and spoke to the few men present. "Come out," they cried, — "come out to the mine. The thief 's caught at last! and who do you think it is? Saul, Brother Saul himself, the hypocrite! They tracked him to his den, and there they found the barrels and sacks and kegs, but the stuff he 's made away with, most of it. He took it all, every crumb, and us a starving!"

"We 've run in to tell the town," said another. "We 've got him fast, and we 're going to make a sample of him. Come out and see the fun."

"Yes," echoed a third, who lifted a ruffianly face from his short, squat figure, "and we 'll take our own time, too. He 's made us suffer, and now he shall suffer a bit, if I know myself."

The women shuddered as, with an ominous growl, all the men went out together.

"I misdoubt they 'll hang him," said Mrs. Malone, shaking her head as she looked after them.

"Or worse," said the miner's wife.

Then the two departed, and the parson was left alone. Did he cut off the service? No. Deliberately he finished every word of the sermon, sang a hymn, and spoke the final prayer; then, after putting everything in order, he too left the little sanctuary; but he did not go homeward, he took the road to the mine.

"Don't-ee go, sir, don't!" pleaded the Englishwoman, standing in her doorway as he passed. "You won't do no good, sir."

"Maybe not," answered the parson, gently, "but at least I must try."

He entered the forest; the air was still and cold, the snow crackled under his feet, and the pine-trees stretched away in long white aisles. He looked like a pygmy as he hastened on among the forest giants, his step more languid than usual from sternest vigil and fasting.

"Thou proud, evil body, I have conquered thee!" he had said in the cold dawning. And he had; at least, the body answered not again.

The mine was several miles away, and to lighten the journey the little man sang a hymn, his voice sounding through the forest in singular melody. It was an ancient hymn that he sang, written long ago by some cowled monk, and it told in quaint language of the joys of "Paradise! O Paradise!" He did not feel the cold as he sang of the pearly gates.

In the late afternoon his halting feet approached the mine; as he drew near the clearing he heard a sound of many voices shouting together, followed by a single cry, and a momentary silence more fearful than the clamor. The tormentors were at work. The parson ran forwara, and, passing the log-huts which lay between, came out upon the scene. A circle of men stood there around a stake. Fastened by a long rope, crouched the wretched prisoner, his face turned to the color of dough, his coarse features drawn apart like an animal in terror, and his hoarse voice never ceasing its piteous cry, "Have mercy, good gentlemen! Dear gentlemen, have mercy!"

At a little distance a fire of logs was burning, and from the brands scattered around it was evident that the man had served as a target for the fiery missiles; in addition he bore the marks of blows, and his clothes were torn and covered with mud as though he had been dragged roughly over the ground. The lurid light of the fire cast a glow over the faces of the miners; behind rose the Iron Mountain, dark in shadow; and on each side stretched out the ranks of the white-pine trees, like ghosts assembled as silent witnesses against the cruelty of man. The parson rushed forward, broke through the circle, and threw his arms around the prisoner at the stake, protecting him with his slender body.

"If ye kill him, ye must kill me also," he cried, in a ringing voice.

On the border, the greatest crime is robbery. A thief is worse than a murderer; a life does not count so much as life's supplies. It was not for the murderer that the Lynch law was made, but for the thief. For months these Algonquin miners had suffered loss; their goods, their provisions, their clothes, and their precious whiskey had been stolen, day after day, and all search had proved vain; exasperated, several times actually suffering from want, they had heaped up a great store of fury for the thief, — fury increased tenfold when, caught at last, he proved to be no other than Brother Saul, the one man whom they had trusted, the one man whom they had clothed and fed before themselves, the one man from whom they had expected better things. An honest, bloodthirsty wolf in his own skin was an animal they respected; indeed, they were themselves little better. But a wolf in sheep's clothing was utterly abhorrent to their peculiar sense of honor. So they gathered around their prey, and esteemed it rightfully theirs; whiskey had sharpened their enjoyment.

To this savage band, enter the little parson. "What! are ye men?" he cried. "Shame, shame, ye murderers!"

The miners stared at the small figure that defied them, and for the moment their anger gave way before a rough sense of the ludicrous.

"Hear the little man," they cried. "Hurrah, Peter! Go ahead!"

But they soon wearied of his appeal and began to answer back.

"What are clothes or provisions to a life?" said the minister.

"Life ain't worth much without 'em, Parson," replied a miner. "He took all we had, and we 've gone cold and hungry 'long of him, and he knowed it. And all the time we was a giving him of the best, and a believing his praying and his preaching."

"If he is guilty, let him be tried by the legal authorities."

"We 're our own legal 'thorities, Parson."

"The country will call you to account."

"The country won't do nothing of the kind. Much the country cares for us poor miners, frozen up here in the woods! Stand back, Parson. Why should you bother about Saul? You always hated him."

"Never! never!" answered the parson, earnestly.

"You did too, and he knowed it. 'T was because he was dirty, and could n't mince his words as you do."

The parson turned to the crouching figure at his side. "Friend," he said, "if this is true, — and the heart is darkly deceitful and hides from man his own worst sins, — I humbly ask your forgiveness."

"O come! None of your gammon," said another miner, impatiently. "Saul did n't care whether you liked him or not, for he knowed you was only a coward."

"'Fraid of a dog! 'Fraid of a dog!" shouted half a dozen voices; and a frozen twig struck the parson's cheek, and drew blood.

"Why, he 's got blood!" said one. "I never thought he had any."

"Come, Parson," said a friendly miner, advancing from the circle, "we don't want to hurt *you*, but you might as well understand that we 're the masters here."

"And if ye are the masters, then be just. Give the criminal to me; I will myself take him to the nearest judge, the nearest jail, and deliver him up."

"He 'll be more likely to deliver *you* up, I reckon, Parson."

"Well, then, send a committee of your own men with me —"

"We 've got other things to do besides taking long journeys over the ice to 'commodate thieves, Parson. Leave the man to us."

"And to torture? Men, men, ye would not treat a beast so!"

"A beast don't steal our food and whiskey," sang out a miner.

"Stand back! stand back!" shouted several voices. "You 're too little to fight, Parson."

"But not too little to die," answered the minister, throwing up his arms towards the sky.

For an instant his words held the men in check; they looked at each other, then at him.

"Think of yourselves," continued the minister. "Are ye without fault? If ye murder this man, ye are worse than he is."

But here the minister went astray in his appeal, and ran against the views of the border.

"Worse! Worse than a sneaking thief! Worse than a praying hypocrite who robs the very men that feed him! Look here, we won't stand that! Sheer off, or take the consequences." And a burning brand struck the parson's coat, and fell on the head of the crouching figure at his side, setting fire to its hair. Instantly the parson extinguished the light flame, and drew the burly form closer within his arms, so that the two stood as one. "Not one, but both of us," he cried.

A new voice spoke next, the voice of the oldest miner, the most hardened reprobate there. "Let go that rascal, Parson. He 's the fellow that lamed you last spring. He set the trap himself; I seen him a doing it."

Involuntarily, for a moment, Herman Peters drew back; the trap set at the chapel door, the deliberate, cruel intention, the painful injury, and its life-long result, brought the angry color to his pale face. The memory was full of the old bitterness.

But Saul, feeling himself deserted, dragged his

miserable body forward, and clasped the parson's knees. With desperate hands he clung, and he was not repulsed. Without a word the parson drew him closer, and again faced the crowd.

"Why, the man 's a downright fool!" said the old miner. "That Saul lamed him for life, and all for nothing, and still he stands by him. The man 's mad!"

"I am not mad," answered the parson, and his voice rung out clear and sweet. "But I am a minister of the great God who has said to men, 'Thou shalt do no murder.' O men! O brothers! look back into your own lives. Have ye no crimes, no sins to be forgiven? Can ye expect mercy when ye give none? Let this poor creature go, and it shall be counted unto you for goodness. Ye, too, must some time die; and when the hour comes, as it often comes, in lives like yours, with sudden horror, ye will have this good deed to remember. For charity — which is mercy — shall cover a multitude of sins."

He ceased, and there was a momentary pause. Then a stern voice answered, "Facts won't alter, Parson. The man is a thief, and must be punished. Your talk may do for women-folks, not for us."

"Women-folks!" repeated the ruffian-faced man who had made the women shudder at the chapel. "He 's a sly fox, this parson! He did n't go out to meet Rosie Ray at the Grotter yesterday, O no!"

"Liar!" shouted a man, who had been standing in the shadow on the outskirts of the crowd, taking, so far, no part in the scene. He forced himself to the front; it was Steven Long, his face dark with passion.

"No liar at all, Steve," answered the first. "I seen 'em there with my own eyes; they had things to eat and everything. Just ask the parson."

"Yes, ask the parson," echoed the others; and with the shifting humor of the border, they stopped to laugh over the idea. "Ask the parson."

Steven Long stepped forward and confronted the little minister. His strong hands were clinched, his blood was on fire with jealousy. The bull-dog followed his master, and smelled around the parson's gaiters,—the same poor old shoes, his only pair, now wet with melted snow. The parson glanced down apprehensively.

"'Fraid of a dog! 'Fraid of a dog!" shouted the miners, again laughing uproariously. The fun was better than they had anticipated.

"Is it true?" demanded Steven Long, in a hoarse voice. "Did you meet that girl at the Grotter yesterday?"

"I did meet Rosamond Ray at the Grotto yesterday," answered the parson; "but—"

He never finished the sentence. A fragment of iron ore struck him on the temple. He fell, and died, his small body lying across the thief, whom he still protected even in death.

The murder was not avenged; Steven Long was left to go his own way. But as the thief was also allowed to depart unmolested, the principles of border justice were held to have been amply satisfied.

The miners attended the funeral in a body, and even deputed one of their number to read the Episcopal burial service over the rough pine coffin, since there was no one else to do it. They brought out the chapel prayer-books, found the places, and followed as well as they could; for "he thought a deal of them books. Don't you remember how he was always carrying 'em backward and forward, poor little chap!"

The Chapel of St. John and St. James was closed for the season. In the summer a new missionary arrived; he was not ritualistic, and before the year was out he married Rosamond Ray.

JEANNETTE.

BEFORE the war for the Union, in the times of the old army, there had been peace throughout the country for thirteen years. Regiments existed in their officers, but the ranks were thin,—the more so the better, since the United States possessed few forts and seemed in chronic embarrassment over her military children, owing to the flying foot-ball of public opinion, now "standing army pro," now "standing army con," with more or less allusion to the much-enduring Cæsar and his legions, the ever-present ghost of the political arena.

In those days the few forts were full and much state was kept up; the officers were all graduates of West Point, and their wives graduates of the first families. They prided themselves upon their antecedents; and if there was any aristocracy in the country, it was in the circles of army life.

Those were pleasant days,—pleasant for the old soldiers who were resting after Mexico,—pleasant for young soldiers destined to die on the plains of

Gettysburg or the cloudy heights of Lookout Mountain. There was an *esprit de corps* in the little band, a dignity of bearing, and a ceremonious state, lost in the great struggle which came afterward. That great struggle now lies ten years back; yet, to-day, when the silver-haired veterans meet, they pass it over as a thing of the present, and go back to the times of the "old army."

Up in the northern straits, between blue Lake Huron, with its clear air, and gray Lake Michigan, with its silver fogs, lies the bold island of Mackinac. Clustered along the beach, which runs around its half-moon harbor, are the houses of the old French village, nestling at the foot of the cliff rising behind, crowned with the little white fort, the stars and stripes floating above it against the deep blue sky. Beyond, on all sides, the forest stretches away, cliffs finishing it abruptly, save one slope at the far end of the island, three miles distant, where the British landed in 1812. That is the whole of Mackinac.

The island has a strange sufficiency of its own; it satisfies; all who have lived there feel it. The island has a wild beauty of its own; it fascinates; all who have lived there love it. Among its aromatic cedars, along the aisles of its pine-trees, in the gay company of its maples, there is companionship. On its bald northern cliffs, bathed in sunshine and swept by the pure breeze, there is exhilaration.

Many there are, bearing the burden and heat of the day, who look back to the island with the tears that rise but do not fall, the sudden longing despondency that comes occasionally to all, when the tired heart cries out, "O, to escape, to flee away, far, far away, and be at rest!"

In 1856 Fort Mackinac held a major, a captain, three lieutenants, a chaplain, and a surgeon, besides those subordinate officers who wear stripes on their sleeves, and whose rank and duties are mysterious to the uninitiated. The force for this array of commanders was small, less than a company; but what it lacked in quantity it made up in quality, owing to the continual drilling it received.

The days were long at Fort Mackinac; happy thought! drill the men. So when the major had finished, the captain began, and each lieutenant was watching his chance. Much state was kept up also. Whenever the major appeared, "Commanding officer; guard, present arms," was called down the line of men on duty, and the guard hastened to obey, the major acknowledging the salute with stiff precision. By day and by night sentinels paced the walls. True, the walls were crumbling, and the whole force was constantly engaged in propping them up, but none the less did the sentinels pace with dignity. What was it to the captain if, while he sternly inspected the muskets in the block-house, the lieutenant, with a detail of men, was hard at work strengthening its underpinning? None the less did he inspect. The sally-port, mended but imposing; the flag-staff with its fair-weather and storm flags; the frowning iron grating; the sidling white causeway, constantly falling down and as constantly repaired, which led up to the main entrance; the well-preserved old cannon, — all showed a strict military rule. When the men were not drilling they were propping up the fort, and when they were not propping up the fort they were drilling. In the early days, the days of the first American commanders, military roads had been made through the forest, — roads even now smooth and solid, although trees of a second growth meet overhead. But that was when the fort was young and stood firmly on its legs. In 1856 there was no time for road-making, for when military duty was over there was always more or less mending to keep the whole fortification from sliding down hill into the lake.

On Sunday there was service in the little chapel, an upper room overlooking the inside parade-ground. Here the kindly Episcopal chaplain read the chapters about Balaam and Balak, and always made the same impressive pause after "Let me die the death of the righteous, and let my last end be like his." (Dear old man! he has gone. Would that our last end might indeed be like his!) Not that the chaplain confined his reading to the Book of Numbers; but as those chapters are appointed for the August Sundays, and as it was in August that the summer visitors came to Mackinac, the little chapel is in many minds associated with the patient Balak, his seven altars, and his seven rams.

There was state and discipline in the fort even on Sundays; bugle-playing marshalled the congregation in, bugle-playing marshalled them out. If the sermon was not finished, so much the worse for the sermon, but it made no difference to the bugle; at a given moment it sounded, and out marched all the soldiers, drowning the poor chaplain's hurrying voice with their tramp down the stairs. The officers attended service in full uniform, sitting erect and dignified in the front seats. We used to smile at the grand air they had, from the stately gray-haired major down to the youngest lieutenant fresh from the Point. But brave hearts were beating under those fine uniforms; and when the great struggle came, one and all died on the field in the front of the battle. Over the grave of the commanding officer is inscribed "Major-General," over the captain's is "Brigadier," and over each young lieutenant is "Colonel." They gained their promotion in death.

I spent many months at Fort Mackinac with Archie; Archie was my nephew, a young lieutenant. In the short, bright summer came the visitors from below; all the world outside is "below" in island vernacular. In the long winter the little white fort looked out over unbroken ice-fields, and watched for the moving black dot of the dog-train bringing the mails from the mainland. One January day I had been out walking on the snow-crust, breathing the cold, still air, and, returning within the walls to our quarters, I found my little parlor already occupied. Jeannette was there, petite Jeanneton, the fisherman's daughter. Strange beauty sometimes results from a mixed descent, and this girl had French, English, and Indian blood in her veins, the three races mixing and intermixing among her ancestors, according to the custom of the Northwestern border. A bold profile delicately finished, heavy blue-black hair, light blue eyes looking out unexpectedly from under black lashes and brows; a fair white skin, neither the rose-white of the blonde nor the cream-white of the Oriental brunette; a rounded form with small hands and feet, — showed the mixed beauties of three nationalities. Yes, there could be no doubt but that Jeannette was singularly lovely, albeit ignorant utterly. Her dress was as much of a *mélange* as her ancestry: a short skirt of military blue, Indian leggins and moccasins, a red jacket and little red cap embroidered with beads. The thick braids of her hair hung down her back, and on the lounge lay a large blanket-mantle lined with fox-skins and ornamented with the plumage of birds. She had come to teach me bead-work; I had already taken several lessons to while away the time, but found myself an awkward scholar.

"*Bonjou', madame*," she said, in her patois of broken English and degenerate French. "Pretty here."

My little parlor had a square of carpet, a hearth-fire of great logs, Turkey-red curtains, a lounge and arm-chair covered with chintz, several prints on the cracked walls, and a number of books, — the whole well used and worn, worth perhaps twenty dollars in any town below, but ten times twenty in icy Mackinac. I began the bead-work, and Jeannette was laughing at my mistakes, when the door opened, and our surgeon came in, pausing to warm his hands before going up to his room in the attic. A taciturn man was our surgeon, Rodney Prescott, not popular in the merry garrison circle, but a favorite of mine; the Puritan, the New-Englander, the Bostonian, were as plainly written upon his face as the French and Indian were written upon Jeannette.

"Sit down, Doctor," I said.

He took a seat and watched us carelessly, now and then smiling at Jeannette's chatter as a giant might smile upon a pygmy. I could see that the child was putting on all her little airs to attract his attention; now the long lashes swept the cheeks, now they were raised suddenly, disclosing the unexpected blue eyes; the little moccasined feet must be warmed on the fender, the braids must be swept back with an impatient movement of the hand and shoulder, and now and then there was a coquettish arch of the red lips, less than a pout, what she herself would have called "*une p'tite moue.*" Our surgeon watched this pantomime unmoved.

"Is n't she beautiful?" I said, when, at the expiration of the hour, Jeannette disappeared, wrapped in her mantle.

"No; not to my eyes."

"Why, what more can you require, Doctor? Look at her rich coloring, her hair —"

"There is no mind in her face, Mrs. Corlyne."

"But she is still a child."

"She will always be a child; she will never mature," answered our surgeon, going up the steep stairs to his room above.

Jeannette came regularly, and one morning, tired of the bead-work, I proposed teaching her to read. She consented, although not without an incentive in the form of shillings; but, however gained, my scholar gave to the long winter a new interest. She learned readily; but as there was no foundation, I was obliged to commence with A, B, C.

"Why not teach her to cook?" suggested the major's fair young wife, whose life was spent in hopeless labors with Indian servants, who, sooner or later, ran away in the night with spoons and the family apparel.

"Why not teach her to sew?" said Madame Captain, wearily raising her eyes from the pile of small garments before her.

"Why not have her up for one of our sociables?" hazarded our most dashing lieutenant, twirling his mustache.

"Frederick!" exclaimed his wife, in a tone of horror: she was aristocratic, but sharp in outlines.

"Why not bring her into the church? Those French half-breeds are little better than heathen," said the chaplain.

Thus the high authorities disapproved of my educational efforts. I related their comments to Archie, and added, "The surgeon is the only one who has said nothing against it."

"Prescott? O, he 's too high and mighty to notice anybody, much less a half-breed girl. I never saw such a stiff, silent fellow; he looks as though he had swallowed all his straightlaced Puritan ancestors. I wish he 'd exchange."

"Gently, Archie —"

"O, yes, without doubt; certainly, and amen! I know *you* like him, Aunt Sarah," said my handsome boy-soldier, laughing.

The lessons went on. We often saw the surgeon during study hours, as the stairway leading to his room opened out of the little parlor. Sometimes he would stop awhile and listen as Jeannette slowly read, "The good boy likes his red top"; "The good girl can sew a seam"; or watched her awkward attempts to write her name, or add a one and a two. It was slow work, but I persevered, if from no other motive than obstinacy. Had not they all prophesied a failure? When wearied with the dull routine, I gave an oral lesson in poetry. If the rhymes were of the chiming, rhythmic kind, Jeannette learned rapidly, catching the verses as one catches a tune, and repeating them with a spirit and dramatic gesture all her own. Her favorite was Macaulay's "Ivry." Beautiful she looked, as, standing in the centre of the room, she rolled out the sonorous lines, her French accent giving a charming foreign coloring to the well-known verses: —

> "Now by the lips of those ye love, fair gentlemen of France,
> Charge for the golden lilies, — upon them with the lance!
> A thousand spurs are striking deep, a thousand spears in rest,
> A thousand knights are pressing close behind the snow-white crest;
> And in they burst, and on they rushed, while, like a guiding star,
> Amidst the thickest carnage blazed the helmet of Navarre."

And yet, after all my explanations, she only half understood it; the "knights" were always "nights" in her mind, and the "thickest carnage" was always the "thickest carriage."

One March day she came at the appointed hour, soon after our noon dinner. The usual clear winter sky was clouded, and a wind blew the snow from the trees where it had lain quietly month after month. "Spring is coming," said the old sergeant that morning, as he hoisted the storm-flag; "it 's getting wild-like."

Jeannette and I went through the lessons, but toward three o'clock a north-wind came sweeping over the Straits and enveloped the island in a whirling snow-storm, partly eddies of white splinters torn from the ice-bound forest, and partly a new fall of round snow pellets careering along on the gale, quite unlike the soft, feathery flakes of early winter. "You cannot go home now, Jeannette," I said, looking out through the little west window; our cottage stood back on the hill, and from this side window we could see the Straits, going down toward far Waugoschance; the steep fort-hill outside the wall; the long meadow, once an Indian burial-place, below; and beyond on the beach the row of cabins inhabited by the French fishermen, one of them the home of my pupil. The girl seldom went round the point into the village; its one street and a half seemed distasteful to her. She climbed the stone-wall on the ridge behind her cabin, took an Indian trail through the grass in summer, or struck across on the snow-crust in winter, ran up the steep side of the fort-hill like a wild chamois, and came into the garrison enclosure with a careless nod to the admiring sentinel, as she passed under the rear entrance. These French half-breeds, like the gypsies, were not without a pride of their own. They held themselves aloof from the Irish of

Shanty-town, the floating sailor population of the summer, and the common soldiers of the garrison. They intermarried among themselves, and held their own revels in their beach-cabins during the winter, with music from their old violins, dancing and songs, French ballads with a chorus after every two lines, quaint *chansons* handed down from voyageur ancestors. Small respect had they for the little Roman Catholic church beyond the old Agency garden; its German priest they refused to honor; but, when stately old Father Piret came over to the island from his hermitage in the Chenaux, they ran to meet him, young and old, and paid him reverence with affectionate respect. Father Piret was a Parisian, and a gentleman; nothing less would suit these far-away sheep in the wilderness!

Jeannette Leblanc had all the pride of her class; the Irish saloon-keeper with his shining tall hat, the loud-talking mate of the lake schooner, the trim sentinel pacing the fort walls, were nothing to her, and this somewhat incongruous hauteur gave her the air of a little princess.

On this stormy afternoon the captain's wife was in my parlor preparing to return to her own quarters with some coffee she had borrowed. Hearing my remark she said, "O, the snow won't hurt the child, Mrs. Corlyne; she must be storm-proof, living down there on the beach! Duncan can take her home."

Duncan was the orderly, a factotum in the garrison.

"*Non,*" said Jeannette, tossing her head proudly as the door closed behind the lady, "I wish not of Duncan; I go alone."

It happened that Archie, my nephew, had gone over to the cottage of the commanding officer to decorate the parlor for the military sociable; I knew he would not return, and the evening stretched out before me in all its long loneliness. "Stay, Jeannette," I said. "We will have tea together here, and when the wind goes down, old Antoine shall go back with you." Antoine was a French wood-cutter, whose cabin clung half-way down the fort-hill like a swallow's nest.

Jeannette's eyes sparkled; I had never invited her before; in an instant she had turned the day into a high festival. "Braid hair?" she asked, glancing toward the mirror; "*faut que je m' fasse belle.*" And the long hair came out of its close braids, enveloping her in its glossy dark waves, while she carefully smoothed out the bits of red ribbon that served as fastenings. At this moment the door opened, and the surgeon, the wind, and a puff of snow came in together. Jeannette looked up, smiling and blushing; the falling hair gave a new softness to her face, and her eyes were as shy as the eyes of a wild fawn.

Only the previous day I had noticed that Rodney Prescott listened with marked attention to the captain's cousin, a Virginia lady, as she advanced a theory that Jeannette had negro blood in her veins. "Those quadroon girls often have a certain kind of plebeian beauty like this pet of yours, Mrs. Corlyne," she said, with a slight sniff of her high-bred, pointed nose. In vain I exclaimed, in vain I argued; the garrison ladies were all against me, and, in their presence, not a man dared come to my aid; and the surgeon even added, "I wish I could be sure of it."

"Sure of the negro blood?" I said, indignantly.

"Yes."

"But Jeannette does not look in the least like a quadroon."

"Some of the quadroon girls are very handsome, Mrs. Corlyne," answered the surgeon, coldly.

"O yes!" said the high-bred Virginia lady. "My brother has a number of them about his place, but we do not teach them to read, I assure you. It spoils them."

As I looked at Jeannette's beautiful face, her delicate eagle profile, her fair skin and light blue eyes, I recalled this conversation with vivid indignation. The surgeon, at least, should be convinced of his mistake. Jeannette had never looked more brilliant; probably the man had never really scanned her features, — he was such a cold, unseeing creature; but to-night he should have a fair opportunity, so I invited him to join our storm-bound tea-party. He hesitated.

"Ah, do, Monsieur Rodenai," said Jeannette, springing forward. "I sing for you, I dance; but, no, you not like that. *Bien,* I tell your fortune then." The young girl loved company. A party of three, no matter who the third, was to her infinitely better than two.

The surgeon stayed.

A merry evening we had before the hearth-fire. The wind howled around the block-house and rattled the flag-staff, and the snow pellets sounded on the window-panes, giving that sense of warm comfort within that comes only with the storm. Our servant had been drafted into service for the military sociable, and I was to prepare the evening meal myself.

"Not tea," said Jeannette, with a wry face; "tea,—*c'est médecine!*" She had arranged her hair in fanciful braids, and now followed me to the kitchen, enjoying the novelty like a child. "*Café?*" she said. "O, please, madame! *I* make it."

The little shed kitchen was cold and dreary, each plank of its thin walls rattling in the gale with a dismal creak; the wind blew the smoke down the chimney, and finally it ended in our bringing everything into the cosey parlor, and using the hearth fire, where Jeannette made coffee and baked little cakes over the coals.

The meal over, Jeannette sang her songs, sitting on the rug before the fire,—*Le Beau Voyageur, Les*

Neiges de la Cloche, ballads in Canadian patois sung to minor airs brought over from France two hundred years before.

The surgeon sat in the shade of the chimney-piece, his face shaded by his hand, and I could not discover whether he saw anything to admire in my *protégée*, until, standing in the centre of the room, she gave us "Ivry" in glorious style. Beautiful she looked as she rolled out the lines:—

"And if my standard-bearer fall, as fall full well he may,—
For never saw I promise yet of such a bloody fray,—
Press where ye see my white plume shine amidst the ranks of war,
And be your oriflamme to-day the helmet of Navarre."

Rodney sat in the full light now, and I secretly triumphed in his rapt attention.

"Something else, Jeannette," I said, in the pride of my heart. Instead of repeating anything I had taught her, she began in French:—

"'Marie, enfin quitte l'ouvrage,
Voici l'étoile du berger.'
—'Ma mère, un enfant du village
Languit captif chez l'étranger;
Pris sur mer, loin de sa patrie,
Il s'est rendu,—mais le dernier.'
File, file, pauvre Marie,
Pour secourir le prisonnier;
File, file, pauvre Marie,
File, file, pour le prisonnier.

"'Pour lui je filerais moi-même
Mon enfant,—mais—j'ai tant vieilli!'

— 'Envoyez à celui que j'aime
Tout le gain par moi recueilli.
Rose à sa noce en vain me prie ;—
Dieu ! j'entends le ménétrier !'
File, file, pauvre Marie,
Pour secourir le prisonnier ;
File, file, pauvre Marie,
File, file, pcur le prisonnier.

" 'Plus près du feu file, ma chère ;
La nuit vient refroidir le temps.'
— 'Adrien, m'a-t-on dit, ma mère,
Gémit dans des cachots flottants.
On repousse la main flétrie
Qu'il étend vers un pain grossier.'
File, file, pauvre Marie,
Pour secourir le prisonnier ;
File, file, pauvre Marie,
File, file, pour le prisonnier." *

Jeannette repeated these lines with a pathos so real that I felt a moisture rising in my eyes.

"Where did you learn that, child?" I asked.

"Father Piret, madame."

"What is it?"

"*Je n' sais.*"

"It is Béranger,—'The Prisoner of War,'" said Rodney Prescott. "But you omitted the last verse, mademoiselle; may I ask why?"

"More sad so," answered Jeannette. "Marie she die now."

* "Le Prisonnier de Guerre," Béranger.

"You wish her to die?"

"*Mais oui:* she die for love; *c'est beau!*"

And there flashed a glance from the girl's eyes that thrilled through me, I scarcely knew why. I looked toward Rodney, but he was back in the shadow again.

The hours passed. "I must go," said Jeannette, drawing aside the curtain. Clouds were still driving across the sky, but the snow had ceased falling, and at intervals the moon shone out over the cold white scene; the March wind continued on its wild career toward the south.

"I will send for Antoine," I said, rising, as Jeannette took up her fur mantle.

"The old man is sick to-day," said Rodney. "It would not be safe for him to leave the fire to-night. I will accompany mademoiselle."

Pretty Jeannette shrugged her shoulders. "*Mais, monsieur,*" she answered, "I go over the hill."

"No, child; not to-night," I said decidedly. "The wind is violent, and the cliff doubly slippery after this ice-storm. Go round through the village."

"Of course we shall go through the village," said our surgeon, in his calm, authoritative way. They started. But in another minute I saw Jeannette fly by the west window, over the wall, and across the snowy road, like a spirit, disappearing down the steep bank, now slippery with glare ice. Another minute, and Rodney Prescott followed in her track.

With bated breath I watched for the reappearance of the two figures on the white plain, one hundred and fifty feet below; the cliff was difficult at any time, and now in this ice! The moments seemed very long, and, alarmed, I was on the point of arousing the garrison, when I spied the two dark figures on the snowy plain below, now clear in the moonlight, now lost in the shadow. I watched them for some distance; then a cloud came, and I lost them entirely.

Rodney did not return, although I sat late before the dying fire. Thinking over the evening, the idea came to me that perhaps, after all, he did admire my *protégée*, and, being a romantic old woman, I did not repel the fancy; it might go a certain distance without harm, and an idyl is always charming, doubly so to people cast away on a desert island. One falls into the habit of studying persons very closely in the limited circle of garrison life.

But, the next morning, the Major's wife gave me an account of the sociable. "It was very pleasant," she said. "Toward the last Dr. Prescott came in, quite unexpectedly. I had no idea he could be so agreeable. Augusta can tell you how charming he was!"

Augusta, a young lady cousin, of pale blond complexion, neutral opinions, and irreproachable manners, smiled primly. My idyl was crushed!

The days passed. The winds, the snows, and the high-up fort remained the same. Jeannette came and went, and the hour lengthened into two or three; not that we read much, but we talked more. Our surgeon did not again pass through the parlor; he had ordered a rickety stairway on the outside wall to be repaired, and we could hear him going up and down its icy steps as we sat by the hearth-fire. One day I said to him, "My *protégée* is improving wonderfully. If she could have a complete education, she might take her place with the best in the land."

"Do not deceive yourself, Mrs. Corlyne," he answered. "It is only the shallow French quickness."

"Why do you always judge the child so harshly, Doctor?"

"Do *you* take her part, Aunt Sarah?" (For sometimes he used the title which Archie had made so familiar.)

"Of course I do, Rodney. A poor, unfriended girl living in this remote place, against a United States surgeon with the best of Boston behind him."

"I wish you would tell me that every day, Aunt Sarah," was the reply I received. It set me musing, but I could make nothing of it. Troubled without knowing why, I suggested to Archie that he should endeavor to interest our surgeon in the fort gayety; there was something for every night in the merry little circle, — games, suppers, tableaux, music, theatricals, readings, and the like.

"Why, he's in the thick of it already, Aunt Sarah,"

said my nephew. "He 's devoting himself to Miss Augusta; she sings 'The Harp that once —' to him every night."

("The Harp that once through Tara's Halls" was Miss Augusta's dress-parade song. The Major's quarters not being as large as the halls aforesaid, the melody was somewhat overpowering.)

"O, does she?" I thought, not without a shade of vexation. But the vague anxiety vanished.

The real spring came at last, — the rapid, vivid spring of Mackinac. Almost in a day the ice moved out, the snows melted, and the northern wild-flowers appeared in the sheltered glens. Lessons were at an end, for my scholar was away in the green woods. Sometimes she brought me a bunch of flowers; but I seldom saw her; my wild bird had flown back to the forest. When the ground was dry and the pine droppings warmed by the sun, I, too, ventured abroad. One day, wandering as far as the Arched Rock, I found the surgeon there, and together we sat down to rest under the trees, looking off over the blue water flecked with white caps. The Arch is a natural bridge over a chasm one hundred and fifty feet above the lake, — a fissure in the cliff which has fallen away in a hollow, leaving the bridge by itself far out over the water. This bridge springs upward in the shape of an arch; it is fifty feet long, and its width is in some places two feet, in others only a few inches, — a narrow, dizzy pathway hanging between sky and water.

"People have crossed it," I said.

"Only fools," answered our surgeon, who despised foolhardiness. "Has a man nothing better to do with his life than risk it for the sake of a silly feat like that? I would not so much as raise my eyes to see any one cross."

"O yes, you would, Monsieur Rodenai," cried a voice behind us. We both turned and caught a glimpse of Jeannette as she bounded through the bushes and out to the very centre of the Arch, where she stood balancing herself and laughing gayly. Her form was outlined against the sky; the breeze swayed her skirt; she seemed hovering over the chasm. I watched her, mute with fear; a word might cause her to lose her balance; but I could not turn my eyes away, I was fascinated with the sight. I was not aware that Rodney had left me until he, too, appeared on the Arch, slowly finding a foothold for himself and advancing toward the centre. A fragment of the rock broke off under his foot and fell into the abyss below.

"Go back, Monsieur Rodenai," cried Jeannette, seeing his danger.

"Will *you* come back too, Jeannette?"

"*Moi? C'est aut' chose,*" answered the girl, gayly tossing her pretty head.

"Then I shall come out and carry you back, wilful child," said the surgeon.

A peal of laughter broke from Jeannette as he spoke,

and then she began to dance on her point of rock, swinging herself from side to side, marking the time with a song. I held my breath; her dance seemed unearthly; it was as though she belonged to the Prince of the Powers of the Air.

At length the surgeon reached the centre and caught the mocking creature in his arms: neither spoke, but I could see the flash of their eyes as they stood for an instant motionless. Then they struggled on the narrow foothold and swayed over so far that I buried my face in my trembling hands, unable to look at the dreadful end. When I opened my eyes again all was still; the Arch was tenantless, and no sound came from below. Were they, then, so soon dead? Without a cry? I forced myself to the brink to look down over the precipice; but while I stood there, fearing to look, I heard a sound behind me in the woods. It was Jeannette singing a gay French song. I called to her to stop. "How could you?" I said severely, for I was still trembling with agitation.

"*Ce n'est rien*, madame. I cross l'Arche when I had five year. *Mais*, Monsieur Rodenai le Grand, he raise his eye to look *this* time, I think," said Jeannette, laughing triumphantly.

"Where is he?"

"On the far side, gone on to Scott's Pic [Peak]. *Féroce, O féroce, comme un loupgarou! Ah! c'est joli, ça!*" And, overflowing with the wildest glee, the girl danced along through the woods in front of me, now pausing to look at something in her hand, now laughing, now shouting like a wild creature, until I lost sight of her. I went back to the fort alone.

For several days I saw nothing of Rodney. When at last we met, I said, "That was a wild freak of Jeannette's at the Arch."

"Planned, to get a few shillings out of us."

"O Doctor! I do not think she had any such motive," I replied, looking up deprecatingly into his cold, scornful eyes.

"Are you not a little sentimental over that ignorant, half-wild creature, Aunt Sarah?"

"Well," I said to myself, "perhaps I am!"

The summer came, sails whitened the blue straits again, steamers stopped for an hour or two at the island docks, and the summer travellers rushed ashore to buy "Indian curiosities," made by the nuns in Montreal, or to climb breathlessly up the steep fort-hill to see the pride and panoply of war. Proud was the little white fort in those summer days; the sentinels held themselves stiffly erect, the officers gave up lying on the parapet half asleep, the best flag was hoisted daily, and there was much bugle-playing and ceremony connected with the evening gun, fired from the ramparts at sunset; the hotels were full, the boarding-house keepers were in their annual state of wonder over the singular taste of these people from "below," who actually preferred a miserable white-fish to the best of beef brought up on ice all the way from Buffalo! There were picnics and walks, and much confusion of historical dates respecting Father Marquette and the irrepressible, omnipresent Pontiac. The fort officers did much escort duty; their buttons gilded every scene. Our quiet surgeon was foremost in everything.

"I am surprised! I had no idea Dr. Prescott was so gay," said the Major's wife.

"I should not think of calling him gay," I answered.

"Why, my dear Mrs. Corlyne! He is going all the time. Just ask Augusta."

Augusta thereupon remarked that society, to a certain extent, was beneficial; that she considered Dr. Prescott much improved; really, he was now very "nice."

I silently protested against the word. But then I was not a Bostonian.

One bright afternoon I went through the village, round the point into the French quarter, in search of a laundress. The fishermen's cottages faced the west; they were low and wide, not unlike scows drifted ashore and moored on the beach for houses. The little windows had gay curtains fluttering in the breeze, and the rooms within looked clean and cheery; the rough walls were adorned with the spoils of the fresh-water seas, shells, green stones, agates, spar, and curiously shaped pebbles; occasionally there was a stuffed water-bird, or a bright-colored print, and always a violin. Black-eyed children played in the water which bordered their narrow beach-gardens; and slender women, with shining black hair, stood in their doorways knitting. I found my laundress, and then went on to Jeannette's home, the last house in the row. From the mother, a Chippewa woman, I learned that Jeannette was with her French father at the fishing-grounds off Drummond's Island.

"How long has she been away?" I asked.

"Veeks four," replied the mother, whose knowledge of English was confined to the price-list of white-fish and blueberries, the two articles of her traffic with the boarding-house keepers.

"When will she return?"

"*Je n' sais.*"

She knitted on, sitting in the sunshine on her little doorstep, looking out over the western water with tranquil content in her beautiful, gentle eyes. As I walked up the beach I glanced back several times to see if she had the curiosity to watch me; but no, she still looked out over the western water. What was I to her? Less than nothing. A white-fish was more.

A week or two later I strolled out to the Giant's Stairway and sat down in the little rock chapel. There was a picnic at the Lovers' Leap, and I had that side of the island to myself. I was leaning back, half asleep, in the deep shadow, when the sound of voices roused me; a birch-bark canoe was passing close in shore, and two were in it,—Jeannette and our surgeon. I could not hear their words, but I noticed Rodney's expression as he leaned forward. Jeannette was paddling slowly; her cheeks were flushed, and her eyes brilliant. Another moment, and a point hid them from my view. I went home troubled.

"Did you enjoy the picnic, Miss Augusta?" I said, with assumed carelessness, that evening. "Dr. Prescott was there, as usual, I suppose?"

"He was not present, but the picnic was highly enjoyable," replied Miss Augusta, in her even voice and impartial manner.

"The Doctor has not been with us for some days," said the major's wife, archly; "I suspect he does not like Mr. Piper."

Mr. Piper was a portly widower, of sanguine complexion, a Chicago produce-dealer, who was supposed to admire Miss Augusta, and was now going through a course of "The Harp that once."

The last days of summer flew swiftly by; the surgeon held himself aloof; we scarcely saw him in the garrison circles, and I no longer met him in my rambles.

"Jealousy!" said the major's wife.

September came. The summer visitors fled away homeward; the remaining "Indian curiosities" were stored away for another season; the hotels were closed, and the forests deserted; the bluebells swung unmolested on their heights, and the plump Indian-pipes grew in peace in their dark corners. The little white fort, too, began to assume its winter manners; the storm-flag was hoisted; there were evening fires upon the broad hearth-stones; the chaplain, having finished everything about Balak, his seven altars and seven rams, was ready for chess-problems; books and papers were ordered; stores laid in, and anxious inquiries made as to the "habits" of the new mail-carrier, — for the mail-carrier was the hero of the winter, and if his "habits" led him to whiskey, there was danger that our precious letters might be dropped all along the northern curve of Lake Huron.

Upon this quiet matter-of-course preparation, suddenly, like a thunderbolt from a clear sky, came orders to leave. The whole garrison, officers and men, were ordered to Florida.

In a moment all was desolation. It was like being ordered into the Valley of the Shadow of Death. Dense everglades, swamp-fevers, malaria in the air, poisonous underbrush, and venomous reptiles and insects, and now and then a wily unseen foe picking off the men, one by one, as they painfully cut out roads through the thickets, — these were the features of military life in Florida at that period. Men who would have marched boldly to the cannon's mouth, officers who would have headed a forlorn hope, shrank from the deadly swamps.

Families must be broken up, also; no women, no children, could go to Florida. There were tears and the sound of sobbing in the little white fort, as the poor wives, all young mothers, hastily packed their few possessions to go back to their fathers' houses, fortunate if they had fathers to receive them. The husbands went about in silence, too sad for words. Archie kept up the best courage; but he was young, and had no one to leave save me.

The evening of the fatal day — for the orders had come in the early dawn — I was alone in my little parlor, already bare and desolate with packing-cases. The wind had been rising since morning, and now blew furiously from the west. Suddenly the door burst open and the surgeon entered. I was shocked at his appearance, as, pale, haggard, with disordered hair and clothing, he sank into a chair, and looked at me in silence.

"Rodney, what is it?" I said.

He did not answer, but still looked at me with that strange gaze. Alarmed, I rose and went toward him, laying my hand on his shoulder with a motherly touch. I loved the quiet, gray-eyed youth next after Archie.

"What is it, my poor boy? Can I help you?"

"O Aunt Sarah, perhaps you can, for *you* know her."

"Her?" I repeated, with sinking heart.

"Yes. Jeannette."

I sat down and folded my hands; trouble had come, but it was not what I apprehended, — the old story of military life, love, and desertion; the ever-present ballad of the "gay young knight who loves and rides away." This was something different.

"I love her, — I love her madly, in spite of myself," said Rodney, pouring forth his words with feverish rapidity. "I know it is an infatuation, I know it is utterly unreasonable, and yet — I love her. I have striven against it, I have fought with myself, I have written out elaborate arguments wherein I have clearly demonstrated the folly of such an affection, and I have compelled myself to read them over slowly, word for word, when alone in my own room, and yet — I love her! Ignorant, I know she would shame me; shallow, I know she could not satisfy me; as a wife she would inevitably drag me down to misery, and yet — I love her! I had not been on the island a week before I saw her, and marked her beauty. Months before you invited her to the fort I had become infatuated with her singular loveliness; but, in some respects, a race of the blood-royal could not be prouder than these French fishermen. They will accept your money, they will cheat you, they will tell you lies for an extra shilling; but make one step toward a simple acquaintance, and the door will be shut in your face. They will bow down before you as a customer, but they will not have you for a friend. Thus I found it impossible to reach Jeannette. I do not say that I tried, for all the time I was fighting myself; but I went far enough to see the barriers. It seemed a fatality that you should take a fancy to her, have her here, and ask me to admire her, — admire the face that haunted me by day and by night, driving me mad with its beauty.

"I realized my danger, and called to my aid all the pride of my race. I said to my heart, 'You shall not love this ignorant half-breed girl to your ruin.' I reasoned with myself, and said, 'It is only because you are isolated on this far-away island. Could you present this girl to your mother? Could she be a companion for your sisters?' I was beginning to gain a firmer control over myself, in spite of her presence, when you unfolded your plan of education. Fatality again. Instantly a crowd of hopes surged up. The education you began, could I not finish? She was but young; a few years of careful teaching might work wonders. Could I not train this forest flower so that it could take its place in the garden? But, when I actually saw this full-grown woman unable to add the simplest sum or write her name correctly, I was again ashamed of my infatuation. It is one thing to talk of ignorance, it is another to come face to face with it. Thus I wavered, at one moment ready to give up all for pride, at another to give up all for love.

"Then came the malicious suggestion of negro blood.

Could it be proved, I was free; that taint I could not pardon. [And here, even as the surgeon spoke, I noticed this as the peculiarity of the New England Abolitionist. Theoretically he believed in the equality of the enslaved race, and stood ready to maintain the belief with his life, but practically he held himself entirely aloof from them; the Southern creed and practice were the exact reverse.] I made inquiries of Father Piret, who knows the mixed genealogy of the little French colony as far back as the first voyageurs of the fur trade, and found — as I, shall I say hoped or feared? — that the insinuation was utterly false. Thus I was thrown back into the old tumult.

"Then came that evening in this parlor when Jeannette made the coffee and baked little cakes over the coals. Do you remember the pathos with which she chanted *File, file, pauvre Marie; File, file, pour le prisonnier?* Do you remember how she looked when she repeated 'Ivry'? Did that tender pity, that ringing inspiration, come from a dull mind and shallow heart? I was avenged of my enforced disdain, my love gave itself up to delicious hope. She was capable of education, and then —! I made a pretext of old Antoine's cough in order to gain an opportunity of speaking to her alone; but she was like a thing possessed, she broke from me and sprang over the icy cliff, her laugh coming back on the wind as I followed her down the dangerous slope. On she rushed, jumping from rock to rock, waving her hand in wild glee when the moon shone out, singing and shouting with merry scorn at my desperate efforts to reach her. It was a mad chase, but only on the plain below could I come up with her. There, breathless and eager, I unfolded to her my plan of education. I only went so far as this: I was willing to send her to school, to give her opportunities of seeing the world, to provide for her whole future. I left the story of my love to come afterward. She laughed me to scorn. As well talk of education to the bird of the wilderness! She rejected my offers, picked up snow to throw in my face, covered me with her French sarcasms, danced around me in circles, laughed, and mocked, until I was at a loss to know whether she was human. Finally, as a shadow darkened the moon, she fled away; and when it passed she was gone, and I was alone on the snowy plain.

"Angry, fierce, filled with scorn for myself, I determined resolutely to crush out my senseless infatuation. I threw myself into such society as we had; I assumed an interest in that inane Miss Augusta; I read and studied far into the night; I walked until sheer fatigue gave me tranquillity; but all I gained was lost in that encounter at the Arch: you remember it? When I saw her on that narrow bridge, my love burst its bonds again, and, senseless as ever, rushed to save her,—to save her, poised on her native rocks, where every inch was familiar from childhood! To save her, — sure-footed and light as a bird! I caught her. She struggled in my arms, angrily, as an imprisoned animal might struggle, but — so beautiful! The impulse came to me to spring with her into the gulf below, and so end the contest forever. I might have done it, — I cannot tell, — but, suddenly, she wrenched herself out of my arms and fled over the Arch, to the farther side. I followed, trembling, blinded, with the violence of my emotion. At that moment I was ready to give up my life, my soul, into her hands.

"In the woods beyond she paused, glanced over her shoulder toward me, then turned eagerly. '*Voilà*,' she said, pointing. I looked down and saw several silver pieces that had dropped from my pocket as I sprang over the rocks, and, with an impatient gesture, I thrust them aside with my foot.

"'*Non*,' she cried, turning toward me and stooping eagerly, — 'so much! O, so much! See! four shillings!' Her eyes glistened with longing as she held the money in her hand and fingered each piece lovingly.

"The sudden revulsion of feeling produced by her words and gesture filled me with fury. 'Keep it, and buy yourself a soul if you can!' I cried; and turning away, I left her with her gains.

"'*Merci, monsieur*,' she answered gayly, all unmindful of my scorn; and off she ran, holding her treasure tightly clasped in both hands. I could hear her singing far down the path.

"It is a bitter thing to feel a scorn for yourself! Did I love this girl who stooped to gather a few shillings from under my feet? Was it, then, impossible for me to conquer this ignoble passion? No; it could not and it should not be! I plunged again into all the gayety; I left myself not one free moment; if sleep came not, I forced it to come with opiates; Jeannette had gone to the fishing-grounds, the weeks passed, I did not see her. I had made the hardest struggle of all, and was beginning to recover my self-respect when, one day, I met her in the woods with some children; she had returned to gather blueberries. I looked at her. She was more gentle than usual, and smiled. Suddenly, as an embankment which has withstood the storms of many winters gives way at last in a calm summer night, I yielded. Without one outward sign, I laid down my arms. Myself knew that the contest was over, and my other self rushed to her feet.

"Since then I have often seen her; I have made plan after plan to meet her; I have — O degrading thought! — paid her to take me out in her canoe, under the pretence of fishing. I no longer looked forward; I lived only in the present, and thought only of when and where I could see her. Thus it has been until this morning, when the orders came. Now, I am brought face to face with reality; I must go; can I leave her behind? For hours I have been wandering in the woods. Aunt Sarah, — it is of no use, — I cannot live without her; I must marry her."

"Marry Jeannette!" I exclaimed.

"Even so."

"An ignorant half-breed?"

"As you say, an ignorant half-breed."

"You are mad, Rodney."

"I know it."

I will not repeat all I said; but, at last, silenced, if not convinced, by the power of this great love, I started with him out into the wild night to seek Jeannette. We went through the village and round the point, where the wind met us, and the waves broke at our feet with a roar. Passing the row of cabins, with their twinkling lights, we reached the home of Jeannette and knocked at the low door. The Indian mother opened it. I entered, without a word, and took a seat near the hearth, where a drift-wood fire was burning. Jeannette came forward with a surprised look. "You little think what good fortune is coming to you, child," I thought, as I noted her coarse dress and the poor furniture of the little room.

Rodney burst at once into his subject.

"Jeannette," he said, going toward her, "I have come to take you away with me. You need not go to school; I have given up that idea, — I accept you as you are. You shall have silk dresses and ribbons, like the ladies at the Mission-House this summer. You shall see all the great cities, you shall hear beautiful music. You shall have everything you want, — money, bright shillings, as many as you wish. See! Mrs. Corlyne has come with me to show you that it is true. This morning we had orders to leave Mackinac; in a few days we must go. But — listen, Jeannette; I will marry you. You shall be my wife. Do not look so startled. I mean it; it is really true."

"*Qu'est-ce-que-c'est?*" said the girl, bewildered by the rapid, eager words.

"Dr. Prescott wishes to marry you, child," I explained, somewhat sadly, for never had the disparity between them seemed so great. The presence of the Indian mother, the common room, were like silent protests.

"Marry!" ejaculated Jeannette.

"Yes, love," said the surgeon, ardently. "It is quite true; you shall be my wife. Father Piret shall marry us. I will exchange into another regiment, or, if necessary, I will resign. Do you understand what I am saying, Jeannette? See! I give you my hand, in token that it is true."

But, with a quick bound, the girl was across the room. "What!" she cried. "You think I marry *you?* Have you not heard of Baptiste? Know, then, that I love one finger of him more than all you, ten times, hundred times."

"Baptiste?" repeated Rodney.

"*Oui, mon cousin,* Baptiste, the fisherman. We marry soon — *tenez* — *la fête de Saint André.*"

Rodney looked bewildered a moment, then his face cleared. "Oh! a child engagement? That is one of your customs, I know. But never fear; Father Piret will absolve you from all that. Baptiste shall have a fine new boat; he will let you off for a handful of silver-pieces. Do not think of that, Jeannette, but come to me —"

"*Je vous abhorre; je vous déteste,*" cried the girl with fury as he approached. "Baptiste not love me? He love me more than boat and silver dollar, — more than all the world! And I love him; I die for him! *Allez-vous-en, traître!*"

Rodney had grown white; he stood before her, motionless, with fixed eyes.

"Jeannette," I said in French, "perhaps you do not understand. Dr. Prescott asks you to marry him; Father Piret shall marry you, and all your friends shall come. Dr. Prescott will take you away from this hard life; he will make you rich; he will support your father and mother in comfort. My child, it is wonderful good fortune. He is an educated gentleman, and loves you truly."

"What is that to me?" replied Jeannette, proudly. "Let him go, I care not." She paused a moment. Then, with flashing eyes, she cried, "Let him go with his fine new boat and silver dollars! He does not believe me? See, then, how I despise him!" And, rushing forward, she struck him on the cheek.

Rodney did not stir, but stood gazing at her while the red mark glowed on his white face.

"You know not what love is," said Jeannette, with indescribable scorn. "You! *You! Ah, mon Baptiste, où es-tu?* But thou wilt kill him, — kill him for his boats and silver dollars!"

"Child!" I said, startled by her fury.

"I am not a child. *Je suis femme, moi!*" replied Jeannette, folding her arms with haughty grace. "*Allez!*" she said, pointing toward the door. We were dismissed. A queen could not have made a more royal gesture.

Throughout the scene the Indian mother had not stopped her knitting.

In four days we were afloat, and the little white fort was deserted. It was a dark afternoon, and we sat clustered on the stern of the steamer, watching the flag come slowly down from its staff in token of the departure of the commanding officer. "Isle of Beauty, fare thee well," sang the major's fair young wife, with the sound of tears in her sweet voice.

"We shall return," said the officers. But not one of them ever saw the beautiful island again.

Rodney Prescott served a month or two in Florida,

"taciturn and stiff as ever," Archie wrote. Then he resigned suddenly, and went abroad. He has never returned, and I have lost all trace of him, so that I cannot say, from any knowledge of my own, how long the feeling lived, — the feeling that swept me along in its train down to the beach-cottage that wild night.

Each man who reads this can decide for himself.

Each woman has decided already.

Last year I met an islander on the cars, going eastward. It was the first time he had ever been "below"; but he saw nothing to admire, that dignified citizen of Mackinac!

"What has become of Jeannette Leblanc?" I asked.

"Jeannette? O, she married that Baptiste, a lazy, good-for-nothing fellow! They live in the same little cabin round the point, and pick up a living most anyhow for their tribe of young ones."

"Are they happy?"

"Happy?" repeated my islander, with a slow stare. "Well, I suppose they are, after their fashion; I don't know much about them. In my opinion, they are a shiftless set, those French half-breeds round the point."

THE OLD AGENCY.

"The buildings of the United States Indian Agency on the island of Mackinac were destroyed by fire December 31, at midnight." — *Western Newspaper Item.*

THE old house is gone then! But it shall not depart into oblivion unchronicled. One who has sat under its roof-tree, one who remembers well its rambling rooms and wild garden, will take the pen to write down a page of its story. It is only an episode, one of many; but the others are fading away, or already buried in dead memories under the sod. It was a quaint, picturesque old place, stretching back from the white limestone road that bordered the little port, its overgrown garden surrounded by an ancient stockade ten feet in height, with a massive, slow-swinging gate in front, defended by loopholes. This stockade bulged out in some places and leaned in at others; but the veteran posts, each a tree sharpened to a point, did not break their ranks, in spite of decrepitude; and the Indian warriors, could they have returned from their happy hunting-grounds, would have found the brave old fence of the Agency a sturdy barrier still. But the Indian warriors could not return. The United States agent had long ago moved to Lake Superior, and the deserted residence, having only a mythical owner, left without repairs year after year, and under a cloud of confusion as regarded taxes, titles, and boundaries, became a sort of flotsam property, used by various persons, but belonging legally to no one. Some tenant, tired of swinging the great gate back and forth, had made a little sally port alongside, but otherwise the place remained unaltered; a broad garden with a central avenue of cherry-trees, on each side dilapidated arbors, overgrown paths, and heart-shaped beds, where the first agents had tried to cultivate flowers, and behind the limestone cliffs crowned with cedars. The house was large on the ground, with wings and various additions built out as if at random; on each side and behind were rough outside chimneys clamped to the wall; in the roof over the central part dormer-windows showed a low second story; and here and there at irregular intervals were outside doors, in some cases opening out into space, since the high steps which once led up to them had fallen down, and remained as they fell, heaps of stones on the ground below. Within were suites of rooms, large and small, showing traces of workmanship elaborate for such a remote locality; the ceilings, patched with rough mortar, had been originally decorated with moulding, the doors were ornamented with scroll-work, and the two large apartments on each side of the entrance-hall possessed chimney-pieces and central hooks for chandeliers. Beyond and behind stretched out the wings; coming to what appeared to be the end of the house on the west, there unexpectedly began a new series of rooms turning toward the north, each with its outside door; looking for a corresponding labyrinth on the eastern side, there was nothing but a blank wall. The blind stairway went up in a kind of dark well, and once up it was a difficult matter to get down without a plunge from top to bottom, since the undefended opening was just where no one would expect to find it. Sometimes an angle was so arbitrarily walled up that you felt sure there must be a secret chamber there, and furtively rapped on the wall to catch the hollow echo within. Then again you opened a door, expecting to step out into the wilderness of a garden, and found yourself in a set of little rooms running off on a tangent, one after the other, and ending in a windowless closet and an open cistern. But the Agency gloried in its irregularities, and defied criticism. The original idea of its architect — if there was any — had vanished; but his work remained, a not unpleasing variety to summer visitors accustomed to city houses, all built with a definite purpose, and one front door.

After some years of wandering in foreign lands, I

returned to my own country, and took up the burden of old associations whose sadness time had mercifully softened. The summer was over; September had begun, but there came to me a great wish to see Mackinac once more; to look again upon the little white fort where I had lived with Archie, my soldier nephew, killed at Shiloh. The steamer took me safely across Erie, up the brimming Detroit River, through the enchanted region of the St. Clair flats, and out into broad Lake Huron; there, off Thunder Bay, a gale met us, and for hours we swayed between life and death. The season for pleasure travelling was over; my fellow-passengers, with one exception, were of that class of Americans who, dressed in cheap imitations of fine clothes, are forever travelling, travelling, — taking the steamers not from preference, but because they are less costly than an all-rail route. The thin, listless men, in ill-fitting black clothes and shining tall hats, sat on the deck in tilted chairs, hour after hour, silent and dreary; the thin, listless women, clad in raiment of many colors, remained upon the fixed sofas in the cabin hour after hour, silent and weary. At meals they ate indiscriminately everything within range, but continued the same, a weary, dreary, silent band. The one exception was an old man, tall and majestic, with silvery hair and bright, dark eyes, dressed in the garb of a Roman Catholic priest, albeit slightly tinged with frontier innovations. He came on board at Detroit, and as soon as we were under way he exchanged his hat for a cloth cap embroidered with Indian bead-work; and when the cold air, precursor of the gale, struck us on Huron, he wrapped himself in a large capote made of skins, with the fur inward.

In times of danger formality drops from us. During those long hours, when the next moment might have brought death, this old man and I were together; and when at last the cold dawn came, and the disabled steamer slowly ploughed through the angry water around the point, and showed us Mackinac in the distance, we discovered that the island was a mutual friend, and that we knew each other, at least by name; for the silver-haired priest was Father Piret, the hermit of the Chenaux. In the old days, when I was living at the little white fort, I had known Father Piret by reputation, and he had heard of me from the French half-breeds around the point. We landed. The summer hotels were closed, and I was directed to the old Agency, where occasionally a boarder was received by the family then in possession. The air was chilly, and a fine rain was falling, the afterpiece of the equinoctial; the wet storm-flag hung heavily down over the fort on the height, and the waves came in sullenly. All was in sad accordance with my feelings as I thought of the past and its dead, while the slow tears of age moistened my eyes. But the next morning Mackinac awoke, robed in autumn splendor; the sunshine poured down, the straits sparkled back, the forest glowed in scarlet, the larches waved their wild, green hands, the fair-weather flag floated over the little fort, and all was as joyous as though no one had ever died; and indeed it is in glorious days like these that we best realize immortality.

I wandered abroad through the gay forest to the Arch, the Lovers' Leap, and old Fort Holmes, whose British walls had been battered down for pastime, so that only a caved-in British cellar remained to mark the spot. Returning to the Agency, I learned that Father Piret had called to see me.

"I am sorry that I missed him," I said; "he is a remarkable old man."

The circle at the dinner-table glanced up with one accord. The little Methodist minister with the surprised eyes looked at me more surprised than ever; his large wife groaned audibly. The Baptist colporteur peppered his potatoes until they and the plate were black; the Presbyterian doctor, who was the champion of the Protestant party on the island, wished to know if I was acquainted with the latest devices of the Scarlet Woman in relation to the county school-fund.

"But, my friends," I replied, "Father Piret and I both belong to the past. We discuss not religion, but Mackinac; not the school-fund, but the old associations of the island, which is dear to both of us."

The four looked at me with distrust; they saw nothing dear about the island, unless it was the price of fresh meat; and as to old associations, they held themselves above such nonsense. So, one and all, they took beef and enjoyed a season of well-regulated conversation, leaving me to silence and my broiled white-fish; as it was Friday, no doubt they thought the latter a rag of popery.

Very good rags.

But my hostess, a gentle little woman, stole away from these bulwarks of Protestantism in the late afternoon, and sought me in my room, or rather series of rooms, since there were five opening one out of the other, the last three unfurnished, and all the doorless doorways staring at me like so many fixed eyes, until, oppressed by their silent watchfulness, I hung a shawl over the first opening and shut out the whole gazing suite.

"You must not think, Mrs. Corlyne, that we islanders do not appreciate Father Piret," said the little woman, who belonged to one of the old island families, descendants of a chief factor of the fur trade. "There has been some feeling lately against the Catholics —"

"Roman Catholics, my dear," I said with Anglican particularity.

"But we all love and respect the dear old man as a father."

"When I was living at the fort, fifteen years ago, I heard occasionally of Father Piret," I said, "but he seemed to be almost a mythic personage. What is his history?"

"No one knows. He came here fifty years ago, and after officiating on the island a few years, he retired to a little Indian farm in the Chenaux, where he has lived ever since. Occasionally he holds a service for the half-breeds at Point St. Ignace, but the parish of Mackinac proper has its regular priest, and Father Piret apparently does not hold even the appointment of missionary. Why he remains here—a man educated, refined, and even aristocratic—is a mystery. He seems to be well provided with money; his little house in the Chenaux contains foreign books and pictures, and he is very charitable to the poor Indians. But he keeps himself aloof, and seems to desire no intercourse with the world beyond his letters and papers, which come regularly, some of them from France. He seldom leaves the Straits; he never speaks of himself; always he appears as you saw him, carefully dressed and stately. Each summer when he is seen on the street, there is more or less curiosity about him among the summer visitors, for he is quite unlike the rest of us Mackinac people. But no one can discover anything more than I have told you, and those who have persisted so far as to sail over to the Chenaux either lose their way among the channels, or if they find the house, they never find him; the door is locked, and no one answers."

"Singular," I said. "He has nothing of the hermit about him. He has what I should call a courtly manner."

"That is it," replied my hostess, taking up the word; "some say he came from the French court, — a nobleman exiled for political offences; others think he is a priest under the ban; and there is still a third story, to the effect that he is a French count, who, owing to a disappointment in love, took orders and came to this far-away island, so that he might seclude himself forever from the world."

"But no one really knows?"

"Absolutely nothing. He is beloved by all the real old island families, whether they are of his faith or not; and when he dies the whole Strait, from Bois Blanc light to far Waugoschance, will mourn for him."

At sunset the Father came again to see me; the front door of my room was open, and we seated ourselves on the piazza outside. The roof of bark thatch had fallen away, leaving the bare beams overhead twined with brier-roses; the floor and house side were frescoed with those lichen-colored spots which show that the gray planks have lacked paint for many long years; the windows had wooden shutters fastened back with irons shaped like the letter S, and on the central door was a brass knocker, and a plate bearing the words, "United States Agency."

"When I first came to the island," said Father Piret,

"this was *the* residence *par excellence.* The old house was brave with green and white paint then; it had candelabra on its high mantles, brass andirons on its many hearthstones, curtains for all its little windows, and carpets for all its uneven floors. Much cooking went on, and smoke curled up from all these outside chimneys. Those were the days of the fur trade, and Mackinac was a central mart. Hither twice a year came the bateaux from the Northwest, loaded with furs; and in those old, decaying warehouses on the back street of the village were stored the goods sent out from New York, with which the bateaux were loaded again, and after a few days of revelry, during which the improvident voyagers squandered all their hard-earned gains, the train returned westward into 'the countries,' as they called the wilderness beyond the lakes, for another six months of toil. The officers of the little fort on the height, the chief factors of the fur company, and the United States Indian agent, formed the feudal aristocracy of the island; but the agent had the most imposing mansion, and often have I seen the old house shining with lights across its whole broadside of windows, and gay with the sound of a dozen French violins. The garden, now a wilderness, was the pride of the island. Its prim arbors, its spring and spring-house, its flower-beds, where, with infinite pains, a few hardy plants were induced to blossom; its cherry-tree avenue, whose early red fruit the short summer could scarcely ripen; its annual attempts at vegetables, which never came to maturity, — formed topics for conversation in court circles. Potatoes then as now were left to the mainland Indians, who came over with their canoes heaped with the fine, large thin-jacketed fellows, bartering them all for a loaf or two of bread and a little whiskey.

"The stockade which surrounds the place was at that day a not unnecessary defence. At the time of the payments the island swarmed with Indians, who came from Lake Superior and the Northwest, to receive the government pittance. Camped on the beach as far as the eye could reach, these wild warriors, dressed in all their savage finery, watched the Agency with greedy eyes, as they waited for their turn. The great gate was barred, and sentinels stood at the loopholes with loaded muskets; one by one the chiefs were admitted, stalked up to the office, — that wing on the right, — received the allotted sum, silently selected something from the displayed goods, and as silently departed, watched by quick eyes, until the great gate closed behind them. The guns of the fort were placed so as to command the Agency during payment time; and when, after several anxious, watchful days and nights, the last brave had received his portion, and the last canoe started away toward the north, leaving only the comparatively peaceful mainland Indians behind, the island drew a long breath of relief."

"Was there any real danger?" I asked.

"The Indians are ever treacherous," replied the Father. Then he was silent, and seemed lost in revery. The pure, ever-present breeze of Mackinac played in his long silvery hair, and his bright eyes roved along the wall of the old house; he had a broad forehead, noble features, and commanding presence, and as he sat there, recluse as he was, — aged, alone, without a history, with scarcely a name or a place in the world, — he looked, in the power of his native-born dignity, worthy of a royal coronet.

"I was thinking of old Jacques," he said, after a long pause. "He once lived in these rooms of yours, and died on that bench at the end of the piazza, sitting in the sunshine, with his staff in his hand."

"Who was he?" I asked. "Tell me the story, Father."

"There is not much to tell, madame; but in my mind he is so associated with this old house, that I always think of him when I come here, and fancy I see him on that bench.

"When the United States agent removed to the Apostle Islands, at the western end of Lake Superior, this place remained for some time uninhabited. But one winter morning smoke was seen coming out of that great chimney on the side; and in the course of the day several curious persons endeavored to open the main gate, at that time the only entrance. But the gate was barred within, and as the high stockade was slippery with ice, for some days the mystery remained unsolved. The islanders, always slow, grow torpid in the winter like bears; they watched the smoke in the daytime and the little twinkling light by night; they talked of spirits both French and Indian as they went their rounds, but they were too indolent to do more. At length the fort commandant heard of the smoke, and saw the light from his quarters on the height. As government property, he considered the Agency under his charge, and he was preparing to send a detail of men to examine the deserted mansion in its ice-bound garden, when its mysterious occupant appeared in the village; it was an old man, silent, gentle, apparently French. He carried a canvas bag, and bought a few supplies of the coarsest description, as though he was very poor. Unconscious of observation, he made his purchases and returned slowly homeward, barring the great gate behind him. Who was he? No one knew. Whence and when came he? No one could tell.

"The detail of soldiers from the fort battered at the gate, and when the silent old man opened it they followed him through the garden, where his feet had made a lonely trail over the deep snow, round to the side door. They entered, and found some blankets on the floor, a fire of old knots on the hearth, a long narrow box tied with a rope; his poor little supplies stood in one corner, — bread, salted fish, and a few potatoes,—and over the fire hung a rusty tea-kettle, its many holes carefully plugged with bits of rag. It was a desolate scene; the old man in the great rambling empty house in the heart of an arctic winter. He said little, and the soldiers could not understand his language; but they left him unmolested, and going back to the fort, they told what they had seen. Then the major went in person to the Agency, and gathered from the stranger's words that he had come to the island over the ice in the track of the mail-carrier; that he was an emigrant from France on his way to the Red River of the North, but his strength failing, owing to the intense cold, he had stopped at the island, and seeing the uninhabited house, he had crept into it, as he had not enough money to pay for a lodging elsewhere. He seemed a quiet, inoffensive old man, and after all the islanders had had a good long slow stare at him, he was left in peace, with his little curling smoke by day and his little twinkling light by night, although no one thought of assisting him; there is a strange coldness of heart in these northern latitudes.

"I was then living at the Chenaux; there was a German priest on the island; I sent over two half-breeds every ten days for the mail, and through them I heard of the stranger at the Agency. He was French, they said, and it was rumored in the saloons along the frozen docks that he had seen Paris. This warmed my heart; for, madame, I spent my youth in

Paris, — the dear, the beautiful city! So I came over to the island in my dog-sledge; a little thing is an event in our long, long winter. I reached the village in the afternoon twilight, and made my way alone to the Agency; the old man no longer barred his gate, and swinging it open with difficulty, I followed the trail through the snowy silent garden round to the side door of this wing, — the wing you occupy. I knocked; he opened; I greeted him, and entered. He had tried to furnish his little room with the broken relics of the deserted dwelling; a mended chair, a stool, a propped-up table, a shelf with two or three battered tin dishes, and some straw in one corner comprised the whole equipment, but the floor was clean, the old dishes polished, and the blankets neatly spread over the straw which formed the bed. On the table the supplies were ranged in order; there was a careful pile of knots on one side of the hearth, and the fire was evidently husbanded to last as long as possible. He gave me the mended chair, lighted a candle-end stuck in a bottle, and then seating himself on the stool, he gazed at me in his silent way until I felt like an uncourteous intruder. I spoke to him in French, offered my services; in short, I did my best to break down the barrier of his reserve; there was something pathetic in the little room and its lonely occupant, and, besides, I knew by his accent that we were both from the banks of the Seine.

"Well, I heard his story, — not then, but afterward; it came out gradually during the eleven months of our acquaintance; for he became my friend, — almost the only friend of fifty years. I am an isolated man, madame. It must be so. God's will be done!"

The Father paused, and looked off over the darkening water; he did not sigh, neither was his calm brow clouded, but there was in his face what seemed to me a noble resignation, and I have ever since felt sure that the secret of his exile held in it a self-sacrifice; for only self-sacrifice can produce that divine expression.

Out in the straits shone the low-down green light of a schooner; beyond glimmered the mast-head star of a steamer, with the line of cabin lights below, and away on the point of Bois Blanc gleamed the steady radiance of the lighthouse showing the way into Lake Huron; the broad overgrown garden cut us off from the village, but above on the height we could see the lighted windows of the fort, although still the evening sky retained that clear hue that seems so much like daylight when one looks aloft, although the earth lies in dark shadows below. The Agency was growing indistinct even to our near eyes; its white chimneys loomed up like ghosts, the shutters sighed in the breeze, and the planks of the piazza creaked causelessly. The old house was full of the spirits of memories, and at twilight they came abroad and bewailed themselves. "The place is haunted," I said, as a distant door groaned drearily.

"Yes," replied Father Piret, coming out of his abstraction, "and this wing is haunted by my old French friend. As time passed and the spring came, he fitted up in his fashion the whole suite of five rooms. He had his parlor, sleeping-room, kitchen, and store-room, the whole furnished only with the articles I have already described, save that the bed was of fresh green boughs instead of straw. Jacques occupied all the rooms with ceremonious exactness; he sat in the parlor, and I too must sit there when I came; in the second room he slept and made his careful toilet, with his shabby old clothes; the third was his kitchen and dining-room; and the fourth, that little closet on the right, was his store-room. His one indulgence was coffee; coffee he must and would have, though he slept on straw and went without meat. But he cooked to perfection in his odd way, and I have often eaten a dainty meal in that little kitchen, sitting at the propped-up table, using the battered tin dishes, and the clumsy wooden spoons fashioned with a jack-knife. After we had become friends Jacques would accept occasional aid from me, and it gave me a warm pleasure to think that I had added something to his comfort, were it only a little sugar, butter, or a pint of milk. No one disturbed the old man; no orders came from Washington respecting the Agency property, and the major had not the heart to order him away. There were more than houses enough for the scanty population of the island,

and only a magnate could furnish these large rambling rooms. So the soldiers were sent down to pick the red cherries for the use of the garrison, but otherwise Jacques had the whole place to himself, with all its wings, outbuildings, arbors, and garden beds.

"But I have not told you all. The fifth apartment in the suite — the square room with four windows and an outside door — was the old man's sanctuary; here were his precious relics, and here he offered up his devotions, half Christian, half pagan, with never-failing ardor. From the long narrow box which the fort soldiers had noticed came an old sabre, a worn and faded uniform of the French grenadiers, a little dried sprig, its two withered leaves tied in their places with thread, and a coarse woodcut of the great Napoleon; for Jacques was a soldier of the Empire. The uniform hung on the wall, carefully arranged on pegs as a man would wear it, and the sabre was brandished from the empty sleeve as though a hand held it; the woodcut framed in green, renewed from day to day, pine in the winter, maple in the summer, occupied the opposite side, and under it was fastened the tiny withered sprig, while on the floor below was a fragment of buffalo-skin which served the soldier for a stool when he knelt in prayer. And did he pray to Napoleon, you ask? I hardly know. He had a few of the Church's prayers by heart, but his mind was full of the Emperor as he repeated them, and his eyes were fixed upon the picture as though it was the face of a saint. Discovering this, I labored hard to bring him to a clearer understanding of the faith; but all in vain. He listened to me patiently, even reverently, although I was much the younger; at intervals he replied, 'Oui, mon père,' and the next day he said his prayers to the dead Emperor as usual. And this was not the worst; in place of an amen, there came a fierce imprecation against the whole English nation. After some months I succeeded in persuading him to abandon this termination; but I always suspected that it was but a verbal abandonment, and that, mentally, the curse was as strong as ever.

"Jacques had been a soldier of the Empire, as it is called, — a grenadier under Napoleon; he had loved his General and Emperor in life, and adored him in death with the affectionate pertinacity of a faithful dog. One hot day during the German campaign, Napoleon, engaged in conference with some of his generals, was disturbed by the uneasy movements of his horse; looking around for some one to brush away the flies, he saw Jacques, who stood at a short distance watching his Emperor with admiring eyes. Always quick to recognize the personal affection he inspired, Napoleon signed to the grenadier to approach. 'Here, mon brave,' he said, smiling; 'get a branch and keep the flies from my horse a few moments.' The proud soldier obeyed; he heard the conversation of the Emperor; he kept the flies from his horse. As he talked, Napoleon idly plucked a little sprig from the branch as it came near his hand, and played with it; and when, the conference over, with a nod of thanks to Jacques, he rode away, the grenadier stopped, picked up the sprig fresh from the Emperor's hand, and placed it carefully in his breast-pocket. The Emperor had noticed him; the Emperor had called him 'mon brave'; the Emperor had smiled upon him. This was the glory of Jacques's life. How many times have I listened to the story, told always in the same words, with the same gestures in the same places! He remembered every sentence of the conversation he had heard, and repeated them with automatic fidelity, understanding nothing of their meaning; even when I explained their probable connection with the campaign, my words made no impression upon him, and I could see that they conveyed no idea to his mind. He was made for a soldier; brave and calm, he reasoned not, but simply obeyed, and to this blind obedience there was added a heart full of affection which, when concentrated upon the Emperor, amounted to idolatry. Napoleon possessed a singular personal power over his soldiers; they all loved him, but Jacques adored him.

"It was an odd, affectionate animal," said Father Piret, dropping unconsciously into a French idiom to express his meaning. "The little sprig had been kept as a talisman, and no saintly relic was ever more honored; the Emperor had touched it!

"Grenadier Jacques made one of the ill-fated Russian army, and, although wounded and suffering, he still endured until the capture of Paris. Then, when Napoleon retired to Elba, he fell sick from grief, nor did he recover until the Emperor returned, when, with thousands of other soldiers, our Jacques hastened to his standard, and the hundred days began. Then came Waterloo. Then came St. Helena. But the grenadier lived on in hope, year after year, until the Emperor died,—died in exile, in the hands of the hated English. Broken-hearted, weary of the sight of his native land, he packed his few possessions, and fled away over the ocean, with a vague idea of joining a French settlement on the Red River; I have always supposed it must be the Red River of the South; there are French there. But the poor soldier was very ignorant; some one directed him to these frozen regions, and he set out; all places were alike to him now that the Emperor had gone from earth. Wandering as far as Mackinac on his blind pilgrimage, Jacques found his strength failing, and crept into this deserted house to die. Recovering, he made for himself a habitation from a kind of instinct, as a beaver might have done. He gathered together the wrecks of furniture, he hung up his treasures, he had his habits for every hour of the day; soldier-like, everything was done by rule. At a particular hour it was his custom to sit on that bench in the sunshine, wrapped in his blankets in the winter, in summer in his shirt-sleeves with his one old coat carefully hung on that peg; I can see him before me now. On certain days he would wash his few poor clothes, and hang them out on the bushes to dry; then he would patiently mend them with his great brass thimble and coarse thread. Poor old garments! they were covered with awkward patches.

"At noon he would prepare his one meal; for his breakfast and supper were but a cup of coffee. Slowly and with the greatest care the materials were prepared and the cooking watched. There was a savor of the camp, a savor of the Paris café, and a savor of originality; and often, wearied with the dishes prepared by my half-breeds, I have come over to the island to dine with Jacques, for the old soldier was proud of his skill, and liked an appreciative guest. And I — But it is not my story I tell."

"O Father Piret, if you could but —"

"Thanks, madame. To others I say, 'What would you? I have been here since youth; you know my life.' But to you I say, there was a past; brief, full, crowded into a few years; but I cannot tell it; my lips are sealed! Again, thanks for your sympathy, madame. And now I will go back to Jacques.

"We were comrades, he and I; he would not come over to the Chenaux; he was unhappy if the routine of his day was disturbed, but I often stayed a day with him at the Agency, for I too liked the silent house. It has its relics, by the way. Have you noticed a carved door in the back part of the main building? That was brought from the old chapel on the mainland, built as early as 1700. The whole of this locality is sacred ground in the history of our Church. It was first visited by our missionaries in 1670, and over at Point St. Ignace the dust which was once the mortal body of Father Marquette lies buried. The exact site of the grave is lost; but we know that in 1677 his Indian converts brought back his body, wrapped in birch-bark, from the eastern shore of Lake Michigan, where he died, to his beloved mission of St. Ignace. There he was buried in a vault under the little log-church. Some years later the spot was abandoned, and the resident priests returned to Montreal. We have another little Indian church there now, and the point is forever consecrated by its unknown grave. At various times I told Jacques the history of this strait, — its islands, and points; but he evinced little interest. He listened with some attention to my account of the battle which took place on Dousman's farm, not far from the British Landing; but when he found that the English were victorious, he muttered a great oath and refused to hear more. To him the English were fiends incarnate. Had they not slowly murdered his Emperor on their barren rock in the sea?

"Only once did I succeed in interesting the old soldier. Then, as now, I received twice each year a package of foreign pamphlets and papers; among them came, that summer, a German ballad, written by that strange being, Henri Heine. I give it to you in a later English translation:—

THE GRENADIERS.

To the land of France went two grenadiers,
  From a Russian prison returning;
But they hung down their heads on the German frontiers,
  The news from the fatherland learning.

For there they both heard the sorrowful tale,
  That France was by fortune forsaken:
That her mighty army was scattered like hail,
  And the Emperor, the Emperor taken.

Then there wept together the grenadiers,
  The sorrowful story learning;
And one said, "O woe!" as the news he hears,
  "How I feel my old wound burning!"

The other said, "The song is sung,
  And I wish that we both were dying!
But at home I 've a wife and a child,—they 're young,
  On me, and me only, relying."

"O, what is a wife or a child to me?
  Deeper wants all my spirit have shaken:
Let them beg, let them beg, should they hungry be!
  My Emperor, my Emperor taken!

"But I beg you, brother, if by chance
  You soon shall see me dying,
Then take my corpse with you back to France:
  Let it ever in France be lying.

"The cross of honor with crimson band
  Shall rest on my heart as it bound me:
Give me my musket in my hand,
  And buckle my sword around me.

"And there I will lie and listen still,
  In my sentry coffin staying,
Till I feel the thundering cannon's thrill,
  And horses tramping and neighing.

"Then my Emperor will ride well over my grave,
  'Mid sabres' bright slashing and fighting,
And I'll rise all weaponed up out of my grave,
  For the Emperor, the Emperor fighting!"

"This simple ballad went straight to the heart of old Jacques; tears rolled down his cheeks as I read, and he would have it over and over again. 'Ah! that comrade was happy,' he said. '*He* died when the Emperor was only *taken*. I too would have gone to my grave smiling, could I have thought that my Emperor would come riding over it with all his army around him again! But he is dead,—my Emperor is dead! Ah! that comrade was a happy man; he died! He did not have to stand by while the English —may they be forever cursed!—slowly, slowly murdered him,—murdered the great Napoleon! No; that comrade died. Perhaps he is with the Emperor now, —that comrade-grenadier.'

"To be with his Emperor was Jacques's idea of heaven.

"From that moment each time I visited the Agency I must repeat the verses again and again; they became a sort of hymn. Jacques had not the capacity to learn the ballad, although he so often listened to it, but the seventh verse he managed to repeat after a fashion of his own, setting it to a nondescript tune, and crooning it about the house as he came and went on his little rounds. Gradually he altered the words, but I could not make out the new phrases as he muttered them over to himself, as if trying them.

"'What is it you are saying, Jacques?' I asked.

"But he would not tell me. After a time I discovered that he had added the altered verse to his prayers; for always when I was at the Agency I went with him to his sanctuary, if for no other purpose than to prevent the uttered imprecation that served as amen for the whole. The verse, whatever it was, came in before this.

"So the summer passed. The vague intention of going on to the Red River of the North had faded away, and Jacques lived along on the island as though he had never lived anywhere else. He grew wonted to the Agency, like some old family cat, until he seemed to belong to the house, and all thought of disturbing him was forgotten. 'There is Jacques out washing his clothes,' 'There is Jacques going to buy his coffee,' 'There is Jacques sitting on the piazza,' said the islanders; the old man served them instead of a clock.

"One dark autumn day I came over from the Chenaux to get the mail. The water was rough, and my boat, tilted far over on one side, skimmed the crests of the waves in the daring fashion peculiar to the Mackinac craft; the mail-steamer had not come in, owing to the storm outside, and I went on to the Agency to see Jacques. He seemed as usual, and we had dinner over the little fire, for the day was chilly; the meal over, my host put everything in order again in his methodical way, and then retired to his sanctuary for prayers. I followed, and stood in the doorway while he knelt. The room was dusky, and the uniform with its outstretched sabre looked like a dead soldier leaning against the wall; the face of Napoleon opposite seemed to gaze down on Jacques as he knelt, as though listening. Jacques muttered his prayers, and I responded Amen! then, after a silence, came the altered verse; then, with a quick glance toward me, another silence, which I felt sure contained the unspoken curse. Gravely he led the way back to the kitchen — for, owing to the cold, he allowed me to dispense with the parlor, — and there we spent the afternoon together, talking, and watching for the mail-boat. 'Jacques,' I said, 'what is that verse you have added to your prayers? Come, my friend, why should you keep it from me?'

"'It is nothing, mon père,—nothing,' he replied. But again I urged him to tell me; more to pass away the time than from any real interest. 'Come,' I said, 'it may be your last chance. Who knows but that I may be drowned on my way back to the Chenaux?'

"'True,' replied the old soldier, calmly. 'Well, then, here it is, mon père: my death-wish. Voilà!'

"'Something you wish to have done after death?'

"'Yes.'

"'And who is to do it?'

"'My Emperor.'

"'But, Jacques, the Emperor is dead.'

"'He will have it done all the same, mon père.'

"In vain I argued; Jacques was calmly obstinate. He had mixed up his Emperor with the stories of the Saints; why should not Napoleon do what they had done?

"'What is the verse, any way?' I said at last.

"'It is my death-wish, as I said before, mon père.' And he repeated the following. He said it in French, for I had given him a French translation, as he knew nothing of German; but I will give you the English, as he had altered it:—

'The Emperor's face with its green leaf band
Shall rest on my heart that loved him so.
Give me the sprig in my dead hand,
My uniform and sabre around me.
Amen.'

"So prays Grenadier Jacques.

"The old soldier had sacrificed the smooth metre; but I understood what he meant.

"The storm increased, and I spent the night at the Agency, lying on the bed of boughs, covered with a blanket. The house shook in the gale, the shutters rattled, and all the floors near and far creaked as though feet were walking over them. I was wakeful and restless, but Jacques slept quietly, and did not stir until daylight broke over the stormy water, showing the ships scudding by under bare poles, and the distant mail-boat laboring up toward the island through the heavy sea. My host made his toilet, washing and shaving himself carefully, and putting on his old clothes as though going on parade. Then came breakfast, with a stew added in honor of my presence; and as by this time the steamer was not far from Round Island, I started down toward the little post-office, anxious to receive some expected letters. The steamer came in slowly, the mail was distributed slowly, and I stopped to read my letters before returning. I had a picture-paper for Jacques, and as I looked out across the straits, I saw that the storm was over, and decided to return to the Chenaux in the afternoon, leaving word with my half-breeds to have the sail-boat in readiness at three o'clock. The sun was throwing out a watery gleam as, after the lapse of an hour or two, I walked up the limestone road and entered the great gate of the Agency. As I came through the garden along the cherry-tree avenue I saw Jacques sitting on that bench in the sun, for this was his hour for sunshine; his staff was in his hand, and he was leaning back against the side of the house with his eyes closed, as if in revery. 'Jacques, here is a picture-paper for you,' I said, laying my hand on his shoulder. He did not answer. He was dead.

"Alone, sitting in the sunshine, apparently without a struggle or a pang, the soul of the old soldier had departed. Whither? We know not. But — smile if you will, madame — I trust he is with his Emperor."

I did not smile; my eyes were too full of tears.

"I buried him, as he wished," continued Father Piret, "in his old uniform, with the picture of Napoleon laid on his breast, the sabre by his side, and the withered sprig in his lifeless hand. He lies in our little cemetery on the height, near the shadow of the great cross; the low white board tablet at the head of the mound once bore the words 'Grenadier Jacques,' but the rains and the snows have washed away the painted letters. It is as well."

The priest paused, and we both looked toward the empty bench, as though we saw a figure seated there, staff in hand. After a time my little hostess came out on to the piazza, and we all talked together of the island and its past. "My boat is waiting," said Father Piret at length; "the wind is fair, and I must return to the Chenaux to-night. This near departure is my excuse for coming twice in one day to see you, madame."

"Stay over, my dear sir," I urged. "I too shall leave in another day. We may not meet again."

"Not on earth; but in another world we may," answered the priest, rising as he spoke.

"Father, your blessing," said the little hostess in a low tone, after a quick glance toward the many windows through which the bulwarks of Protestantism might be gazing. But all was dark, both without and within, and the Father gave his blessing to both of us, fervently, but with an apostolic simplicity. Then he left us, and I watched his tall form, crowned with silvery hair, as he passed down the cherry-tree avenue. Later in the evening the moon came out, and I saw a Mackinac boat skimming by the house, its white sails swelling full in the fresh breeze.

"That is Father Piret's boat," said my hostess. "The wind is fair; he will reach the Chenaux before midnight."

A day later, and I too sailed away. As the steamer bore me southward, I looked back toward the island with a sigh. Half hidden in its wild green garden I saw the old Agency; first I could distinguish its whole rambling length; then I lost the roofless piazza, then the dormer-windows, and finally I could only discern the white chimneys, with their crumbling crooked tops. The sun sank into the Strait off Waugoschance, the evening gun flashed from the little fort on the height, the shadows grew dark and darker, the island turned into green foliage, then a blue outline, and finally there was nothing but the dusky water.

MISERY LANDING.

TOWARD the western end of Lake Superior there is a group of islands, twenty-three in number, called the "Twelve Apostles." One more and the Apostles might have had two apiece. But although Apostles taken together, officially, as it were, they have personal names of a very different character, such as "Cat," "Eagle," "Bear," "Devil," etc. Whether the Jesuit fathers who first explored this little archipelago had any symbolical ideas connected with these animals we know not, but they were wise enough to appreciate the beauty of the group, and established a little church and Indian college upon the southernmost point of the southernmost island as early as 1680. A village grew slowly into existence on this point, — very slowly, since one hundred and ninety-two years later it was still a village, and less than a village; the Catholic church and adjoining buildings, the house of the Indian agent, and the United States warehouse, stored full at payment time, one store, and the cabins of the fishermen and trappers, comprised the whole. Two miles to the eastward rose a bold promontory, running far out into the bay, and forming the horizon line on that side. Perched upon the edge of this promontory, outlined against the sky, stood a solitary house. The pine forest stopped abruptly behind it, the cliff broke off abruptly in front, and for a long distance up and down the coast there was no beach or landing-place. This spot was "Misery Landing," so called because there was no landing there, not even a miserable one, — at least that was what John Jay said when he first saw the place. The inconsistency pleased him, and forthwith he ordered a cabin built on the edge of the cliff, taking up his abode meanwhile in the village, and systematically investigating the origin of the name. He explored the upper circle, consisting of the Indian agent, the storekeeper, and the priests; but they could tell him nothing. A priest more imaginative than the rest hastily improvised a legend about some miserable sinner, but John refused to accept the obvious fraud. The second circle, consisting of fishermen, voyageurs, and half-breed trappers, knew nothing save the fact that the name belonged to the point before their day. The third circle, consisting of unadulterated Indian, produced the item that the name was given by a white man as long ago as the days of their great-grandfathers. Who the white man was and what his story no one knew, and John was at liberty to imagine anything he pleased. The cabin built, he took possession of his eyrie. It was fortified by a high stockade across the land side; the other three sides were sheer cliffs rising from the deep water. Directly in front of the house, however, a rope-ladder was suspended over the cliff, strongly fastened at the top, but hanging loose at the bottom within two feet of the water; so, in spite of nature's obstacles, he had a landing-place at Misery after all. Extracts from his diary will best tell his story:—

"*June* 15, 1872.—Settled at last in my cabin at Misery Landing. Now, indeed, I feel myself free from the frivolity, the hypocrisy, the evil, the cowardice, and the falsity of the world. Now I can live close to nature; now I can throw off the habits of cities, and mentally and physically be a man; not a puppet, not a fashion-plate, but a man! Here I have all that life holds of real worth, the sun, the free winds of heaven, the broad water, the woods, the flowers, the birds, and the wild animals, whom I welcome as my fellows. True-Heart, my dog, shall be my companion,—ah, how much more trustworthy than a human friend!

"*June* 16.—Have cooked and eaten my solitary supper, and now, with Sweet-Silence, my pipe, breathing out fragrance, and True-Heart lying at my feet, I take up my pen. First I will describe my cabin. The people of the village are full of wonder over its marvels, and the stockade is none too high to keep them out.

They cannot understand why I have no gate. 'Don't you see, we never can come out to call on you in the evening if we have to take a boat, come round by water, and climb up that dizzy ladder,' they say. It never occurs to them that possibly that is what I intend. My cabin is made of logs, well chinked and plastered; it is one large square room, with a deep chimney at each end, the western half curtained off as a sleeping-apartment. There is only one door, and that is in front, where there are also two large windows looking off over the lake; on the other three sides the windows are high up, and filled with painted glass. I can look out only upon the boundless water, and only toward the eastward. In this respect I am as devout as any ascetic. The question arises, Did n't the ascetics have the best of it, after all? I am inclined to think they fled away into the wilderness to get rid of feminine frivolity and falsity, just as I have done; they were ashamed of their own weakness, just as I am; and they resolved to have nothing to do with the accursed beautiful images, who are fickle because such is their nature. Why should we expect vanes to remain stationary?

"I have a luxurious bed, a hair-mattress suspended in a hammock. Here, when the red curtains are down and the fire has burned into red coals, I fall asleep, lulled by the sighing of the wind among the pine-trees, the rush of the rain upon the roof, or the boom of the surf at the foot of the cliffs. Ah, Misery Landing, thou art indeed a rest for the weary!

"*June* 17. — I have been looking over my books, and smiling at their selection; they represent eras in my life. There 's St. Francis de Sales, Thomas à Kempis, a quantity of mediæval Latin hymns, together with Tennyson's 'Sir Galahad,' superbly illustrated. Heaven help me! I thought I was a Sir Galahad myself once upon a time. But I got bravely over that, it seems, since the next series is 'all for love.' O Petrarch, and ye of that ilk, how I sighed over your pages! Then comes a dash of French, cynical, exquisite in detail, glittering, brilliant, — the refinement of selfishness; then a soar into the cloud-land of Germany, and a wrestle with philosophy, coming down into modern rationalism, Darwin, Huxley, and the like, each phase represented by a single volume, the one which for some unexplained reason happened to impress me the most. And what is the last book of all? Bret Harte. Not his verse, but his deep-hearted prose. After all, as long as I can read his pages, I cannot be so bad as I seem, since, to my idea, there is more of goodness and generosity and courage in his words than in many a sermon. He shows us the good in the heart of the outcast. I wonder if I am an outcast.

"*June* 29. — It is a fine thing to have money. Poverty *pur et simple* is not adapted to the cultivation of either soul, mind, or body. I have been cultivating the last named. The truth is, I felt blue, and so I ordered out the hunters and fishermen, sent for old Lize the cook, and held a royal feast. It lasted for days, Indian fashion. I did nothing but eat, sleep, and smoke. Sweet-Silence and True-Heart were my companions; the riffraff who ate the fragments camped outside in the forest, and Lize had orders to throw them supplies over the stockade. She herself was ordered not to speak, and to depart at nightfall, leaving a store of well-cooked viands behind her. With my rare old wines, my delicate canned, potted, and preserved stores of all kinds, I passed a luxurious week. I thought of Francesca: she would have entered into it with all her heart, (by the way, has she a heart?) but she would have required velvet robes and a chair draped with ermine before she would condescend to give herself as an adjunct to the scene. Sybarite! But why should I cast scorn upon her? Can she help her nature? She is so beautiful that she seeks luxury as a rose seeks sunshine. Ease is the natural condition of her being. Is it any wonder, then, that she longed for my wealth? But I had the insane fancy to be loved for myself alone; and so, having found her out, I left her forever.

"*July* 9.—I have been studying the wild-flowers of this region; equipped for botanizing, I have spent days in the forest. I shall commence a complete collection. This is indeed living close to nature.

"*July* 15.—Flowers are but inanimate things, after all, the toys of vegetation. It has been said that all naturalists are what they are because they have been the victims of some heart disappointment, which means, I suppose, that they take up with the less because they cannot have the greater.

"*July* 20.—Thoreau found the climbing fern, and I, too, have found a rare and unique plant! Who knows but that it may carry my name down to posterity!

"*July* 25.—It is n't rare at all. It is the same old Indian pipe, or monotropa, masquerading under a new disguise. And as to posterity, who cares for it? As the Englishman said in Parliament, 'My lords and gentlemen, I hear a great deal said here about posterity, but let me ask, frankly, what has posterity ever done for us?'

"*August* 1.—They say you can teach birds to come at your call. There was a bird girl in Teverino, I remember. Will begin to-day.

"*August* 15.—It can't be done. Am going fishing.

"*August* 16.—On the whole, I don't like fishing. Dying agonies are not cheerful. Have been painting a little for the first time in months. It seems as if poverty was the *sine qua non* in painting: all great artists are poor.

"*August* 25.—Painting for days. Have painted

Francesca as she looked that night at the opera. She was leaning forward, with parted lips and starry eyes, her golden hair shining on the velvet of her robe, a rose-flush on her cheek, pearls on her full white throat. I sat in the shadow watching her. 'She is moved by the pathos of the scene,' I thought, as I noted the absorbed expression. I spoke to her, and drew out the whole. 'O, the perfection of that drapery!' she murmured; 'the exquisite pattern of that lace!'

"*August* 26. — There is no doubt but that she was royally beautiful. I could have stood it, I think, or rather I fear, if she had condescended so far as even to pretend to love me. But she simply did not know how. A woman of more brain would have deceived me, but Francesca never tried. No merit to her, though, for that. Am going hunting.

"*September* 1. — In the village to-day. For curiosity, went into the old Catholic church. It is anchored down to the rocks, covered with lichen on the outside, and decked with tinsel within. The priests were chanting horribly out of tune, and the ignorant, dirty congregation mumbled their prayers while they stared open-mouthed at me. There was a homely little girl kneeling near me who did not glance up, the only person who did not. A homely woman is a complete mistake, always: a woman should always be beautiful, as a man should always be strong.

"*September* 5. — The homely little girl was there

again to-day. She is slight, thin, and dark; her features are irregular; her dark hair braided closely around her small head. Ah! what glorious waves of gold flowed over Francesca's shoulders!

"*September* 10. — The fall storms are upon us; the wind is howling overhead, and the waves roaring below. But what a strange sense of comfort there is in it all! I was sitting before the fire last evening smoking Sweet-Silence, and deep in a delicious revery. Suddenly there came a knock at the door. I was startled. The rain was pouring down in torrents; it seemed as though no human foot could have climbed the swaying ladder in front of my hermitage. I opened the door, half hoping that the Prince of the Powers of the Air had come to pay me a visit, and I resolved to entertain him royally. But no mighty, potent spirit was on my threshold; only a slim youth, drenched and pallid, with large pale eyes and pinched features. He said nothing, but gazed at me imploringly, while the water dripped from every bony angle. Evidently this was no devil of jovial tastes; he was more like a washed-out cherub in the process of awkward growth toward full angelhood.

"'What do you want?' I said. He did not answer, and somewhat roughly I drew him in; I never could endure to see anything shiver. Then I closed the door, and resumed my warm seat and Sweet-Silence, turning my back upon the interloper; he was welcome to everything save my own personality,—let him warm himself and eat or sleep, but me he must not approach. But minutes passed; the creature neither moved nor spoke, and his very silence was more offensive to me than loud-tongued importunity. At length it so wrought upon me that, angry with myself for being unable to banish his miserable presence from my thoughts, I turned sharply around and confronted him. He had not moved, standing on the exact spot where I had left him, shivering and dumb, with the rain dripping in chilly little pools upon the floor. There were holes in his wet old boots; I could see his blue-white skin gleaming through; he had no stockings, and no shirt under his ragged coat, held together over his narrow chest with long thin fingers.

"'Stop shivering, you horrible image of despair,' I called out.

"'Please, sir, I can't help it,' he answered, humbly. Well, of course I went to work; I knew I should all the time,—I always do. I got him into warm dry clothes, I fed him, I made him drink spiced wine, I gave him my own easy-chair. Then, stretching out fleecy stockings and slippers upon the hearth, in the plenitude of warmth and comfort, gradually the creature unfolded all his lank length, and thawed into speech. His name was George Washington Brown, his tribe Yankee, his state orphanage, his condition poverty, his trouble a malarial chill and fever, which haunted him and devoured what poor strength his rapid growth had left. On the mainland hunting, the storm had kept him until, his provisions exhausted, half fainting with hunger, he essayed to cross back to the village; but his sail was torn away, he lost an oar, and, drifting hopelessly, chance sent him ashore on the iron-bound coast just where my rope-ladder struck his face in the darkness of the stormy night. He knew then where he was. He had been drifting twenty-four hours. The ascent was perilous, for the ladder swung him about like a cork on a line, but desperately he clung, and so reached my door at last. Poor wretch! It was a sight to see him take in comfort at every pore. 'You may stay until the storm goes down,' I said.

"*September* 15. — The storm has gone down, but he is here still.

"*September* 18. — He knows nothing. He cannot read, he cannot write; he has never heard of Shakespeare, of Raphael, of Napoleon, or even of his own sponsor, Washington, beyond the fact that he 'heard tell as how Washington was a wery good sort of a man'; he has never seen anything but Lake Superior, he knows nothing of geography, he has Joshua's ideas of the heavenly bodies, and he believes in ghosts; he has heard of Grant, and vaguely remembers that Lincoln was killed; he has never seen 'niggers,' but is glad, on general principles, that they are free. I have told him that he may stay here a month.

"*September* 28. — I played simple tunes on my violin last evening, and the boy was moved to tears. I shall teach him to play, I think.

"*September* 30. — Another gale. I read aloud last evening. George did not seem much interested in Bret Harte, but was captivated with the pageantry of 'Ivanhoe.' Strange that it should be so, but everywhere it is the cultivated people only who are taken with Bret. But they must be imaginative as well as cultivated; routine people, whether in life or in literature, dislike anything unconventional or new.

"*October* 28. — Have been so occupied that I could not write. George has gone over to the village to church to-day. He is a good Catholic, and I have resisted the temptation to trouble his faith, so far. I drew and colored a picture for him yesterday, and ever since he has been wild to have me paint the likeness of some one in the village. He does not say who, but I suspect it is one of the priests. I am teaching him to read and write.

"*November* 2. — George did not return until the next morning, and then who should the boy bring with him but that homely girl! 'This is Marthy,' he said; 'she 's come to be painted, governor.' To please him, I began. The girl sat down with quiet composure; no fine city lady could have been more unconcerned. She must be about seventeen.

"*November* 7. — George brings her out in the boat every day, and takes her back at night; but ice is forming now, and he must find some other way. While I paint he cooks the dinner, and serves it with the most delicate of my stores. Martha presides at the feast with a quaint little dignity peculiarly her own. She is a colorless, undeveloped child. A picture of her will be like a shadow on the wall.

"*November* 9. — Cold and stormy. I am alone. George has gone to the village. Have been reading Shakespeare. Booth plays Hamlet wonderfully well; but why is it that he never has a fair Ophelia? It looks too much like method in his madness when he leaves her so easily. Ophelia should be slight and young, with timid eyes, and delicate, colorless complexion. She should be without guile, innocent, ignorant of the world. At least that is my idea of her.

"*November* 11. — Little Martha can sing. She has a sweet, fresh, untrained voice, and now while I paint she sings song after song. I am making quite an elaborate picture, after all. It will serve as a souvenir of Misery Landing."

Here the diary ends, and the narrator takes up the tale. One evening in April, five months later, when the wild spring winds were sweeping through the sky, and the snow-drifts were beginning to sink, John Jay and his protégé sat together before the fire in the cabin on the point.

"But, George," said the gentleman, "think of all I offer you, — education, a chance to see the world, a certainty of comfort for all your life. If it is myself you object to, I will leave you entirely independent of me."

"'T is n't you, governor; I'm mighty fond of you. I s'pose ye 're like what my father ud have been ef he 'd lived."

"No, no, George. Your father would have been a much older man than I am. I am not thirty-five yet."

"And I am not twenty-one. What was you like when you was young, governor?"

"Very much what I am now, I suppose."

"O no; that could n't be, you know. Why, you 've got wrinkles, and some gray hairs, and such a tremenjous mus-tash, you have! Marthy says she 's never seen the like."

"She does not admire it?"

"My! no. I say, governor, *she* 's got a nice little face, now has n't she?"

"Really, I am no judge of that style, George. But look, I will show you a lovely lady I once knew. There are many such faces out in the world, and you can see them for yourself if you will go to school and college as I wish."

Rising, the gentleman brought out the glowing picture of Francesca at the opera. The boor gazed at it with wide-open eyes. "It's some queen, I reckon," he said at length.

"No, it is a beautiful lady, and you shall know her, her very self, if you please. Look at the waves of her golden hair, her starry eyes, her velvet skin with its rose-leaf glow. See her head, her bearing, her exquisite royal beauty. Look, look with all your eyes, boy, and think that you too can see and love her."

The boor gazed as the gentleman pointed out each beauty. "It's mighty grand, it's powerful fine," he said at last, drawing a long breath. "But arter all, governor, Marthy is sweeter nor her!"

Another time the conversation ran as follows:—

"Yes, George, that is floating on the Nile, just as I have told you, with the palm-trees, the gorgeous flowers, the brilliant birds, the temples, and the strange Pyramids. You shall see the Bedouins of the desert; you shall ride on Arabian horses; you shall study the secrets of the Old World in their very birthplace. Isn't that better than living forever on this cold coast, with only your own two hands between yourself and starvation?"

George looked down slowly at his hands, spreading them open on his knees for a clearer view. "Can't Marthy go with me, governor?" he said, wistfully.

"I tell you, no. You must give her up. She is

as ignorant as you were before I knew you, and, being a woman, she cannot learn, or rather unlearn."

"Can't women-folks learn?" said George, wonderingly.

"No," thundered the governor; "they are an inferior race; by nature they must be either tyrants or slaves, — tyrants to the weak, slaves to the strong. The wise man chains them down; the chains may be gilded, but none the less must they be chains."

"Well, then, governor," replied the youth, simply, "I'll just take Marthy with me as my slave. It ull do as long as I have her some way; and seeing as we're going to Africa, it ull be all right, won't it?"

"Why do you want her, George?" said the gentleman, abruptly. "She is not beautiful; she is utterly ignorant."

"I know it, governor."

"And she does not love you."

"I know that too," said the boy, dejectedly. "But the point of the thing is just here: she may not love me, but, governor, I love her, — love her so much that I can't live without her."

"Nonsense! Boys always think so. Try it for six months, George, and you'll find I am right."

"Not for six days, governor. I jest could n't," said the youth, in a tone of miserable conviction. The tears stood in his pale eyes, and he shifted his long limbs uneasily.

"Don't squirm," ejaculated the gentleman, sternly, glowering at him over Sweet-Silence. "I'm afraid you're a fool, George," he continued, after a pause.

"I'm afraid so too, governor."

Then John Jay took the girl into his confidence. "What, go away!" she exclaimed. "George to go away! And you, sir?"

"I am quite attached to the boy," said the gentleman, ignoring her question. "Why I call him a boy I scarcely know; I myself am not thirty-five, Martha."

"And I am not seventeen, sir."

"A woman is a woman. But never mind that now. What I want to know is whether you are willing he should go?"

"O yes, sir; it will be for his good. But you?"

"I do not know whether I shall go or not," replied the gentleman, gazing down into the timid, upraised eyes. Then he told her of the outside world, and all its knowledge, all its splendor; this was what he intended for George. The maiden listened, spell-bound.

"It will be beautiful for him," she murmured. "Yes, he must go. I shall make him."

"Will he do as you say, Martha?"

"O yes; he always does!"

"But this time it will be different."

"How different?"

"He must leave you behind."

"O, as to that, sir, *I* do not want to go. I shall tell him so."

"But perhaps *he* will not go without you."

The girl laughed merrily, showing little white teeth like pearls. "Poor old George!" she said, dismissing, as it were, with a wave of her small brown hand the absent boy-lover. Her tone jarred some chord in the gentleman's breast; he rose, bade her good evening ceremoniously, and opened the door. She lingered, but he stood silent. At last, subdued and timid again, she took up her little basket and hurried away. But hours afterward, when John Jay went out, according to his custom, to smoke Sweet-Silence in the open evening air, a small dark object was sitting on the edge of the cliff. He approached; it was Martha.

"O sir," she said, "you are not going away? Say you are not! O say you are not!"

"What if I am?" said the gentleman, abruptly.

"O sir! O —" And the tears came.

"Go home, child!" said the man, leading her toward the stockade. There was a postern-gate there now. She went obediently; but at the edge of the wood she paused, and wiped her eyes with her apron in order to see him plainly as he stood outlined in the gateway against the clear evening sky. The gentleman closed the gate with violence, and went back into the house.

Not one word more said John Jay to his protégé

on the subject of education and travel. But Martha took up the song, and chanted it in every key, with all her woman's wit to aid her. George grew pale and sad and restless. He could settle to nothing; his gun, traps, and tackle, his kettles and frying-pans, his books and music, were all neglected. Every day he saw Martha, and every day she had a new way of presenting the hateful subject. Every day he tried to speak the words that choked him, and every day he failed, and parted from her in silent misery.

One morning they were all together in the cabin.

"When you come back, George, I suppose you 'll have a great mustache, like Mr. Jay's," said Martha, merrily. She had taken the "of-course-you-'re-going-and-it 's-all-settled" tone that day, much to the poor lad's discomfiture.

"I suppose you 'd scarcely say, 'How d' ye do?' then," answered George. Then, with a sudden rush of boldness, "I say, Marthy," he burst forth, "ef I do go, will you give me a kiss for good-by?"

"Of course I will," answered the girl, gayly; and springing up, she tripped across the room, and lightly touched his forehead with her delicate little lips. The boy flushed scarlet, and caught her hands in an attempt at awkward frolicking.

"Give the old governor one too," he said. "Come, I 'll let you."

The "old governor" (ah! so very old!) advanced;

he came close to her; then he stopped. He did not even touch her hand; but for one moment he looked deep down into her upraised eyes. The girl drew a quick, audible breath; then turning, she ran from the house like some shy, startled creature of the woods. They saw her no more that day, nor the next, nor for many days. The boy pined visibly. One evening John Jay said, suddenly, "George, I have changed my mind. Martha shall go with you. You may marry her, and I will care for you both."

"Do you really mean it, governor?"

"Yes; go and tell her so."

Then there was a rush out of the cabin, a headlong climbing down the swinging ladder, a frantic row across the bay, and a wild irruption into the little house on the beach where Martha lived. Half an hour later the same whirlwind came back across the bay and up the ladder, and demanded of the governor, "Are you going with us?"

"No," said the governor, shortly, and the whirlwind departed again. At one o'clock there came a feeble knock at the barred door. There stood the drooping lover, drenched with the rain which had been falling since midnight. "What do you mean by coming out here at this time of night, you uncomfortable object?" said the governor, getting back again into his luxurious bed.

"I did n't know it was late, and I did n't care for

the rain nor nothing," replied the truant, recklessly; "for Marthy she 's gone and said she won't go." And sitting down, he took out his handkerchief and bowed his pale face upon it.

"You goose! the handkerchief is already soaked with rain," said the gentleman, raising himself on his elbow to watch the boy.

"With tears, governor."

"Well, get a dry one, take something to eat and drink, and get into bed as soon as possible. She 'll say 'yes' to-morrow: they 're all alike."

"I don't know any other girl but Marthy, governor, and so I don't know whether they 're all alike or not; but Marthy she 's vowed she won't go with me, and she won't, that 's the end of it! And as for eating, I could n't touch a crumb; my throat 's all choked up."

He climbed into his bunk, and turned his face to the wall. There was no sound; but hours afterward John Jay knew that the boy was still silently weeping. In the morning he went about his tasks, pale and haggard, his eyes sunken, his mouth drawn. A chill came on at breakfast, and he could not eat. As, later, he studied his lesson, the fever rose and mixed with the words, until the page swam before his tired eyes. The gentleman had noted all silently. Now he said, "Go out into the open air, George. Go down into the village and bring back Martha; say that I wish her to come. Take heart, boy. Don't give up so easily."

"So easily! But it ain't so easily, governor, Seems as though something was broken inside of me. How can I go and see Marthy when — when — O, I know I'm humly and poor; but I'd work for her, I'd take such care of her. O governor, perhaps if you was to speak to her!"

"Go and bring her to me," said the gentleman, rising abruptly. In the open air he paced to and fro. Sweet-Silence died out unnoticed while he watched the boat moving toward the village. At length it returned with two in it; but when the girl entered the house, with head erect and defiant eyes, the gentleman sat in his easy-chair, Sweet-Silence breathing out a cloud of incense, and a book before him, the picture of idle contentment.

"How now, little girl," he said, gayly, "what is this I hear? You do not want to go out into the bright world with George, and see all its wonders?"

She answered not a word.

"Are we not a little selfish? It is a bad thing to be selfish, child."

Still no answer.

"Think of all the benefit to George," pursued the gentleman. "Think of all you might see, might know, might be! Why, that is all there is of life, Martha."

"It is *not* all," answered the girl, in a low voice.

"It *is*, if George is with you. — Can you say nothing for yourself, boy?" asked the gentleman, sharply.

For answer the lad threw himself on his knees before her, and caught her hands in his fevered grasp, while he poured out a flood of broken entreaties. The gentleman listened, meanwhile carelessly smoking Sweet-Silence and patting the head of True-Heart laid wistfully upon his knee. (Why should the dog be jealous ?)

"Do, Marthy, do !" pleaded the boy ; and he pressed her hands to his eager lips. The gentleman smiled.

"I never, never will," said the girl, looking, not at her lover, but into the quiet, smiling face across the room. Defiantly she spoke, and drew herself aloof from the boy at her feet.

"Well, then, Martha, if you will not go with George, will you stay here with him ?" said the gentleman. "See, I will give you this house and everything in it. Will it do to commence housekeeping ?"

The boy sprang up with a burst of joy. "Will you, governor ? Will you really ? Do you hear that, Marthy ? You did n't like the thought of travelling out into the big world, dear ; and no wonder. But now you can stay right on here in the place you 're used to, and everything so comfortable. Never mind about Egypt and the palm-trees and things ; they 're nothing alongside of you. And I 'd take such care of you, dear. You would n't have to work a bit ; I 'd hunt and fish and cook too ; I 'd make the fires, and everything. All I want is just to see you sitting by the chimbley when I come home, dear, so pretty and so sweet. O governor, won't we have fine times now, we three together?" And, school-boy fashion, George gave a great bound for joy.

A rose flush had risen in Martha's cheek; her eyes were gentle now. "*I* will keep the house," she said softly, as if to herself, and smiled.

"Yes, you shall," said George; "you shall, my pretty one. Hurrah for the little housekeeper of Misery Landing! Won't it be nice, governor, to find her here when we come in from hunting?"

"Very nice, my boy; only I fear I cannot enjoy the sight with you. But that need make no difference."

"Well, no," replied George, with the frank ingratitude of youth. "But I'm sorry on your own account, governor; we'd have been so comfortable all together. Marthy would have been like a daughter to you."

"Thank you, George; you are very kind. But I must go."

"Soon, governor?"

"I'll stay to see you married, my boy. Suppose we say next Tuesday? I will give a ball, and invite all the village to do you honor."

"Next Tuesday! O my!" ejaculated George in the excess of his joy. Words failed him, but he caught his love in his arms. That at least needed no language.

The girl burst from his embrace. "What!" she cried, in a voice strained high with passion, "I marry you, you ungrateful dog! Never, never, here or anywhere! I will die first!" The door closed after her, and the two men stood gazing at vacancy.

A week later at Misery Landing there is a boy racked with fever; a man nurses him, if not tenderly, at least with exactest care.

"She will not see me,—even see me!" cries the delirious voice. "Marthy! my little Marthy!"

The days pass; the fever lasts, and consumes the small store of strength; still, night and day; the voice of the sick boy never ceases its cry for her he loves. His heart exhausts its last drops in calling her name. At length the burning tide finds nothing more to nourish it, and departs, leaving death to finish the work. The boy is conscious again, but wasted, pale, and pinched, his form under the sheet like a skeleton, his voice a whisper, his hands strangely white and weak. He lies in the luxurious hammock-bed, but notices nothing; his large eyes are closed, his breath labored. The man who watches him so closely is trying every human device to raise him to life again; for three days, for a week, night and day he tends him, administering hour by hour drops of delicate cordial and the small nourishment his feeble frame will bear, laying, as it were, the very atoms in place for a new foundation. But he gains almost nothing, since the hopeless mind he cannot reach, and that is killing the body. In the night he finds the boy weeping; too weak to sob aloud, the great tears on his pale cheeks bear witness to his despair. There came a night when, rousing suddenly from a sleep which had overwhelmed his weary eyes, he thought the boy was dead, so rigid and so motionless seemed the still form under the sheet. He shuddered. Was it death? "I have done all I could," he said to himself, hurriedly, as he had often said it before; but the words failed this time, and he stood face to face for one bare moment with his inmost self. Then, pale as the face before him, he approached the bed, and laid his trembling hand upon the heart. It was still beating. The boy slept.

Calling the old half-breed to keep watch, John Jay rushed out into the night, climbed down the ladder, and rowed the boat swiftly across the bay toward the village. As the sun rose above the eastern woods he reached the beach cottage, and found the girl outside. Without a word he took her hand and led her to the boat. She followed mutely, and in silence they took the journey together, nor paused until they stood in the presence of the sleeping boy. Then the man spoke. "He will die unless you love him, Martha."

"I cannot," answered the girl, bowing her face upon her hands.

"Then, at least let him love you; that will suffice him, poor fellow!"

She did not speak.

"Martha," said the gentleman, bending over her and drawing away her hands, "what I tell you is absolutely true. I have done my best, as far as skill and care can go; but the boy — no, he is a man now — cannot live without you. Look at him. Will you let him die?"

He drew her forward. Hand in hand they stood together and gazed upon the poor pinched face before them; from long habit a tear even in sleep crept from under the closed lids.

"We cannot do this thing, Martha," said the man in a low deep voice. He turned away a moment and left her there alone; then coming back to the bedside, he lifted the sleeper, laid him in her arms, his head resting on her shoulder, and without a word went away into the wide world again, leaving Misery Landing behind him forever.

Two weeks later he presented himself at the door of Francesca's opera-box in the Academy. Francesca was still beautiful, and still Francesca: no "Madame" graced her card.

"Good evening, Mr. Jay," she said, smiling the same old beautiful smile. "You have been away just a year in the wilderness. I hope you have enjoyed yourself?"

"Immensely," answered John.

EPILOGUE.

Place, — Fifth Avenue mansion. *Scene*, — Dinner. *Time*, — 7 P. M.

MRS. JAY. "By the way, John, you have never told me about that Lake Superior hermitage of yours, — Misery Landing, was n't it? I suppose you behaved very badly there."

JOHN JAY. "Of course. I always do, you know. Hand me a peach, please. That claret-colored velvet becomes you admirably, Francesca."

MRS. JAY. "Do you think so? I am so glad. I made a real study of this trimming. But about Misery Landing, John; you never told me — "

JOHN JAY. "And never shall, madame."

SOLOMON.

MIDWAY in the eastern part of Ohio lies the coal country; round-topped hills there begin to show themselves in the level plain, trending back from Lake Erie; afterwards rising higher and higher, they stretch away into Pennsylvania and are dignified by the name of Alleghany Mountains. But no names have they in their Ohio birthplace, and little do the people care for them, save as storehouses for fuel. The roads lie along the slow-moving streams, and the farmers ride slowly over them in their broad-wheeled wagons, now and then passing dark holes in the bank from whence come little carts into the sunshine, and men, like *silhouettes,* walking behind them, with glow-worm lamps fastened in their hat-bands. Neither farmers nor miners glance up towards the hilltops; no doubt they consider them useless mounds, and, were it not for the coal, they would envy their neighbors of the grain-country, whose broad, level fields stretch unbroken through Central Ohio; as, however, the canal-boats go away full, and long lines of coal-cars go away full, and every man's coal-shed is full, and money comes back from the great iron-mills of Pittsburgh, Cincinnati, and Cleveland, the coal country, though unknown in a picturesque point of view, continues to grow rich and prosperous.

Yet picturesque it is, and no part more so than the valley where stands the village of the quaint German Community on the banks of the slow-moving Tuscarawas River. One October day we left the lake behind us and journeyed inland, following the water-courses and looking forward for the first glimpse of rising ground; blue are the waters of Erie on a summer day, red and golden are its autumn sunsets, but so level, so deadly level are its shores that, at times, there comes a longing for the sight of distant hills. Hence our journey. Night found us still in the "Western Reserve." Ohio has some queer names of her own for portions of her territory, the "Fire Lands," the "Donation Grant," the "Salt Section," the "Refugee's Tract," and the "Western Reserve" are names well known, although not found on the maps. Two days more and we came into the coal country; near by were the "Moravian Lands," and at the end of the last day's ride we crossed a yellow bridge over a stream called the "One-Leg Creek."

"I have tried in vain to discover the origin of this name," I said, as we leaned out of the carriage to watch the red leaves float down the slow tide.

"Create one, then. A one-legged soldier, a farmer's pretty daughter, an elopement in a flat-bottomed boat, and a home upon this stream which yields its stores of catfish for their support," suggested Erminia.

"The original legend would be better than that if we could only find it, for real life is always better than fiction," I answered.

"In real life we are all masked; but in fiction the author shows the faces as they are, Dora."

"I do not believe we are all masked, Erminia. I can read my friends like a printed page."

"O, the wonderful faith of youth!" said Erminia, retiring upon her seniority.

Presently the little church on the hill came into view through a vista in the trees. We passed the mill and its flowing race, the blacksmith's shop, the great grass meadow, and drew up in front of the quaint hotel where the trustees allowed the world's people, if uninquisitive and decorous, to remain in the Community for short periods of time, on the payment of three dollars per week for each person. This village was our favorite retreat, our little hiding-place in the hill-country; at that time it was almost as isolated as a solitary island, for the Community owned thousands of outlying acres and held no intercourse with the surrounding townships. Content with their own, unmindful of the rest of the world, these Germans grew steadily richer and richer, solving quietly the problem of co-operative labor, while the French and Americans worked at it in vain with newspapers, orators, and even cannon to aid them. The members of the Community were no ascetic anchorites; each tiled roof covered a home with a thrifty mother and train of grave little children, the girls in short-waisted gowns, kerchiefs, and frilled caps, and the boys in tailed coats, long-flapped vests, and trousers, as soon as they were able to toddle. We liked them all, we liked the life; we liked the mountain-high beds, the coarse snowy linen, and the remarkable counterpanes; we liked the cream-stewed chicken, the Käse-lab, and fresh butter, but, best of all, the hot bretzels for breakfast. And let not the hasty city imagination turn to the hard, salty, sawdust cake in the shape of a broken-down figure eight which is served with lager-beer in saloons and gardens. The Community bretzel was of a delicate flaky white in the inside, shading away into a golden-brown crust of crisp involutions, light as a feather, and flanked by little pats of fresh, unsalted butter, and a deep-blue cup wherein the coffee was hot, the cream yellow, and the sugar broken lumps from the old-fashioned loaf, now alas! obsolete.

We stayed among the simple people and played at shepherdesses and pastorellas; we adopted the hours of the birds, we went to church on Sunday and sang German chorals as old as Luther. We even played at work to the extent of helping gather apples, eating the best, and riding home on top of the loaded four-horse wains. But one day we heard of a new diversion, a sulphur-spring over the hills about two miles from the hotel on land belonging to the Community; and, obeying the fascination which earth's native medicines exercise over all earth's children, we immediately started in search of the nauseous spring. The road wound over the hill, past one of the apple-orchards, where the girls were gathering the red fruit, and then down a little declivity where the track branched off to the Community coal-mine; then a solitary stretch through the thick woods, a long hill with a curve, and at the foot a little dell with a patch of meadow, a brook, and a log-house with overhanging roof, a forlorn house unpainted and desolate. There was not even the blue door which enlivened many of the Community dwellings. "This looks like the huts of the Black Forest," said Erminia. "Who would have supposed that we should find such an antique in Ohio!"

"I am confident it was built by the M. B.'s," I replied. "They tramped, you know, extensively through the State, burying axes and leaving every now and then a mastodon behind them."

"Well, if the Mound-Builders selected this site they showed good taste," said Erminia, refusing, in her afternoon indolence, the argumentum nonsensicum with which we were accustomed to enliven our conversation. It was, indeed, a lovely spot,—the little meadow, smooth and bright as green velvet, the brook chattering over the pebbles, and the hills, gay in red and yellow foliage, rising abruptly on all sides. After some labor we swung open the great gate and entered the yard, crossed the brook on a mossy plank, and followed the path through the grass towards the lonely house. An old shepherd-dog lay at the door of a dilapidated shed, like a block-house, which had once been a stable; he did not bark, but, rising slowly, came along beside us, — a large, gaunt animal that looked at us with such melancholy eyes that Erminia stooped to pat him. Ermine had a weakness for dogs; she herself owned a wild beast of the dog kind that went by the name of the "Emperor Trajan"; and, accompanied by this dignitary, she was accustomed to stroll up the avenues of C——, lost in maiden meditations.

We drew near the house and stepped up on the sunken piazza, but no signs of life appeared. The little loophole windows were pasted over with paper, and the plank door had no latch or handle. I knocked, but no one came. "Apparently it is a haunted house, and that dog is the spectre," I said, stepping back.

"Knock three times," suggested Ermine; "that is what they always do in ghost-stories."

"Try it yourself. My knuckles are not cast-iron."

Ermine picked up a stone and began tapping on the door. "Open sesame," she said, and it opened.

Instantly the dog slunk away to his block-house and a woman confronted us, her dull face lighting up as her eyes ran rapidly over our attire from head to foot. "Is there a sulphur-spring here?" I asked. "We would like to try the water."

"Yes, it's here fast enough in the back hall. Come in, ladies; I'm right proud to see you. From the city, I suppose?"

"From C——," I answered; "we are spending a few days in the Community."

Our hostess led the way through the little hall, and throwing open a back door pulled up a trap in the floor, and there we saw the spring,—a shallow well set in stones, with a jar of butter cooling in its white water. She brought a cup, and we drank. "Delicious," said Ermine. "The true, spoiled-egg flavor! Four cups is the minimum allowance, Dora."

"I reckon it's good for the insides," said the woman, standing with arms akimbo and staring at us. She was a singular creature, with large black eyes, Roman nose, and a mass of black hair tightly knotted on the top of her head, but pinched and gaunt; her yellow forehead was wrinkled with a fixed frown, and her thin lips drawn down in permanent discontent. Her dress was a shapeless linsey-woolsey gown, and home-made list slippers covered her long, lank feet. "Be that the fashion?" she asked, pointing to my short, closely fitting walking-dress.

"Yes," I answered; "do you like it?"

"Well, it does for you, sis, because you 're so little and peaked-like, but it would n't do for me. The other lady, now, don't wear nothing like that; is she even with the style, too?"

"There is such a thing as being above the style, madam," replied Ermine, bending to dip up glass number two.

"Our figgers is a good deal alike," pursued the woman; "I reckon that fashion ud suit me best."

Willowy Erminia glanced at the stick-like hostess. "You do me honor," she said, suavely. "I shall consider myself fortunate, madam, if you will allow me to send you patterns from C——. What are we if not well dressed?"

"You have a fine dog," I began hastily, fearing lest the great, black eyes should penetrate the sarcasm; "what is his name?"

"A stupid beast! He 's none of mine; belongs to my man."

"Your husband?"

"Yes, my man. He works in the coal-mine over the hill."

"You have no children?"

"Not a brat. Glad of it, too."

"You must be lonely," I said, glancing around the desolate house. To my surprise, suddenly the woman burst into a flood of tears, and sinking down on the floor she rocked from side to side, sobbing, and covering her face with her bony hands.

"What can be the matter with her?" I said in alarm; and, in my agitation, I dipped up some sulphur-water and held it to her lips.

"Take away the smelling stuff, — I hate it!" she cried, pushing the cup angrily from her.

Ermine looked on in silence for a moment or two, then she took off her neck-tie, a bright-colored Roman scarf, and threw it across the trap into the woman's lap. "Do me the favor to accept that trifle, madam," she said, in her soft voice.

The woman's sobs ceased as she saw the ribbon; she fingered it with one hand in silent admiration, wiped her wet face with the skirt of her gown, and then suddenly disappeared into an adjoining room, closing the door behind her.

"Do you think she is crazy?" I whispered.

"O no; merely pensive."

"Nonsense, Ermine! But why did you give her that ribbon?"

"To develop her æsthetic taste," replied my cousin, finishing her last glass, and beginning to draw on her delicate gloves.

Immediately I began gulping down my neglected dose; but so vile was the odor that some time was required for the operation, and in the midst of my struggles our hostess reappeared. She had thrown on an old dress of plaid delaine, a faded red ribbon was tied over her head, and around her sinewed throat reposed the Roman scarf pinned with a glass brooch.

"Really, madam, you honor us," said Ermine, gravely.

"Thankee, marm. It 's so long since I 've had on anything but that old bag, and so long since I 've seen anything but them Dutch girls over to the Community, with their wooden shapes and wooden shoes, that it sorter come over me all 't onct what a miserable life I 've had. You see, I ain't what I looked like; now I 've dressed up a bit I feel more like telling you that I come of good Ohio stock, without a drop of Dutch blood. My father, he kep' a store in Sandy, and I had everything I wanted until I must needs get crazy over Painting Sol at the Community. Father, he would n't hear to it, and so I ran away; Sol, he turned out good for nothing to work, and so here I am, yer see, in spite of all his pictures making me out the Queen of Sheby."

"Is your husband an artist?" I asked.

"No, miss. He 's a coal-miner, he is. But he used to like to paint me all sorts of ways. Wait, I 'll show yer." Going up the rough stairs that led into the attic, the woman came back after a moment with a number of sheets of drawing-paper which she hung up along the walls with pins for our inspection. They were all portraits of the same face, with brick-red cheeks, enormous black eyes, and a profusion of shining black hair hanging down over plump white shoulders; the costumes were various, but the faces were the same. I gazed in silence, seeing no likeness to anything earthly. Erminia took out her glasses and scanned the pictures slowly.

"Yourself, madam, I perceive," she said, much to my surprise.

"Yes, 'm, that 's me," replied our hostess, complacently. "I never was like those yellow-haired girls over to the Community. Sol allers said my face was real rental."

"Rental?" I repeated, inquiringly.

"Oriental, of course," said Ermine. "Mr. — Mr. Solomon is quite right. May I ask the names of these characters, madam?"

"Queen of Sheby, Judy, Ruth, Esthy, Po-co-hon-tus, Goddessaliberty, Sunset, and eight Octobers, them with the grapes. Sunset 's the one with the red paint behind it like clouds."

"Truly a remarkable collection," said Ermine. "Does Mr. Solomon devote much time to his art?"

"No, not now. He could n't make a cent out of it, so he 's took to digging coal. He painted all them when we was first married, and he went a journey all the way to Cincinnati to sell 'em. First he was going to buy me a silk dress and some ear-rings, and, after that, a farm. But pretty soon home he come on a canal-boat, without a shilling, and a bringing all the pictures back with him! Well, then he tried most everything, but he never could keep to any one trade, for he 'd just as lief quit work in the middle of the forenoon and go to painting; no boss 'll stand that, you know. We kep' a going down, and I had to sell the few things my father give me when he found I was married whether or no, — my chany, my feather-beds, and my nice clothes, piece by piece. I held on to the big looking-glass for four years, but at last it had to go, and then I just gave up and put on a linsey-woolsey gown. When a girl's spirit 's once broke, she don't care for nothing, you know; so, when the Community offered to take Sol back as coal-digger, I just said, 'Go,' and we come." Here she tried to smear the tears away with her bony hands, and gave a low groan.

"Groaning probably relieves you," observed Ermine.

"Yes, 'm. It 's kinder company like, when I 'm all alone. But you see it 's hard on the prettiest girl in Sandy to have to live in this lone lorn place. Why, ladies, you might n't believe it, but I had open-work stockings, and feathers in my winter bunnets before I was married!" And the tears broke forth afresh.

"Accept my handkerchief," said Ermine; "it will serve your purpose better than fingers."

The woman took the dainty cambric and surveyed it curiously, held at arm's length. "Reg'lar thistle-down, now, ain't it?" she said; "and smells like a locust-tree blossom."

"Mr. Solomon, then, belonged to the Community?" I asked, trying to gather up the threads of the story.

"No, he did n't either; he 's no Dutchman, I reckon, he 's a Lake County man, born near Painesville, he is."

"I thought you spoke as though he had been in the Community."

"So he had; he did n't belong, but he worked for 'em since he was a boy, did middling well, in spite of the painting, until one day, when he come over to Sandy on a load of wood and seen me standing at the door. That was the end of him," continued the woman, with an air of girlish pride; "he could n't work no more for thinking of me."

"*Où la vanité va-t-elle se nicher?*" murmured Ermine, rising. "Come, Dora; it is time to return."

As I hastily finished my last cup of sulphur-water, our hostess followed Ermine towards the door. "Will you have your handkercher back, marm?" she said, holding it out reluctantly.

"It was a free gift, madam," replied my cousin; "I wish you a good afternoon."

"Say, will yer be coming again to-morrow?" asked the woman as I took my departure.

"Very likely; good by."

The door closed, and then, but not till then, the melancholy dog joined us and stalked behind until we had crossed the meadow and reached the gate. We passed out and turned up the hill; but looking back we saw the outline of the woman's head at the upper window, and the dog's head at the bars, both watching us out of sight.

In the evening there came a cold wind down from the north, and the parlor, with its primitive ventilators, square openings in the side of the house, grew chilly. So a great fire of soft coal was built in the broad Franklin stove, and before its blaze we made good cheer, nor needed the one candle which flickered on the table behind us. Cider fresh from the mill, carded gingerbread, and new cheese crowned the scene, and during the evening came a band of singers, the young people of the Community, and sang for us the song of the Lorelei, accompanied by home-made violins and flageolets. At length we were left alone, the candle had burned out, the house door was barred, and the peaceful Community was asleep; still we two sat together with our feet upon the hearth, looking down into the glowing coals.

> "Ich weisz nicht was soll es bedeuten
> Dasz ich so traurig bin,"

I said, repeating the opening lines of the Lorelei; "I feel absolutely blue to-night."

"The memory of the sulphur-woman," suggested Ermine.

"Sulphur-woman! What a name!"

"Entirely appropriate, in my opinion."

"Poor thing! How she longed with a great longing for the finery of her youth in Sandy."

"I suppose from those barbarous pictures that she was originally in the flesh," mused Ermine; "at present she is but a bony outline."

"Such as she is, however, she has had her romance," I answered. "She is quite sure that there was one to love her; then let come what may, she has had her day."

"Misquoting Tennyson on such a subject!" said Ermine, with disdain.

"A man 's a man for all that and a woman 's a woman too," I retorted. "You are blind, cousin, blinded with pride. That woman has had her tragedy, as real and bitter as any that can come to us."

"What have you to say for the poor man, then?" exclaimed Ermine, rousing to the contest. "If there is a tragedy at the sulphur-house, it belongs to the sulphur-man, not to the sulphur-woman."

"He is not a sulphur-man, he is a coal-man; keep to your bearings, Ermine."

"I tell you," pursued my cousin, earnestly, "that I pitied that unknown man with inward tears all the while I sat by that trap-door. Depend upon it, he had his dream, his ideal; and this country girl with her great eyes and wealth of hair represented the beautiful to his hungry soul. He gave his whole life and hope into her hands, and woke to find his goddess a common wooden image."

"Waste sympathy upon a coal-miner!" I said, imitating my cousin's former tone.

"If any one is blind, it is you," she answered, with gleaming eyes. "That man's whole history stood revealed in the selfish complainings of that creature. He had been in the Community from boyhood, therefore of course he had no chance to learn life, to see its art-treasures. He has been shipwrecked, poor soul, hopelessly shipwrecked."

"She too, Ermine."

"She!"

"Yes. If he loved pictures, she loved her chany and her feather-beds, not to speak of the big looking-glass. No doubt she had other lovers, and might have lived in a red brick farmhouse with ten unopened front windows and a blistered front door. The wives of men of genius are always to be pitied; they do not soar into the crowd of feminine admirers who circle round the husband, and they are therefore called 'grubs,' 'worms of the earth,' 'drudges,' and other sweet titles."

"Nonsense," said Ermine, tumbling the arched coals into chaos with the poker; "it 's after midnight, let us go up stairs." I knew very well that my beautiful cousin enjoyed the society of several poets, painters, musicians, and others of that ilk, without concerning herself about their stay-at-home wives.

The next day the winds were out in battle array, howling over the Strasburg hills, raging up and down the river, and whirling the colored leaves wildly along the lovely road to the One-Leg Creek. Evidently there could be no rambling in the painted woods that day, so we went over to old Fritz's shop, played on his home-made piano, inspected the woolly horse who turned his crank patiently in an underground den, and set in motion all the curious little images which the carpenter's deft fingers had wrought. Fritz belonged to the Community, and knew nothing of the outside world; he had a taste for mechanism, which showed itself in many labor-saving devices, and with it all he was the roundest, kindest little man, with bright eyes like a canary-bird.

"Do you know Solomon the coal-miner?" asked Ermine, in her correct, well-learned German.

"Sol Bangs? Yes, I know him," replied Fritz, in his Würtemberg dialect.

"What kind of a man is he?"

"Good for nothing," replied Fritz, placidly.

"Why?"

"Wrong here"; tapping his forehead.

"Do you know his wife?" I asked.

"Yes."

"What kind of a woman is she?"

"Too much tongue. Women must not talk much."

"Old Fritz touched us both there," I said, as we ran back laughing to the hotel through the blustering wind. "In his opinion, I suppose, we have the popular verdict of the township upon our two *protégés*, the sulphur-woman and her husband."

The next day opened calm, hazy, and warm, the perfection of Indian summer; the breezy hill was outlined in purple, and the trees glowed in rich colors. In the afternoon we started for the sulphur-spring without shawls or wraps, for the heat was almost oppressive; we loitered on the way through the still woods, gathering the tinted leaves, and wondering why no poet has yet arisen to celebrate in fit words the glories of the American autumn. At last we reached the turn whence the lonely house came into view, and at the bars we saw the dog awaiting us.

"Evidently the sulphur-woman does not like that melancholy animal," I said, as we applied our united strength to the gate.

"Did you ever know a woman of limited mind who liked a large dog?" replied Ermine. "Occasionally such a woman will fancy a small cur; but to appreciate a large, noble dog requires a large, noble mind."

"Nonsense with your dogs and minds," I said, laughing. "Wonderful! There is a curtain."

It was true. The paper had been removed from

one of the windows, and in its place hung some white drapery, probably part of a sheet rigged as a curtain.

Before we reached the piazza the door opened, and our hostess appeared. "Glad to see yer, ladies," she said. "Walk right in this way to the keeping-room."

The dog went away to his block-house, and we followed the woman into a room on the right of the hall; there were three rooms, beside the attic above. An Old-World German stove of brick-work occupied a large portion of the space, and over it hung a few tins, and a clock whose pendulum swung outside; a table, a settle, and some stools completed the furniture; but on the plastered walls were two rude brackets, one holding a cup and saucer of figured china, and the other surmounted by a large bunch of autumn leaves, so beautiful in themselves and so exquisitely arranged that we crossed the room to admire them.

"Sol fixed 'em, he did," said the sulphur-woman; "he seen me setting things to rights, and he would do it. I told him they was trash, but he made me promise to leave 'em alone in case you should call again."

"Madam Bangs, they would adorn a palace," said Ermine, severely.

"The cup is pretty too," I observed, seeing the woman's eyes turn that way.

"It 's the last of my chany," she answered, with pathos in her voice, — "the very last piece."

As we took our places on the settle we noticed the brave attire of our hostess. The delaine was there; but how altered! Flounces it had, skimped, but still flounces, and at the top was a collar of crochet cotton reaching nearly to the shoulders; the hair, too, was braided in imitation of Ermine's sunny coronet, and the Roman scarf did duty as a belt around the large flat waist.

"You see she tries to improve," I whispered, as Mrs. Bangs went into the hall to get some sulphur-water for us.

"Vanity," answered Ermine.

We drank our dose slowly, and our hostess talked on and on. Even I, her champion, began to weary of her complainings. "How dark it is!" said Ermine at last, rising and drawing aside the curtain. "See, Dora, a storm is close upon us."

We hurried to the door, but one look at the black cloud was enough to convince us that we could not reach the Community hotel before it would break, and somewhat drearily we returned to the keeping-room, which grew darker and darker, until our hostess was obliged to light a candle. "Reckon you 'll have to stay all night; I 'd like to have you, ladies," she said. "The Community ain't got nothing covered to send after you, except the old king's coach, and I misdoubt they won't let that out in such a storm, steps and all. When it begins to rain in this valley, it do rain, I can tell you; and from the way it 's begun, 't won't stop 'fore morning. You just let me send the Roarer over to the mine, he 'll tell Sol; Sol can tell the Community folks, so they 'll know where you be."

I looked somewhat aghast at this proposal, but Ermine listened to the rain upon the roof a moment, and then quietly accepted; she remembered the long hills of tenacious red clay, and her kid boots were dear to her.

"The Roarer, I presume, is some faithful kobold who bears your message to and from the mine," she said, making herself as comfortable as the wooden settle would allow.

The sulphur-woman stared. "Roarer 's Sol's old dog," she answered, opening the door; "perhaps one of you will write a bit of a note for him to carry in his basket. — Roarer, Roarer!"

The melancholy dog came slowly in, and stood still while she tied a small covered basket around his neck.

Ermine took a leaf from her tablets and wrote a line or two with the gold pencil attached to her watch-chain.

"Well now, you do have everything handy, I do declare," said the woman, admiringly.

I glanced at the paper.

"MR. SOLOMON BANGS: My cousin Theodora Wentworth and myself have accepted the hospitality of your house for the night. Will you be so good as to send tidings of our safety to the Community, and oblige,

"ERMINIA STUART."

The Roarer started obediently out into the rain-storm with his little basket; he did not run, but walked slowly, as if the storm was nothing compared to his settled melancholy.

"What a note to send to a coal-miner!" I said, during a momentary absence of our hostess.

"Never fear; it will be appreciated," replied Ermine.

"What is this king's carriage of which you spoke?" I asked, during the next hour's conversation.

"O, when they first come over from Germany, they had a sort of a king; he knew more than the rest, and he lived in that big brick house with dormel-winders and a cuperler, that stands next the garden. The carriage was hisn, and it had steps to let down, and curtains and all; they don't use it much now he 's dead. They 're a queer set anyhow! The women look like meal-sacks. After Sol seen me, he could n't abide to look at 'em."

Soon after six we heard the great gate creak.

"That 's Sol," said the woman, "and now of course Roarer 'll come in and track all over my floor." The hall door opened and a shadow passed into the opposite room, two shadows, — a man and a dog.

"He 's going to wash himself now," continued the wife; "he 's always washing himself, just like a horse."

"New fact in natural history, Dora love," observed Ermine.

After some moments the miner appeared, — a tall, stooping figure with high forehead, large blue eyes, and long thin yellow hair; there was a singularly lifeless expression in his face, and a far-off look in his eyes. He gazed about the room in an absent way, as though he scarcely saw us. Behind him stalked the Roarer, wagging his tail slowly from side to side.

"Now, then, don't yer see the ladies, Sol? Where 's yer manners?" said his wife, sharply.

"Ah, — yes, — good evening," he said, vaguely. Then his wandering eyes fell upon Ermine's beautiful face, and fixed themselves there with strange intentness.

"You received my note, Mr. Bangs?" said my cousin in her soft voice.

"Yes, surely. You are Erminia," replied the man, still standing in the centre of the room with fixed eyes. The Roarer laid himself down behind his master, and his tail, still wagging, sounded upon the floor with a regular tap.

"Now then, Sol, since you 've come home, perhaps you 'll entertain the ladies while I get supper," quoth Mrs. Bangs; and forthwith began a clatter of pans.

The man passed his long hand abstractedly over his forehead. "Eh," he said with long-drawn utterance,— "eh-h? Yes, my rose of Sharon, certainly, certainly."

"Then why don't you do it?" said the woman, lighting the fire in the brick stove.

"And what will the ladies please to do?" he answered, his eyes going back to Ermine.

"We will look over your pictures, sir," said my cousin, rising; "they are in the upper room, I believe."

A great flush rose in the painter's thin cheeks. "Will you," he said eagerly,—"will you? Come!"

"It 's a broken-down old hole, ladies; Sol will never let me sweep it out. Reckon you 'll be more comfortable here," said Mrs. Bangs, with her arms in the flour.

"No, no, my lily of the valley. The ladies will come with me; they will not scorn the poor room."

"A studio is always interesting," said Ermine, sweeping up the rough stairs behind Solomon's candle. The dog followed us, and laid himself down on an old mat, as though well accustomed to the place. "Eh-h, boy, you came bravely through the storm with the lady's note," said his master, beginning to light candle after candle. "See him laugh!"

"Can a dog laugh?" I asked.

"Certainly; look at him now. What is that but a grin of happy contentment? Don't the Bible say, 'grin like a dog'?"

"You seem much attached to the Roarer."

"Tuscarora, lady, Tuscarora. Yes, I love him well. He has been with me through all, and he has watched the making of all my pictures; he always lies there when I paint."

By this time a dozen candles were burning on shelves and brackets, and we could see all parts of the attic studio. It was but a poor place, unfloored in the corners where the roof slanted down, and having no ceiling but the dark beams and thatch; hung upon the walls were the pictures we had seen, and many others, all crude and highly colored, and all representing the same face, — the sulphur-woman in her youth, the poor artist's only ideal. He showed us these one by one, handling them tenderly, and telling us, in his quaint language, all they symbolized. "This is Ruth, and denoteth the power of hope," he said. "Behold Judith, the queen of revenge. And this dear one is Rachel, for whom Jacob served seven years, and they seemed unto him but a day, so well he loved her." The light shone on his pale face, and we noticed the far-off look in his eyes, and the long, tapering fingers coming out from the hard-worked, broad palm. To me it was a melancholy scene, the poor artist with his daubs and the dreary attic.

But Ermine seemed eagerly interested; she looked at the staring pictures, listened to the explanations, and at last she said gently, "Let me show you something of perspective, and the part that shadows play in a pictured face. Have you any crayons?"

No; the man had only his coarse paints and lumps of charcoal; taking a piece of the coal in her delicate hand, my cousin began to work upon a sheet of drawing-paper attached to the rough easel. Solomon watched her intently, as she explained and demonstrated some of the rules of drawing, the lights and shades, and the manner of representing the different features and curves. All his pictures were full faces, flat and unshaded; Ermine showed him the power of the profile and the three-quarter view. I grew weary of watching them, and pressing my face against the little window gazed out into the night; steadily the rain came down and the hills shut us in like a well. I thought of our home in C——, and its bright lights, warmth, company, and life. Why should we come masquerading out among the Ohio hills at this late season? And then I remembered that it was because Ermine would come; she liked such expeditions, and from childhood I had always followed her lead. "*Dux nascitur*, etc., etc." Turning away from the gloomy night, I looked towards the easel again; Solomon's cheeks were deeply flushed, and his eyes shone like stars. The lesson went on, the merely mechanical hand explaining its art to the ignorant fingers of genius. Ermine had taken lessons all her life, but she had never produced an original picture, only copies.

At last the lesson was interrupted by a voice from below, "Sol, Sol, supper 's ready!" No one stirred until, feeling some sympathy for the amount of work which my ears told me had been going on below, I woke up the two enthusiasts and took them away from the easel down stairs into the keeping-room, where a loaded table and a scarlet hostess bore witness to the truth of my surmise. Strange things we ate that night, dishes unheard of in towns, but not unpalatable. Ermine had the one china cup for her corn-coffee; her grand air always secured her such favors. Tuscarora was there and ate of the best, now and then laying his shaggy head on the table, and, as his master said, "smiling at us"; evidently the evening was his gala time. It was nearly nine when the feast was ended, and I immediately proposed retiring to bed, for, having but little art enthusiasm, I dreaded a vigil in that dreary attic. Solomon looked disappointed, but I ruthlessly carried off Ermine to the opposite room, which we afterwards suspected was the apartment of our hosts, freshened and set in order in our honor. The sound of the rain on the piazza roof lulled us soon to sleep, in spite of the strange surroundings; but more than once I woke and wondered where I was, suddenly remembering the lonely house in its lonely valley with a shiver of discomfort. The next morning we woke at our usual hour, but some time after the miner's departure; breakfast was awaiting us in the keeping-room, and our hostess said that an ox-team from the Community would come for us before nine. She seemed sorry to part with us, and refused any remuneration for our stay; but none the less did we promise ourselves to send some dresses and even ornaments from C——, to feed that poor, starving love of finery. As we rode away in the ox-cart, the Roarer looked wistfully after us through the bars; but his melancholy mood was upon him again, and he had not the heart even to wag his tail.

As we were sitting in the hotel parlor, in front of our soft-coal fire in the evening of the following day, and discussing whether or no we should return to the city within the week, the old landlord entered without his broad-brimmed hat, — an unusual attention, since he was a trustee and a man of note in the Community, and removed his hat for no one nor nothing; we even suspected that he slept in it.

"You know Zolomon Barngs," he said, slowly.

"Yes," we answered.

"Well, he 's dead. Kilt in de mine." And putting on the hat, removed, we now saw, in respect for death, he left the room as suddenly as he had entered it. As it happened, we had been discussing the couple, I, as usual, contending for the wife, and Ermine, as usual, advocating the cause of the husband.

"Let us go out there immediately to see her, poor woman!" I said, rising.

"Yes, poor man, we will go to him!" said Ermine.

"But the man is dead, cousin."

"Then he shall at least have one kind, friendly glance before he is carried to his grave," answered Ermine, quietly.

In a short time we set out in the darkness, and dearly did we have to pay for the night-ride; no one could understand the motive of our going, but money was money, and we could pay for all peculiarities. It was a dark night, and the ride seemed endless as the oxen moved slowly on through the red-clay mire. At last we reached the turn and saw the little lonely house with its upper room brightly lighted.

"He is in the studio," said Ermine; and so it proved. He was not dead, but dying; not maimed, but poisoned by the gas of the mine, and rescued too late for recovery. They had placed him upon the floor on a couch of blankets, and the dull-eyed Community doctor stood at his side. "No good, no good," he said; "he must die." And then, hearing of the returning cart, he left us, and we could hear the tramp of the oxen over the little bridge, on their way back to the village.

The dying man's head lay upon his wife's breast, and her arms supported him; she did not speak, but gazed at us with a dumb agony in her large eyes. Ermine knelt down and took the lifeless hand streaked with coal-dust in both her own. "Solomon," she said, in her soft, clear voice, "do you know me?"

The closed eyes opened slowly, and fixed themselves upon her face a moment: then they turned towards the window, as if seeking something.

"It 's the picter he means," said the wife. "He sat up most all last night a doing it."

I lighted all the candles, and Ermine brought forward the easel; upon it stood a sketch in charcoal wonderful to behold,—the same face, the face of the faded wife, but so noble in its idealized beauty that it might have been a portrait of her glorified face in Paradise. It was a profile, with the eyes upturned,—a mere outline, but grand in conception and expression. I gazed in silent astonishment.

Ermine said, "Yes, I knew you could do it, Solomon. It is perfect of its kind." The shadow of a smile stole over the pallid face, and then the husband's fading gaze turned upward to meet the wild, dark eyes of the wife.

"It 's you, Dorcas," he murmured; "that 's how you looked to me, but I never could get it right before." She bent over him, and silently we watched the coming of the shadow of death; he spoke only once, "My rose of Sharon —" And then in a moment he was gone, the poor artist was dead.

Wild, wild was the grief of the ungoverned heart left behind; she was like a mad-woman, and our united strength was needed to keep her from injuring herself in her frenzy. I was frightened, but Ermine's strong little hands and lithe arms kept her down until, exhausted, she lay motionless near her dead husband. Then we carried her down stairs and I watched by the bedside, while my cousin went back to the studio. She was absent some time, and then she came back to keep the vigil with me through the long, still night. At dawn the woman woke, and her face looked aged in the gray light. She was quiet, and took without a word the food we had prepared, awkwardly enough, in the keeping-room.

"I must go to him, I must go to him," she murmured, as we led her back.

"Yes," said Ermine, "but first let me make you tidy. He loved to see you neat." And with deft, gentle touch she dressed the poor creature, arranging the heavy hair so artistically that, for the first time, I saw what she might have been, and understood the husband's dream.

"What is that?" I said, as a peculiar sound startled us.

"It's Roarer. He was tied up last night, but I suppose he's gnawed the rope," said the woman. I opened the hall door, and in stalked the great dog, smelling his way directly up the stairs.

"O, he must not go!" I exclaimed.

"Yes, let him go, he loved his master," said Ermine; "we will go too." So silently we all went up into the chamber of death.

The pictures had been taken down from the walls, but the wonderful sketch remained on the easel, which had been moved to the head of the couch where Solomon lay. His long, light hair was smooth, his face peacefully quiet, and on his breast lay the beautiful bunch of autumn leaves which he had arranged in our honor. It was a striking picture,—the noble face of the sketch above, and the dead face of the artist below. It brought to my mind a design I had once seen, where Fame with her laurels came at last to the door of the poor artist and gently knocked; but he had died the night before!

The dog lay at his master's feet, nor stirred until Solomon was carried out to his grave.

The Community buried the miner in one corner of the lonely little meadow. No service had they and no mound was raised to mark the spot, for such was their custom; but in the early spring we went down again into the valley, and placed a block of granite over the grave. It bore the inscription:—

SOLOMON.

He will finish his work in Heaven.

Strange as it may seem, the wife pined for her artist husband. We found her in the Community trying to work, but so aged and bent that we hardly knew her. Her large eyes had lost their peevish discontent, and a great sadness had taken the place.

"Seems like I could n't get on without Sol," she said, sitting with us in the hotel parlor after work-hours. "I kinder miss his voice, and all them names he used to call me; he got 'em out of the Bible, so they must have been good, you know. He always thought everything I did was right, and he thought no end of my good looks, too; I suppose I 've lost 'em all now. He was mighty fond of me; nobody in all the world cares a straw for me now. Even Roarer would n't stay with me, for all I petted him; he kep' a going out to that meader and a lying by Sol, until, one day, we found him there dead. He just died of sheer loneliness, I reckon. I sha' n't have to stop long I know, because I keep a dreaming of Sol, and he always looks at me like he did when I first knew him. He was a beautiful boy when I first saw him on that load of wood coming into Sandy. Well, ladies, I must go. Thank you kindly for all you 've done for me. And say, Miss Stuart, when I die you shall have that coal picter; no one else 'ud vally it so much."

Three months after, while we were at the sea-shore, Ermine received a long tin case, directed in a peculiar handwriting; it had been forwarded from C——, and contained the sketch and a note from the Community.

"E. STUART: The woman Dorcas Bangs died this day. She will be put away by the side of her husband, Solomon Bangs. She left the enclosed picture, which we hereby send, and which please acknowledge by return of mail.

"JACOB BOLL, *Trustee.*"

I unfolded the wrappings and looked at the sketch. "It is indeed striking," I said. "She must have been beautiful once, poor woman!"

"Let us hope that at least she is beautiful now, for her husband's sake, poor man!" replied Ermine.

Even then we could not give up our preferences.

WILHELMINA.

"AND so, Mina, you will not marry the baker?"

"No; I waits for Gustav."

"How long is it since you have seen him?"

"Three year; it was a three-year regi-mènt."

"Then he will soon be home?"

"I not know," answered the girl, with a wistful look in her dark eyes, as if asking information from the superior being who sat in the skiff, — a being from the outside world where newspapers, the modern Tree of Knowledge, were not forbidden.

"Perhaps he will re-enlist, and stay three years longer," I said.

"Ah, lady, — six year! It breaks the heart," answered Wilhelmina.

She was the gardener's daughter, a member of the Community of German Separatists who live secluded in one of Ohio's rich valleys, separated by their own broad acres and orchard-covered hills from the busy world outside; down the valley flows the tranquil Tuscarawas on its way to the Muskingum, its slow tide rolling through the fertile bottom-lands between stone dikes, and utilized to the utmost extent of carefulness by the thrifty brothers, now working a saw-mill on the bank, now sending a tributary to the flour-mill across the canal, and now branching off in a sparkling race across the valley to turn wheels for two or three factories, watering the great grass-meadow on the way. We were floating on this river in a skiff named by myself Der Fliegende Holländer, much to the slow wonder of the Zoarites, who did not understand how a Dutchman could, nor why he should, fly. Wilhelmina sat before me, her oars idly trailing in the water. She showed a Nubian head above her white kerchief: large-lidded soft brown eyes, heavy braids of dark hair, a creamy skin with purple tints in the lips and brown shadows under the eyes, and a far-off dreamy expression which even the steady, monotonous toil of Community life had not been able to efface. She wore the blue dress and white kerchief of the society, the quaint little calico bonnet lying beside her; she was a small maiden; her slender form swayed in the stiff, short-waisted gown, her feet slipped about in the broad shoes, and her hands, roughened and browned with garden-work, were yet narrow and graceful. From the first we felt sure she was grafted, and not a shoot from the Community stalk. But we could learn nothing of her origin; the Zoarites are not communicative; they fill each day with twelve good hours of labor, and look neither forward nor back. "She is a daughter," said the old gardener in answer to our questions. "Adopted?" I suggested; but he vouchsafed no answer. I liked the little daughter's dreamy face, but she was pale and undeveloped, like a Southern flower growing in Northern soil; the rosy-cheeked, flaxen-haired Rosines, Salomes, and Dorotys, with their broad shoulders and ponderous tread, thought this brown changeling ugly, and pitied her in their slow, good-natured way.

"It breaks the heart," said Wilhelmina again, softly, as if to herself.

I repented me of my thoughtlessness. "In any case he can come back for a few days," I hastened to say. "What regiment was it?"

"The One Hundred and Seventh, lady."

I had a Cleveland paper in my basket, and taking it out I glanced over the war-news column, carelessly, as one who does not expect to find what he seeks. But chance was with us, and gave this item: "The One Hundred and Seventh Regiment, O. V. I., is expected home next week. The men will be paid off at Camp Chase."

"Ah!" said Wilhelmina, catching her breath with a half-sob under her tightly drawn kerchief, — "ah, mein Gustav!"

"Yes, you will soon see him," I answered, bending forward to take the rough little hand in mine; for I was a romantic wife, and my heart went out to all lovers. But the girl did not notice my words or my touch; silently she sat, absorbed in her own emotion, her eyes fixed on the hilltops far away, as though she saw the regiment marching home through the blue June sky.

I took the oars and rowed up as far as the island, letting the skiff float back with the current. Other boats were out, filled with fresh-faced boys in their high-crowned hats, long-waisted, wide-flapped vests of calico, and funny little swallow-tailed coats with buttons up under the shoulder-blades; they appeared unaccountably long in front and short behind, these young Zoar brethren. On the vine-covered dike were groups of mothers and grave little children, and up in the hill-orchards were moving figures, young and old; the whole village was abroad in the lovely afternoon, according to their Sunday custom, which gave the morning to chorals and a long sermon in the little church, and the afternoon to nature, even old Christian, the pastor, taking his imposing white fur hat and tasselled cane for a walk through the Community fields, with the remark, "Thus is cheered the heart of man, and his countenance refreshed."

As the sun sank in the warm western sky, homeward came the villagers from the river, the orchards, and the meadows, men, women, and children, a hardy, simple-minded band, whose fathers, for religion's sake, had taken the long journey from Würtemberg across the ocean to this distant valley, and made it a garden of rest in the wilderness. We, too, landed, and walked up the apple-tree lane towards the hotel.

"The cows come," said Wilhelmina as we heard a distant tinkling; "I must gŏ." But still she lingered. "Der regi-mènt, it come soon, you say?" she asked in a low voice, as though she wanted to hear the good news again and again.

"They will be paid off next week; they cannot be later than ten days from now."

"Ten day! Ah, mein Gustav," murmured the little maiden; she turned away and tied on her stiff bonnet, furtively wiping off a tear with her prim handkerchief folded in a square.

"Why, my child," I said, following her and stooping to look in her face, "what is this?"

"It is nothing; it is for glad, — for very glad," said Wilhelmina. Away she ran as the first solemn cow came into view, heading the long procession meandering slowly towards the stalls. They knew nothing of haste, these dignified Community cows; from stall to pasture, from pasture to stall, in a plethora of comfort, this was their life. The silver-haired shepherd came last with his staff and scrip, and the nervous shepherd-dog ran hither and thither in the hope of finding some cow to bark at; but the comfortable cows moved on in orderly ranks, and he was obliged to dart off on a tangent every now and then, and bark at nothing, to relieve his feelings. Reaching the paved court-yard each cow walked into her own stall, and the milking began. All the girls took part in this work, sitting on little stools and singing together as the milk frothed up in the tin pails; the pails were emptied into tubs, and when the tubs were full the girls bore them on their heads to the dairy, where the milk was poured into a huge strainer, a constant procession of girls with tubs above and the old milk-mother ladling out as fast as she could below. With the bee-hives near by, it was a realization of the Scriptural phrase, "A land flowing with milk and honey."

The next morning, after breakfast, I strolled up the still street, leaving the Wirthshaus with its pointed roof behind me. On the right were some ancient cottages built of crossed timbers filled in with plaster; sundials hung on the walls, and each house had its piazza, where, when the work of the day was over, the families assembled, often singing folk-songs to the music of their home-made flutes and pipes. On the left stood the residence of the first pastor, the reverend man who had led these sheep to their refuge in the wilds of the New World. It was a wide-spreading brick mansion, with a broadside of white-curtained windows, an enclosed glass porch, iron railings, and gilded eaves; a building so stately among the surrounding cottages that it had gained from outsiders the name of the King's Palace, although the good man whose grave remains unmarked in the quiet God's Acre, according to the Separatist custom, was a father to his people, not a king.

Beyond the palace began the Community garden, a large square in the centre of the village filled with flowers and fruit, adorned with arbors and cedar-trees clipped in the form of birds, and enriched with an old-style greenhouse whose sliding glasses were viewed with admiration by the visitors of thirty years ago, who sent their choice plants thither from far and near to be tended through the long, cold lake-country winters. The garden, the cedars, and the greenhouse were all antiquated, but to me none the less charming. The spring that gushed up in one corner, the old-fashioned flowers in their box-bordered beds, larkspur, lady slippers, bachelor's buttons, peonies, aromatic pinks, and all varieties of roses, the arbors with red honeysuckle overhead and tan bark under foot, were all delightful; and I knew, also, that I should find the gardener's daughter at her never-ending task of weeding. This time it was the strawberry bed. "I have come to sit in your pleasant garden, Mina," I said, taking a seat on a shaded bench near the bending figure.

"So?" said Wilhelmina in long-drawn interrogation, glancing up shyly with a smile. She was a child of the sun, this little maiden, and while her blond companions wore always their bonnets or broad-brimmed hats over their precise caps, Wilhelmina, as now, constantly discarded these coverings and sat in the sun basking like a bird of the tropics. In truth, it did not redden her; she was one of those whose coloring comes not from without, but within.

"Do you like this work, Mina?"

"O — so. Good as any."

"Do you like work?"

"Folks must work." This was said gravely, as part of the Community creed.

"Would n't you like to go with me to the city?"

"No; I 's better here."

"But you can see the great world, Mina. You need not work, I will take care of you. You shall have pretty dresses; would n't you like that?" I asked, curious to discover the secret of the Separatist indifference to everything outside.

"Nein," answered the little maiden, tranquilly; "nein, fräulein. Ich bin zufrieden."

Those three words were the key. "I am contented." So were they taught from childhood, and — I was about to say — they knew no better; but, after all, is there anything better to know?

We talked on, for Mina understood English, although many of her mates could chatter only in their Würtemberg dialect, whose provincialisms confused my carefully learned German; I was grounded in Goethe, well read in Schiller, and struggling with Jean Paul, who, fortunately, is "der Einzige," the only; another such would destroy life. At length a bell sounded, and forthwith work was laid aside in the fields, the workshops, and the houses, while all partook of a light repast, one of the five meals with which the long summer day of toil is broken. Flagons of beer had the men afield, with bread and cheese; the women took bread and apple-butter. But Mina did not care for the thick slice which the thrifty house-mother had provided; she had not the steady unfanciful appetite of the Community which eats the same food day after day, as the cow eats its grass, desiring no change.

"And the gardener really wishes you to marry Jacob?" I said as she sat on the grass near me, enjoying the rest.

"Yes. Jacob is good, — always the same."

"And Gustav?"

"Ah, mein Gustav! Lady, *he* is young, tall, — so tall as tree; he run, he sing, his eyes like veilchen there, his hair like gold. If I see him not soon, lady, I die! The year so long, — *so* long they are. Three year without Gustav!" The brown eyes grew dim, and out came the square-folded handkerchief, of colored calico for week-days.

"But it will not be long now, Mina."

"Yes; I hope."

"He writes to you, I suppose?"

"No. Gustav knows not to write, he not like school. But he speak through the other boys, Ernst the verliebte of Rosine, and Peter of Doroty."

"The Zoar soldiers were all young men?"

"Yes; all verliebte. Some are not; they have gone to the Next Country" (died).

"Killed in battle?"

"Yes; on the berge that looks, — what you call, I not know —"

"Lookout Mountain?"

"Yes."

"Were the boys volunteers?" I asked, remembering the Community theory of non-resistance.

"O yes; they volunteer, Gustav the first. *They* not drafted," said Wilhelmina, proudly. For these two words, so prominent during the war, had penetrated even into this quiet valley.

"But did the trustees approve?"

"Apperouve?"

"I mean, did they like it?"

"Ah! they like it not. They talk, they preach in church, they say 'No.' Zoar must give soldiers? So. Then they take money and pay for der substitute; but the boys, they must not go."

"But they went, in spite of the trustees?"

"Yes; Gustav first. They go in night, they walk in woods, over the hills to Brownville, where is der recruiter. The morning come, they gone!"

"They have been away three years, you say? They have seen the world in that time," I remarked half to myself, as I thought of the strange mind-opening and knowledge-gaining of those years to youths brought up in the strict seclusion of the Community..

"Yes; Gustav have seen the wide world," answered Wilhelmina with pride.

"But will they be content to step back into the dull routine of Zoar life?" I thought; and a doubt came that made me scan more closely the face of the girl at my side. To me it was attractive because of its possibilities; I was always fancying some excitement that would bring the color to the cheeks and full lips, and light up the heavy-lidded eyes with soft brilliancy. But would this Gustav see these might-be beauties? And how far would the singularly ugly costume offend eyes grown accustomed to fanciful finery and gay colors?

"You fully expect to marry Gustav?" I asked.

"We are verlobt," answered Mina, not without a little air of dignity.

"Yes, I know. But that was long ago."

"Verlobt once, verlobt always," said the little maiden, confidently.

"But why, then, does the gardener speak of Jacob, if you are engaged to this Gustav?"

"O, fader he like the old, and Jacob is old, thirty

year! His wife is gone to the Next Country. Jacob is a brother, too; he write his name in the book. But Gustav he not do so; he is free."

"You mean that the baker has signed the articles, and is a member of the Community?"

"Yes; but the baker is old, very old; thirty year! Gustav not twenty and three yet; he come home, then he sign."

"And have you signed these articles, Wilhelmina?"

"Yes; all the womens signs."

"What does the paper say?"

"Da ich Unterzeichneter," — began the girl.

"I cannot understand that. Tell me in English."

"Well; you wants to join the Zoar Community of Separatists; you writes your name and says, 'Give me house, victual, and clothes for my work and I join; and I never fernerer Forderung an besagte Gesellschaft machen kann, oder will.'"

"Will never make further demand upon said society," I repeated, translating slowly.

"Yes; that is it."

"But who takes charge of all the money?"

"The trustees."

"Don't they give you any?"

"No; for what? It 's no good," answered Wilhelmina.

I knew that all the necessaries of life were dealt

out to the members of the Community according to their need, and, as they never went outside of their valley, they could scarcely have spent money even if they had possessed it. But, nevertheless, it was startling in this nineteenth century to come upon a sincere belief in the worthlessness of the green-tinted paper we cherish so fondly. "Gustav will have learned its value," I thought, as Mina, having finished the strawberry-bed, started away towards the dairy to assist in the butter-making.

I strolled on up the little hill, past the picturesque bakery, where through the open window I caught a glimpse of the "old, very old Jacob," a serious young man of thirty, drawing out his large loaves of bread from the brick oven with a long-handled rake. It was gingerbread-day also, and a spicy odor met me at the window; so I put in my head and asked for a piece, receiving a card about a foot square, laid on fresh grape-leaves.

"But I cannot eat all this," I said, breaking off a corner.

"O, dat 's noding!" answered Jacob, beginning to knead fresh dough in a long white trough, the village supply for the next day.

"I have been sitting with Wilhelmina," I remarked, as I leaned on the casement, impelled by a desire to see the effect of the name.

"So?" said Jacob, interrogatively.

"Yes; she is a sweet girl."

"So?" (doubtfully.)

"Don't you think so, Jacob?"

"Ye-es. So-so. A leetle black," answered this impassive lover.

"But you wish to marry her?"

"O, ye-es. She young and strong; her fader say she good to work. I have children five; I must have some one in the house."

"O Jacob! Is that the way to talk?" I exclaimed.

"Warum nicht?" replied the baker, pausing in his kneading, and regarding me with wide-open, candid eyes.

"Why not, indeed?" I thought, as I turned away from the window. "He is at least honest, and no doubt in his way he would be a kind husband to little Mina. But what a way!"

I walked on up the street, passing the pleasant house where all the infirm old women of the Community were lodged together, carefully tended by appointed nurses. The aged sisters were out on the piazza sunning themselves, like so many old cats. They were bent with hard, out-door labor, for they belonged to the early days when the wild forest covered the fields now so rich, and only a few log-cabins stood on the site of the tidy cottages and gardens of the present village. Some of them had taken the long journey on foot from Philadelphia westward, four hundred and fifty miles, in the depths of winter. Well might they rest from their labors and sit in the sunshine, poor old souls!

A few days later, my friendly newspaper mentioned the arrival of the German regiment at Camp Chase. "They will probably be paid off in a day or two," I thought, "and another day may bring them here." Eager to be the first to tell the good news to my little favorite, I hastened up to the garden, and found her engaged, as usual, in weeding.

"Mina," I said, "I have something to tell you. The regiment is at Camp Chase; you will see Gustav soon, perhaps this week."

And there, before my eyes, the transformation I had often fancied took place; the color rushed to the brown surface, the cheeks and lips glowed in vivid red, and the heavy eyes opened wide and shone like stars, with a brilliancy that astonished and even disturbed me. The statue had a soul at last; the beauty dormant had awakened. But for the fire of that soul would this expected Pygmalion suffice? Would the real prince fill his place in the long-cherished dreams of this beauty of the wood?

The girl had risen as I spoke, and now she stood erect, trembling with excitement, her hands clasped on her breast, breathing quickly and heavily as though an overweight of joy was pressing down her heart; her eyes were fixed upon my face, but she saw me not.

Strange was her gaze, like the gaze of one walking in sleep. Her sloping shoulders seemed to expand and chafe against the stuff gown as though they would burst their bonds; the blood glowed in her face and throat, and her lips quivered, not as though tears were coming, but from the fulness of unuttered speech. Her emotion resembled the intensest fire of fever, and yet it seemed natural; like noon in the tropics when the gorgeous flowers flame in the white, shadowless heat. Thus stood Wilhelmina, looking up into the sky with eyes that challenged the sun.

"Come here, child," I said; "come here and sit by me. We will talk about it."

But she neither saw nor heard me. I drew her down on the bench at my side; she yielded unconsciously; her slender form throbbed, and pulses were beating under my hands wherever I touched her. "Mina!" I said again. But she did not answer. Like an unfolding rose, she revealed her hidden, beautiful heart, as though a spirit had breathed upon the bud; silenced in the presence of this great love, I ceased speaking, and left her to herself. After a time single words fell from her lips, broken utterances of happiness. I was as nothing; she was absorbed in the One. "Gustav! mein Gustav!" It was like the bird's note, oft repeated, ever the same. So isolated, so intense was her joy, that, as often happens, my mind took refuge in the opposite extreme of commonplace, and I found myself wondering whether she would be able to eat boiled beef and cabbage for dinner, or fill the soft-soap barrel for the laundry-women, later in the day.

All the morning I sat under the trees with Wilhelmina, who had forgotten her life-long tasks as completely as though they had never existed. I hated to leave her to the leather-colored wife of the old gardener, and lingered until the sharp voice came out from the distant house-door, calling, "Veel-hel-*meeny*," as the twelve-o'clock bell summoned the Community to dinner. But as Mina rose and swept back the heavy braids that had fallen from the little ivory stick which confined them, I saw that she was armed *cap-à-pie* in that full happiness from which all weapons glance off harmless.

All the rest of the day she was like a thing possessed. I followed her to the hill-pasture, whither she had gone to mind the cows, and found her coiled up on the grass in the blaze of the afternoon sun, like a little salamander. She was lost in day-dreams, and the decorous cows had a holiday for once in their sober lives, wandering beyond bounds at will, and even tasting the dissipations of the marsh, standing unheeded in the bog up to their sleek knees. Wilhelmina had not many words to give me; her English vocabulary was limited; she had never read a line of romance nor a verse of poetry. The nearest approach to either was the Community hymn-book, containing the Separatist hymns, of which the following lines are a specimen,

> "Ruhe ist das beste Gut
> Dasz man haben kann," —

> "Rest is the best good
> That man can have," —

and which embody the religious doctrine of the Zoar Brethren, although they think, apparently, that the labor of twelve hours each day is necessary to its enjoyment. The "Ruhe," however, refers more especially to their quiet seclusion away from the turmoil of the wicked world outside.

The second morning after this it was evident that an unusual excitement was abroad in the phlegmatic village. All the daily duties were fulfilled as usual at the Wirthshaus: Pauline went up to the bakery with her board, and returned with her load of bread and bretzels balanced on her head; Jacobina served our coffee with her slow precision; and the broad-shouldered, young-faced Lydia patted and puffed up our mountain-high feather-beds with due care. The men went afield at the blast of the horn, the workshops were full and the mills running. But, nevertheless, all was not the same; the air seemed full of mystery; there were whisperings when two met, furtive signals, and an inward excitement glowing in the faces of men, women, and children, hitherto placid as their own sheep. "They have heard the news," I said, after watching the tailor's Gretchen and the blacksmith's Barbara stop to exchange a whisper behind the wood-house. Later in the day we learned that several letters from the absent soldier-boys had been received that morning, announcing their arrival on the evening train. The news had flown from one end of the village to the other; and although the well-drilled hands were all at work, hearts were stirring with the greatest excitement of a lifetime, since there was hardly a house where there was not one expected. Each large house often held a number of families, stowed away in little sets of chambers, with one dining-room in common.

Several times during the day we saw the three trustees conferring apart with anxious faces. The war had been a sore trouble to them, owing to their conscientious scruples against rendering military service. They had hoped to remain non-combatants. But the country was on fire with patriotism, and nothing less than a *bona fide* Separatist in United States uniform would quiet the surrounding towns, long jealous of the wealth of this foreign community, misunderstanding its tenets, and glowing with that zeal against "sympathizers" which kept star-spangled banners flying over every suspected house. "Hang out the flag!" was their cry, and they demanded that Zoar should hang out its soldiers, giving them to understand that if not voluntarily hung out, they would soon be involuntarily hung up! A draft was ordered, and then the young men of the society, who had long chafed against their bonds, broke loose, volunteered, and marched away, principles or no principles, trustees or no trustees. These bold hearts once gone, the village sank into quietude again. Their letters, however, were a source of anxiety, coming as they did from the vain outside world; and the old postmaster, autocrat though he was, hardly dared to suppress them. But he said, shaking his head, that they "had fallen upon troublous times," and handed each dangerous envelope out with a groan. But the soldiers were not skilled penmen; their letters, few and far between, at length stopped entirely. Time passed, and the very existence of the runaways had become a far-off problem to the wise men of the Community, absorbed in their slow calculations and cautious agriculture, when now, suddenly, it forced itself upon them face to face, and they were required to solve it in the twinkling of an eye. The bold hearts were coming back, full of knowledge of the outside world; almost every house would hold one, and the bands of law and order would be broken. Before this prospect the trustees quailed. Twenty years before they would have forbidden the entrance of these unruly sons within their borders; but now they dared not, since even into Zoar had penetrated the knowledge that America was a free country. The younger generation were not as their fathers were; objections had been openly made to the cut of the Sunday coats, and the girls had spoken together of ribbons!

The shadows of twilight seemed very long in falling that night, but at last there was no further excuse for delaying the evening bell, and home came the laborers to their evening meal. There was no moon, a soft mist obscured the stars, and the night was darkened with the excess of richness which rose from the ripening valley-fields and fat bottom-lands along the river. The Community store opposite the Wirthshaus was closed early in the evening, the houses of the trustees were dark, and indeed the village was almost unlighted, as if to hide its own excitement. The entire population was abroad in the night, and one by one the men and boys stole away down the station road, a lovely, winding track on the hillside, following the river on its way down the valley to the little station on the grass-grown railroad, a branch from the main track. As ten o'clock came, the women and girls, grown bold with excitement, gathered in the open space in front of the Wirthshaus, where the lights from the windows illumined their faces. There I saw the broad-shouldered Lydia, Rosine, Doroty, and all the rest, in their Sunday clothes, flushed, laughing, and chattering; but no Wilhelmina.

"Where can she be?" I said.

If she was there, the larger girls concealed her with their buxom breadth; I looked for the slender little maiden in vain.

"Shu!" cried the girls, "de bugle!"

Far down the station road we heard the bugle and saw the glimmering of lights among the trees. On it came, a will-o'-the-wisp procession: first a detachment of village boys each with a lantern or torch, next the returned soldiers winding their bugles,—for, German-like, they all had musical instruments,—then an excited crowd of brothers and cousins loaded with knapsacks, guns, and military accoutrements of all kinds; each man had something, were it only a tin cup, and proudly they marched in the footsteps of their glorious relatives, bearing the spoils of war. The girls set up a shrill cry of welcome as the procession approached, but the ranks continued unbroken until the open space in front of the Wirthshaus was reached; then, at a signal, the soldiers gave three cheers, the villagers joining in with all their hearts and lungs, but wildly and out of time, like the scattering fire of an awkward squad. The sound had never been heard in Zoar before. The soldiers gave a final "Tiger-r-r!" and then broke ranks, mingling with the excited crowd, exchanging greetings and embraces. All talked at once; some wept, some laughed; and through it all silently stood the three trustees on the dark porch in front of the store, looking down upon their wild flock, their sober faces visible in the glare of the torches and lanterns below. The entire population was present; even the babies were held up on the outskirts of the crowd, stolid and staring.

"Where can Wilhelmina be?" I said again.

"Here, under the window; I saw her long ago," replied one of the women.

Leaning against a piazza-pillar, close under my eyes, stood the little maiden, pale and still. I could not disguise from myself that she looked almost ugly among those florid, laughing girls, for her color was gone, and her eyes so fixed that they looked unnaturally large; her somewhat heavy Egyptian features stood out in the bright light, but her small form was lost among the group of broad, white-kerchiefed shoulders, adorned with breast-knots of gay flowers. And had Wilhelmina no flower? She, so fond of blossoms? I looked again; yes, a little white rose, drooping and pale as herself.

But where was Gustav? The soldiers came and went in the crowd, and all spoke to Mina; but where was the One? I caught the landlord's little son as he passed, and asked the question.

"Gustav? Dat 's him," he answered, pointing out a tall, rollicking soldier who seemed to be embracing the whole population in his gleeful welcome. That very soldier had passed Mina a dozen times, flinging a gay greeting to her each time; but nothing more.

After half an hour of general rejoicing, the crowd dispersed, each household bearing off in triumph the hero that fell to its lot. Then the tiled domiciles, where usually all were asleep an hour after twilight, blazed forth with unaccustomed light from every little window; and within we could see the circles, with flagons of beer and various dainties manufactured in secret during the day, sitting and talking together in a manner which, for Zoar, was a wild revel, since it was nearly eleven o'clock! We were not the only outside spectators of this unwonted gayety; several times we met the three trustees stealing along in the shadow from house to house, like anxious spectres in broad-brimmed hats. No doubt they said to each other, "How, how will this end!"

The merry Gustav had gone off by Mina's side, which gave me some comfort; but when in our rounds we came to the gardener's house and gazed through the open door, the little maiden sat apart, and the soldier, in the centre of an admiring circle, was telling stories of the war.

I felt a foreboding of sorrow as I gazed out through the little window before climbing up into my high bed. Lights still twinkled in some of the houses, but a white mist was rising from the river, and the drowsy, long-drawn chant of the summer night invited me to dreamless sleep.

The next morning I could not resist questioning Jacobina, who also had her lover among the soldiers, if all was well.

"O yes. They stay, — all but two. We 's married next mont."

"And the two?"

"Karl and Gustav."

"And Wilhelmina!" I exclaimed.

"O, she let him go," answered Jacobina, bringing fresh coffee.

"Poor child! How does she bear it?"

"O, so. She cannot help. She say noding."

"But the trustees, will they allow these young men to leave the Community?"

"They cannot help," said Jacobina. "Gustav and Karl write not in the book; they free to go. Wilhelmina marry Jacob; it 's joost the same; all r-r-ight," added Jacobina, who prided herself upon her English, caught from visitors at the Wirthshaus table.

"Ah! but it is not just the same," I thought as I went up to the garden to find my little maiden. She was not there; the leathery mother said she was out on the hills with the cows.

"So Gustav is going to leave the Community," I said in German.

"Yes, better so. He is an idle, wild boy. Now, Veelhelmeeny can marry the baker, a good steady man."

"But Mina does not like him," I suggested.

"Das macht nichts," answered the leathery mother.

Wilhelmina was not in the pasture; I sought for her everywhere, and called her name. The poor child had hidden herself, and whether she heard me or not, she did not respond. All day she kept herself aloof; I almost feared she would never return; but in the late twilight a little figure slipped through the garden-gate and took refuge in the house before I could speak; for I was watching for the child, apparently the only one, though a stranger, to care for her sorrow.

"Can I not see her?" I said to the leathery mother, following to the door.

"Eh, no; she 's foolish; she will not speak a word; she has gone off to bed," was the answer.

For three days I did not see Mina, so early did she flee away to the hills and so late return. I followed her to the pasture once or twice, but she would not show herself, and I could not discover her hiding-place. The fourth day I learned that Gustav and Karl were to leave the village in the afternoon, probably forever. The other soldiers had signed the articles presented by the anxious trustees, and settled down into the old routine, going afield with the rest, although still heroes of the hour; they were all to be married in August. No doubt the hardships of their campaigns among the Tennessee mountains had taught them that the rich valley was a home not to be despised; nevertheless, it was evident that the flowers of the flock were those who were about departing, and that in Gustav and Karl the Community lost its brightest spirits. Evident to us; but, possibly, the Community cared not for bright spirits.

I had made several attempts to speak to Gustav; this morning I at last succeeded. I found him polishing his bugle on the garden bench.

"Why are you going away, Gustav?" I asked. "Zoar is a pleasant little village."

"Too slow for me, miss."

"The life is easy, however; you will find the world a hard place."

"I don't mind work, ma'am, but I do like to be free. I feel all cramped up here, with these rules and bells; and, besides, I could n't stand those trustees; they never let a fellow alone."

"And Wilhelmina? If you do go, I hope you will take her with you, or come for her when you have found work."

"O no, miss. All that was long ago. It 's all over now."

"But you like her, Gustav?"

"O, so. She 's a good little thing, but too quiet for me."

"But she likes you," I said desperately, for I saw no other way to loosen this Gordian knot.

"O no, miss. She got used to it, and has thought of it all these years; that 's all. She 'll forget about it, and marry the baker."

"But she does not like the baker."

"Why not? He 's a good fellow enough. She 'll like him in time. It 's all the same. I declare it 's too bad to see all these girls going on in the same old way, in their ugly gowns and big shoes! Why, ma'am, I could n't take Mina outside, even if I wanted to; she 's too old to learn new ways, and everybody would laugh at her. She could n't get along a day. Besides," said the young soldier, coloring up to his eyes, "I don't mind telling you that — that there 's some one else. Look here, ma'am." And he put into my hand a card photograph representing a pretty girl, over-dressed, and adorned with curls and gilt jewelry. "That 's Miss Martin," said Gustav with pride; "Miss Emmeline Martin, of Cincinnati. I 'm going to marry Miss Martin."

As I held the pretty, flashy picture in my hand, all my castles fell to the ground. My plan for taking Mina home with me, accustoming her gradually to other clothes and ways, teaching her enough of the world to enable her to hold her place without pain, my hope that my husband might find a situation for Gustav in some of the iron-mills near Cleveland, in short, all the idyl I had woven, was destroyed. If it had not been for this red-cheeked Miss Martin in her gilt beads! "Why is it that men will be such fools?" I thought. Up sprung a memory of the curls and ponderous jet necklace I sported at a certain period of my existence, when John — I was silenced, gave Gustav his picture, and walked away without a word.

At noon the villagers, on their way back to work, paused at the Wirthshaus to say good by; Karl and Gustav were there, and the old woolly horse had already gone to the station with their boxes. Among the others came Christine, Karl's former affianced, heart-whole and smiling, already betrothed to a new lover; but no Wilhelmina. Good wishes and farewells were exchanged, and at last the two soldiers started away, falling into the marching step, and watched with furtive satisfaction by the three trustees, who stood together in the shadow of the smithy, apparently deeply absorbed in a broken-down cask.

It was a lovely afternoon, and I, too, strolled down the station road embowered in shade. The two soldiers were not far in advance. I had passed the flour-mill on the outskirts of the village and was approaching the old quarry, when a sound startled me; out from the rocks in front rushed a little figure, and crying, "Gustav, mein Gustav!" fell at the soldier's feet. It was Wilhelmina.

I ran forward and took her from the young men; she lay in my arms as if dead. The poor child was sadly changed; always slender and swaying, she now looked thin and shrunken, her skin had a strange, dark pallor, and her lips were drawn in as if from pain. I could see her eyes through the large-orbed thin lids, and the brown shadows beneath extended down into the cheeks.

"Was ist's?" said Gustav, looking bewildered. "Is she sick?"

I answered "Yes," but nothing more. I could see that he had no suspicion of the truth, believing as he did that the "good fellow" of a baker would do very well for this "good little thing" who was "too quiet" for him. The memory of Miss Martin sealed my lips. But if it had not been for that pretty, flashy picture, would I not have spoken!

"You must go; you will miss the train," I said, after a few minutes. "I will see to Mina."

But Gustav lingered. Perhaps he was really troubled to see the little sweetheart of his boyhood in such desolate plight; perhaps a touch of the old feeling came back; and perhaps, also, it was nothing of the kind, and, as usual, my romantic imagination was carrying me away. At any rate, whatever it was, he stooped over the fainting girl.

"She looks bad," he said, "very bad. I wish — But she 'll get well and marry the baker. Good by, Mina." And bending his tall form, he kissed her colorless cheek, and then hastened away to join the impatient Karl; a curve in the road soon hid them from view.

Wilhelmina had stirred at his touch; after a moment her large eyes opened slowly; she looked around as if dazed, but all at once memory came back, and she started up with the same cry, "Gustav, mein Gustav!" I drew her head down on my shoulder to stifle the sound; it was better the soldier should not hear it, and its anguish thrilled my own heart also. She had not the strength to resist me, and in a few minutes I knew that the young men were out of hearing as they strode on towards the station and out into the wide world.

The forest was solitary, we were beyond the village; all the afternoon I sat under the trees with the stricken girl. Again, as in her joy, her words were few; again, as in her joy, her whole being was involved. Her little rough hands were cold, a film had gathered over her eyes; she did not weep, but moaned to herself, and all her senses seemed blunted. At nightfall I took her home, and the leathery mother received her with a frown; but the child was beyond caring, and crept away, dumbly, to her room.

The next morning she was off to the hills again, nor could I find her for several days. Evidently, in spite of my sympathy, I was no more to her than I should have been to a wounded fawn. She was a mixture of the wild, shy creature of the woods and the deep-loving woman of the tropics; in either case I could be but small comfort. When at last I did see her, she was apathetic and dull; her feelings, her senses, and her intelligence seemed to have gone within, as if preying upon her heart. She scarcely listened to my proposal to take her with me; for, in my pity, I had suggested it, in spite of its difficulties.

"No," she said, mechanically, "I 's better here"; and fell into silence again.

A month later a friend went down to spend a few days in the valley, and upon her return described to us the weddings of the whilom soldiers. "It was really a pretty sight," she said, "the quaint peasant dresses and the flowers. Afterwards, the band went round the village playing their odd tunes, and all had a holiday. There were two civilians married also; I mean two young men who had not been to the war. It seems that two of the soldiers turned their backs upon the Community and their allotted brides, and marched away; but the Zoar maidens are not romantic, I fancy, for these two deserted ones were betrothed again and married, all in the short space of four weeks."

"Was not one Wilhelmina, the gardener's daughter, a short, dark girl?" I asked.

"Yes."

"And she married Jacob the baker?"

"Yes."

The next year, weary of the cold lake-winds, we left the icy shore and went down to the valley to meet the coming spring, finding her already there, decked with vines and flowers. A new waitress brought us our coffee.

"How is Wilhelmina?" I asked.

"Eh, — Wilhelmina? O, she not here now; she gone to the Next Country," answered the girl in a matter-of-fact way. "She die last October, and Jacob he haf anoder wife now."

In the late afternoon I asked a little girl to show me Wilhelmina's grave in the quiet God's Acre on the hill. Innovation was creeping in, even here; the later graves had mounds raised over them, and one had a little head-board with an inscription in ink.

Wilhelmina lay apart, and some one, probably the old gardener, who had loved the little maiden in his silent way, had planted a rose-bush at the head of the mound. I dismissed my guide and sat there alone in the sunset, thinking of many things, but chiefly of this: "Why should this great wealth of love have been allowed to waste itself? Why is it that the greatest power, unquestionably, of this mortal life should so often seem a useless gift?"

No answer came from the sunset clouds, and as twilight sank down on the earth I rose to go. "I fully believe," I said, as though repeating a creed, "that this poor, loving heart, whose earthly body lies under this mound, is happy now in its own loving way. It has not been changed, but the happiness it longed for has come. How, we know not; but the God who made Wilhelmina understands her. He has given unto her not rest, not peace, but an active, living joy."

I walked away through the wild meadow, under whose turf, unmarked by stone or mound, lay the first pioneers of the Community, and out into the forest road, untravelled save when the dead passed over it to their last earthly home. The evening was still and breathless, and the shadows lay thick on the grass as I looked back. But I could still distinguish the little mound with the rose-bush at its head, and, not without tears, I said, "Farewell, poor Wilhelmina; farewell."

ST. CLAIR FLATS.

IN September, 1855, I first saw the St. Clair Flats. Owing to Raymond's determination, we stopped there.

"Why go on?" he asked. "Why cross another long, rough lake, when here is all we want?"

"But no one ever stops here," I said.

"So much the better; we shall have it all to ourselves."

"But we must at least have a roof over our heads."

"I presume we can find one."

The captain of the steamer, however, knew of no roof save that covering a little lighthouse set on spiles, which the boat would pass within the half-hour; we decided to get off there, and throw ourselves upon the charity of the lighthouse-man. In the mean time, we sat on the bow with Captain Kidd, our four-legged companion, who had often accompanied us on hunting expeditions, but never before so far westward. It had been rough on Lake Erie, — very rough. We, who had sailed the ocean with composure, found ourselves most inhumanly tossed on the short, chopping waves of this fresh-water sea; we, who alone of all the cabin-list had eaten our four courses and dessert every day on the ocean-steamer, found ourselves here reduced to the depressing diet of a herring and pilot-bread. Captain Kidd, too, had suffered dumbly; even now he could not find comfort, but tried every plank in the deck, one after the other, circling round and round after his tail, dog-fashion, before lying down, and no sooner down than up again for another melancholy wandering about the deck, another choice of planks, another circling, and another failure. We were sailing across a small lake whose smooth waters were like clear green oil; as we drew near the outlet, the low, green shores curved inward and came together, and the steamer entered a narrow, green river.

"Here we are," said Raymond. "Now we can soon land."

"But there is n't any land," I answered.

"What is that, then?" asked my near-sighted companion, pointing toward what seemed a shore.

"Reeds."

"And what do they run back to?"

"Nothing."

"But there must be solid ground beyond?"

"Nothing but reeds, flags, lily-pads, grass, and water, as far as I can see."

"A marsh?"

"Yes, a marsh."

The word "marsh" does not bring up a beautiful picture to the mind, and yet the reality was as beautiful as anything I have ever seen, — an enchanted land, whose memory haunts me as an idea unwritten, a melody unsung, a picture unpainted, haunts the artist, and will not away. On each side and in front, as far as the eye could reach, stretched the low green land which was yet no land, intersected by hundreds of channels, narrow and broad, whose waters were green as their shores. In and out, now running into each other for a moment, now setting off each for himself again, these many channels flowed along with a rippling current; zigzag as they were, they never seemed to loiter, but, as if knowing just where they were going and what they had to do, they found time to take their own pleasant roundabout way, visiting the secluded households of their friends the flags, who, poor souls, must always stay at home. These currents were as clear as crystal, and green as the water-grasses that fringed their miniature shores. The bristling reeds, like companies of free-lances, rode boldly out here and there into the deeps, trying to conquer more territory for the grasses, but the currents were hard to conquer; they dismounted the free-lances, and flowed over their submerged heads; they beat them down with assaulting ripples; they broke their backs so effectually that the bravest had no spirit left, but trailed along, limp and bedraggled. And, if by chance the lances succeeded in stretching their forces across from one little shore to another, then the unconquered currents forced their way between the closely serried ranks of the enemy, and flowed on as gayly as ever, leaving the grasses sitting hopeless on the bank; for they needed solid ground for their delicate feet, these graceful ladies in green.

You might call it a marsh; but there was no mud, no dark slimy water, no stagnant scum; there were no rank yellow lilies, no gormandizing frogs, no swinish mud-turtles. The clear waters of the channels ran over golden sands, and hurtled among the stiff reeds so swiftly that only in a bay, or where protected by a crescent point, could the fair white lilies float in the quiet their serene beauty requires. The flags, who brandished their swords proudly, were martinets down to their very heels, keeping themselves as clean under the water as above, and harboring not a speck of mud on their bright green uniforms. For inhabitants, there were small fish roving about here and there in the clear tide, keeping an eye out for the herons, who, watery as to legs, but venerable and wise of aspect, stood on promontories musing, apparently, on the secrets of the ages.

The steamer's route was a constant curve; through the larger channels of the archipelago she wound, as if following the clew of a labyrinth. By turns she headed toward all the points of the compass, finding a channel where, to our uninitiated eyes, there was no channel, doubling upon her own track, going broadside foremost, floundering and backing, like a whale caught in a shallow. Here, landlocked, she would choose what seemed the narrowest channel of all, and dash recklessly through, with the reeds almost brushing her sides; there she crept gingerly along a broad expanse of water, her paddle-wheels scarcely revolving, in the excess of her caution. Saplings, with their heads of foliage on, and branches adorned with fluttering rags, served as finger-posts to show the way through the watery defiles, and there were many other hieroglyphics legible only to the pilot. "This time, surely, we shall run ashore," we thought again and again, as the steamer glided, head-on, toward an islet; but at the last there was always a quick turn into some unseen strait opening like a secret passage in a castle-wall, and we found ourselves in a new lakelet, heading in the opposite direction. Once we met another steamer, and the two great hulls floated slowly past each other, with engines motionless, so near that the passengers could have shaken hands with each other had they been so disposed. Not that they were so disposed, however; far from it. They gathered on their respective decks and gazed at each other gravely; not a smile was seen, not a word spoken, not the shadow of a salutation given. It was not pride, it was not suspicion; it was the universal listlessness of the travelling American bereft of his business, Othello with his occupation gone. What can such a man do on a steamer? Generally, nothing. Certainly he would never think of any such light-hearted nonsense as a smile or passing bow.

But the ships were, *par excellence,* the bewitched craft, the Flying Dutchmen of the Flats. A brig, with lofty, sky-scraping sails, bound south, came into view of our steamer, bound north, and passed, we hugging the shore to give her room; five minutes afterward the sky-scraping sails we had left behind veered around in front of us again; another five minutes, and there they were far distant on the right; another, and there they were again close by us on the left. For half an hour those sails circled around us, and yet all the time we were pushing steadily forward; this seemed witching work indeed. Again, the numerous schooners thought nothing of sailing overland; we saw them on all sides gliding before the wind, or beating up against it over the meadows as easily as over the water; sailing on grass was a mere trifle to these spirit-barks. All this we saw, as I said before, apparently. But in that adverb is hidden the magic of the St. Clair Flats.

"It is beautiful, — beautiful," I said, looking off over the vivid green expanse.

"Beautiful?" echoed the captain, who had himself taken charge of the steering when the steamer entered the labyrinth,—"I don't see anything beautiful in it!—Port your helm up there; port!"

"Port it is, sir," came back from the pilot-house above.

"These Flats give us more trouble than any other spot on the lakes; vessels are all the time getting aground and blocking up the way, which is narrow enough at best. There 's some talk of Uncle Sam's cutting a canal right through,—a straight canal; but he 's so slow, Uncle Sam is, and I 'm afraid I 'll be off the waters before the job is done."

"A straight canal!" I repeated, thinking with dismay of an ugly utilitarian ditch invading this beautiful winding waste of green.

"Yes, you can see for yourself what a saving it would be," replied the captain. "We could run right through in no time, day or night; whereas, now, we have to turn and twist and watch every inch of the whole everlasting marsh." Such was the captain's opinion. But we, albeit neither romantic nor artistic, were captivated with his "everlasting marsh," and eager to penetrate far within its green fastnesses.

"I suppose there are other families living about here, besides the family at the lighthouse?" I said.

"Never heard of any. They 'd have to live on a raft if they did."

"But there must be some solid ground."

"Don't believe it; it's nothing but one great sponge for miles. — Steady up there; steady!"

"Very well," said Raymond, "so be it. If there is only the lighthouse, at the lighthouse we'll get off, and take our chances."

"You're surveyors, I suppose?" said the captain.

Surveyors are the pioneers of the lake-country, understood by the people to be a set of harmless monomaniacs, given to building little observatories along-shore, where there is nothing to observe; mild madmen, whose vagaries and instruments are equally singular. As surveyors, therefore, the captain saw nothing surprising in our determination to get off at the lighthouse; if we had proposed going ashore on a plank in the middle of Lake Huron, he would have made no objection.

At length the lighthouse came into view, a little fortress perched on spiles, with a ladder for entrance; as usual in small houses, much time seemed devoted to washing, for a large crane, swung to and fro by a rope, extended out over the water, covered with fluttering garments hung out to dry. The steamer lay to, our row-boat was launched, our traps handed out, Captain Kidd took his place in the bow, and we pushed off into the shallows; then the great paddle-wheels revolved again, and the steamer sailed away, leaving us astern, rocking on her waves, and watched listlessly by the passengers until a turn hid us from their view. In the mean time numerous flaxen-haired children had appeared at the little windows of the lighthouse, — too many of them, indeed, for our hopes of comfort.

"Ten," said Raymond, counting heads.

The ten, moved by curiosity as we approached, hung out of the windows so far that they held on merely by their ankles.

"We cannot possibly save them all," I remarked, looking up at the dangling gazers.

"O, they 're amphibious," said Raymond; "web-footed, I presume."

We rowed up under the fortress, and demanded parley with the keeper in the following language: —

"Is your father here?"

"No; but ma is," answered the chorus. — "Ma! ma!"

Ma appeared, a portly female, who held converse with us from the top of the ladder. The sum and substance of the dialogue was that she had not a corner to give us, and recommended us to find Liakim, and have him show us the way to Waiting Samuel's.

"Waiting Samuel's?" we repeated.

"Yes; he 's a kind of crazy man living away over there in the Flats. But there 's no harm in him, and his wife is a tidy housekeeper. You be surveyors, I suppose?"

We accepted the imputation in order to avoid a broadside of questions, and asked the whereabouts of Liakim.

"O, he 's round the point, somewhere there, fishing!"

We rowed on and found him, a little, round-shouldered man, in an old flat-bottomed boat, who had not taken a fish, and looked as though he never would. We explained our errand.

"Did Rosabel Lee tell ye to come to me?" he asked.

"The woman in the lighthouse told us," I said.

"That 's Rosabel Lee, that 's my wife; I 'm Liakim Lee," said the little man, gathering together his forlorn old rods and tackle, and pulling up his anchor.

> "In the kingdom down by the sea
> Lived the beautiful Annabel Lee,"

I quoted, *sotto voce.*

"And what very remarkable feet had she!" added Raymond, improvising under the inspiration of certain shoes, scow-like in shape, gigantic in length and breadth, which had made themselves visible at the top round of the ladder.

At length the shabby old boat got under way, and we followed in its path, turning off to the right through a network of channels, now pulling ourselves along by the reeds, now paddling over a raft of lily-pads, now poling through a winding labyrinth, and now rowing with broad sweeps across the little lake. The sun was sinking, and the western sky grew bright at his coming; there was not a cloud to make mountain-peaks on the horizon, nothing but the level earth below meeting the curved sky above, so evenly and clearly that it seemed as though we could go out there and touch it with our hands. Soon we lost sight of the little lighthouse; then one by one the distant sails sank down and disappeared, and we were left alone on the grassy sea, rowing toward the sunset.

"We must have come a mile or two, and there is no sign of a house," I called out to our guide.

"Well, I don't pretend to know how far it is, exactly," replied Liakim; "we don't know how far anything is here in the Flats, we don't."

"But are you sure you know the way?"

"O my, yes! We've got most to the boy. There it is!"

The "boy" was a buoy, a fragment of plank painted white, part of the cabin-work of some wrecked steamer.

"Now, then," said Liakim, pausing, "you jest go straight on in this here channel till you come to the ninth run from this boy, on the right; take that, and it will lead you right up to Waiting Samuel's door."

"Are n't you coming with us?"

"Well, no. In the first place, Rosabel Lee will be

waiting supper for me, and she don't like to wait; and, besides, Samuel can't abide to see none of us round his part of the Flats."

"But —" I began.

"Let him go," interposed Raymond; "we can find the house without trouble." And he tossed a silver dollar to the little man, who was already turning his boat.

"Thank you," said Liakim. "Be sure you take the ninth run and no other, — the ninth run from this boy. If you make any mistake, you 'll find yourselves miles away."

With this cheerful statement, he began to row back. I did not altogether fancy being left on the watery waste without a guide; the name, too, of our mythic host did not bring up a certainty of supper and beds. "Waiting Samuel," I repeated, doubtfully. "What is he waiting for?" I called back over my shoulder; for Raymond was rowing.

"The judgment-day!" answered Liakim, in a shrill key. The boats were now far apart; another turn, and we were alone.

We glided on, counting the runs on the right: some were wide, promising rivers; others wee little rivulets; the eighth was far away; and, when we had passed it, we could hardly decide whether we had reached the ninth or not, so small was the opening, so choked with weeds, showing scarcely a gleam of water beyond when we stood up to inspect it.

"It is certainly the ninth, and I vote that we try it. It will do as well as another, and I, for one, am in no hurry to arrive anywhere," said Raymond, pushing the boat in among the reeds.

"Do you want to lose yourself in this wilderness?" I asked, making a flag of my handkerchief to mark the spot where we had left the main stream.

"I think we are lost already," was the calm reply. I began to fear we were.

For some distance the "run," as Liakim called it, continued choked with aquatic vegetation, which acted like so many devil-fish catching our oars; at length it widened and gradually gave us a clear channel, albeit so winding and erratic that the glow of the sunset, our only beacon, seemed to be executing a waltz all round the horizon. At length we saw a dark spot on the left, and distinguished the outline of a low house. "There it is," I said, plying my oars with renewed strength. But the run turned short off in the opposite direction, and the house disappeared. After some time it rose again, this time on our right, but once more the run turned its back and shot off on a tangent. The sun had gone, and the rapid twilight of September was falling around us; the air, however, was singularly clear, and, as there was absolutely nothing to make a shadow, the darkness came on evenly over the level green. I was growing anxious, when a third time the house appeared, but the wilful run passed by it, although so near that we could distinguish its open windows and door. "Why not get out and wade across?" I suggested.

"According to Liakim, it is the duty of this run to take us to the very door of Waiting Samuel's mansion, and it shall take us," said Raymond, rowing on. It did.

Doubling upon itself in the most unexpected manner, it brought us back to a little island, where the tall grass had given way to a vegetable-garden. We landed, secured our boat, and walked up the pathway toward the house. In the dusk it seemed to be a low, square structure, built of planks covered with plaster; the roof was flat, the windows unusually broad, the door stood open, — but no one appeared. We knocked. A voice from within called out, "Who are you, and what do you want with Waiting Samuel?"

"Pilgrims, asking for food and shelter," replied Raymond.

"Do you know the ways of righteousness?"

"We can learn them."

"Will you conform to the rules of this household without murmuring?"

"We will."

"Enter then, and peace be with you!" said the voice, drawing nearer. We stepped cautiously through the dark passage into a room, whose open windows let in sufficient twilight to show us a shadowy figure. "Seat yourselves," it said. We found a bench, and sat down.

"What seek ye here?" continued the shadow.

"Rest!" replied Raymond.

"Hunting and fishing!" I added.

"Ye will find more than rest," said the voice, ignoring me altogether (I am often ignored in this way), — "more than rest, if ye stay long enough, and learn of the hidden treasures. Are you willing to seek for them?"

"Certainly!" said Raymond. "Where shall we dig?"

"I speak not of earthly digging, young man. Will you give me the charge of your souls?"

"Certainly, if you will also take charge of our bodies."

"Supper, for instance," I said, again coming to the front; "and beds."

The shadow groaned; then it called out wearily, "Roxana!"

"Yes, Samuel," replied an answering voice, and a second shadow became dimly visible on the threshold. "The woman will attend to your earthly concerns," said Waiting Samuel. — "Roxana, take them hence." The second shadow came forward, and, without a word, took our hands and led us along the dark passage like two children, warning us now of a step, now of a turn, then of two steps, and finally opening a door and ushering us into a fire-lighted room. Peat was burning upon the wide hearth, and a singing kettle hung above it on a crane; the red glow shone on a rough table, chairs cushioned in bright calico, a loud-ticking clock, a few gayly flowered plates and cups on a shelf, shining tins against the plastered wall, and a cat dozing on a bit of carpet in one corner. The cheery domestic scene, coming after the wide, dusky Flats, the silence, the darkness, and the mystical words of the shadowy Samuel, seemed so real and pleasant that my heart grew light within me.

"What a bright fire!" I said. "This is your domain, I suppose, Mrs. — Mrs. —"

"I am not Mrs.; I am called Roxana," replied the woman, busying herself at the hearth.

"Ah, you are then the sister of Waiting Samuel, I presume?"

"No, I am his wife, fast enough; we were married by the minister twenty years ago. But that was before Samuel had seen any visions."

"Does he see visions?"

"Yes, almost every day."

"Do you see them, also?"

"O no; I'm not like Samuel. He has great gifts, Samuel has! The visions told us to come here; we used to live away down in Maine."

"Indeed! That was a long journey!"

"Yes! And we did n't come straight either. We'd get to one place and stop, and I'd think we were going to stay, and just get things comfortable, when Samuel would see another vision, and we'd have to start on. We wandered in that way two or three years, but at last we got here, and something in the Flats seemed to suit the spirits, and they let us stay."

At this moment, through the half-open door, came a voice.

"An evil beast is in this house. Let him depart."

"Do you mean me?" said Raymond, who had made himself comfortable in a rocking-chair.

"Nay; I refer to the four-legged beast," continued the voice. "Come forth, Apollyon!"

Poor Captain Kidd seemed to feel that he was the person in question, for he hastened under the table with drooping tail and mortified aspect.

"Roxana, send forth the beast," said the voice.

The woman put down her dishes and went toward the table; but I interposed.

"If he must go, I will take him," I said, rising.

"Yes; he must go," replied Roxana, holding open the door. So I ordered out the unwilling Captain, and led him into the passageway.

"Out of the house, out of the house," said Waiting Samuel. "His feet may not rest upon this sacred ground. I must take him hence in the boat."

"But where?"

"Across the channel there is an islet large enough for him; he shall have food and shelter, but here he cannot abide," said the man, leading the way down to the boat.

The Captain was therefore ferried across, a tent was made for him out of some old mats, food was provided, and, lest he should swim back, he was tethered by a long rope, which allowed him to prowl around his domain and take his choice of three runs for drinking-water. With all these advantages, the ungrateful animal persisted in howling dismally as we rowed away. It was company he wanted, and not a "dear little isle of his own"; but then, he was not by nature poetical.

"You do not like dogs?" I said, as we reached our strand again.

"St. Paul wrote, 'Beware of dogs,'" replied Samuel.

"But did he mean —"

"I argue not with unbelievers; his meaning is clear to me, let that suffice," said my strange host, turning away and leaving me to find my way back alone. A delicious repast was awaiting me. Years have gone by, the world and all its delicacies have been unrolled before me, but the memory of the meals I ate in that little kitchen in the Flats haunts me still. That night it was only fish, potatoes, biscuits, butter, stewed fruit, and coffee; but the fish was fresh, and done to the turn of a perfect broil, not burn; the potatoes were fried to a rare crisp, yet tender perfection, not chippy brittleness; the biscuits were light, flaked creamily, and brown on the bottom; the butter freshly churned, without salt; the fruit, great pears, with their cores extracted, standing whole on their dish, ready to melt, but not melted; and the coffee clear and strong, with yellow cream and the old-fashioned, unadulterated loaf-sugar. We ate. That does not express it; we devoured. Roxana waited on us, and warmed up into something like excitement under our praises.

"I *do* like good cooking," she confessed. "It 's about all I have left of my old life. I go over to the mainland for supplies, and in the winter I try all kinds of new things to pass away the time. But Samuel is a poor eater, he is; and so there is n't much comfort in it. I 'm mighty glad you 've come, and I hope you 'll stay as long as you find it pleasant." This we promised to do, as we finished the potatoes and attacked the great jellied pears. "There 's one thing, though," continued Roxana; "you 'll have to come to our service on the roof at sunrise."

"What service?" I asked.

"The invocation. Dawn is a holy time, Samuel says, and we always wait for it; 'before the morning watch,' you know, — it says so in the Bible. Why, my name means 'the dawn,' Samuel says; that 's the reason he gave it to me. My real name, down in Maine, was Maria, — Maria Ann."

"But I may not wake in time," I said.

"Samuel will call you."

"And if, in spite of that, I should sleep over?"

"You would not do that; it would vex him," replied Roxana, calmly.

"Do you believe in these visions, madam?" asked Raymond, as we left the table, and seated ourselves in front of the dying fire.

"Yes," said Roxana; emphasis was unnecessary, — of course she believed.

"How often do they come?"

"Almost every day there is a spiritual presence, but it does not always speak. They come and hold long conversations in the winter, when there is nothing else to do; that, I think, is very kind of them, for in the summer Samuel can fish, and his time is more occupied. There were fishermen in the Bible, you know; it is a holy calling."

"Does Samuel ever go over to the mainland?"

"No, he never leaves the Flats. I do all the business; take over the fish, and buy the supplies. I bought all our cattle," said Roxana, with pride. "I poled them away over here on a raft, one by one, when they were little things."

"Where do you pasture them?"

"Here, on the island; there are only a few acres, to

be sure; but I can cut boat-loads of the best feed within a stone's throw. If we only had a little more solid ground! But this island is almost the only solid piece in the Flats."

"Your butter is certainly delicious."

"Yes, I do my best. It is sold to the steamers and vessels as fast as I make it."

"You keep yourself busy, I see."

"O, I like to work; I could n't get on without it."

"And Samuel?"

"He is not like me," replied Roxana. "He has great gifts, Samuel has. I often think how strange it is that I should be the wife of such a holy man! He is very kind to me, too; he tells me about the visions, and all the other things."

"What things?" said Raymond.

"The spirits, and the sacred influence of the sun; the fiery triangle, and the thousand years of joy. The great day is coming, you know; Samuel is waiting for it."

"Nine of the night. Take thou thy rest. I will lay me down in peace, and sleep, for it is thou, Lord, only, that makest me dwell in safety," chanted a voice in the hall; the tone was deep and not without melody, and the words singularly impressive in that still, remote place.

"Go," said Roxana, instantly pushing aside her half-washed dishes. "Samuel will take you to your room."

"Do you leave your work unfinished?" I said, with some curiosity, noticing that she had folded her hands without even hanging up her towels.

"We do nothing after the evening chant," she said. "Pray go; he is waiting."

"Can we have candles?"

"Waiting Samuel allows no false lights in his house; as imitations of the glorious sun, they are abominable to him. Go, I beg."

She opened the door, and we went into the passage; it was entirely dark, but the man led us across to our room, showed us the position of our beds by sense of feeling, and left us without a word. After he had gone, we struck matches, one by one, and, with the aid of their uncertain light, managed to get into our respective mounds in safety; they were shake-downs on the floor, made of fragrant hay instead of straw, covered with clean sheets and patchwork coverlids, and provided with large, luxurious pillows. O pillow! Has any one sung thy praises? When tired or sick, when discouraged or sad, what gives so much comfort as a pillow? Not your curled-hair brickbats; not your stiff, fluted, rasping covers, or limp cotton cases; but a good, generous, soft pillow, deftly cased in smooth, cool, untrimmed linen! There's a friend for you, a friend who changes not, a friend who soothes all your troubles with a soft caress, a mesmeric touch of balmy forgetfulness.

I slept a dreamless sleep. Then I heard a voice borne toward me as if coming from far over a sea, the waves bringing it nearer and nearer.

"Awake!" it cried; "awake! The night is far spent; the day is at hand. Awake!"

I wondered vaguely over this voice as to what manner of voice it might be, but it came again, and again, and finally I awoke to find it at my side. The gray light of dawn came through the open windows, and Raymond was already up, engaged with a tub of water and crash towels. Again the chant sounded in my ears.

"Very well, very well," I said, testily. "But if you sing before breakfast you'll cry before night, Waiting Samuel."

Our host had disappeared, however, without hearing my flippant speech, and slowly I rose from my fragrant couch; the room was empty save for our two mounds, two tubs of water, and a number of towels hanging on nails. "Not overcrowded with furniture," I remarked.

"From Maine to Florida, from Massachusetts to Missouri, have I travelled, and never before found water enough," said Raymond. "If waiting for the judgment-day raises such liberal ideas of tubs and towels, I would that all the hotel-keepers in the land could be convened here to take a lesson."

Our green hunting-clothes were soon donned, and we went out into the hall; a flight of broad steps led up to the roof; Roxana appeared at the top and beckoned us thither. We ascended, and found ourselves on the flat roof. Samuel stood with his face toward the east and his arms outstretched, watching the horizon; behind was Roxana, with her hands clasped on her breast and her head bowed: thus they waited. The eastern sky was bright with golden light; rays shot upward toward the zenith, where the rose-lights of dawn were retreating down to the west, which still lay in the shadow of night; there was not a sound; the Flats stretched out dusky and still. Two or three minutes passed, and then a dazzling rim appeared above the horizon, and the first gleam of sunshine was shed over the level earth; simultaneously the two began a chant, simple as a Gregorian, but rendered in correct full tones. The words, apparently, had been collected from the Bible:—

"The heavens declare the glory of God—
Joy cometh in the morning!
In them is laid out the path of the sun—
Joy cometh in the morning!
As a bridegroom goeth he forth;
As a strong man runneth his race.
The outgoings of the morning
Praise thee, O Lord!
Like a pelican in the wilderness,
Like a sparrow upon the house-top,
I wait for the Lord.
It is good that we hope and wait,
Wait—wait."

The chant over, the two stood a moment silently, as if in contemplation, and then descended, passing us without a word or sign, with their hands clasped before them as though forming part of an unseen procession. Raymond and I were left alone upon the house-top.

"After all, it is not such a bad opening for a day; and there is the pelican of the wilderness to emphasize it," I said, as a heron flew up from the water, and, slowly flapping his great wings, sailed across to another channel. As the sun rose higher, the birds began to sing; first a single note here and there, then a little trilling solo, and finally an outpouring of melody on all sides, — land-birds and water-birds, birds that lived in the Flats, and birds that had flown thither for breakfast, — the whole waste was awake and rejoicing in the sunshine.

"What a wild place it is!" said Raymond. "How boundless it looks! One hill in the distance, one dark line of forest, even one tree, would break its charm. I have seen the ocean, I have seen the prairies, I have seen the great desert, but this is like a mixture of the three. It is an ocean full of land, — a prairie full of water, — a desert full of verdure."

"Whatever it is, we shall find in it fishing and aquatic hunting to our hearts' content," I answered.

And we did. After a breakfast delicious as the supper, we took our boat and a lunch-basket, and set out.

"But how shall we ever find our way back?" I said, pausing as I recalled the network of runs, and the will-o'-the-wisp aspect of the house, the previous evening.

"There is no other way but to take a large ball of cord with you, fasten one end on shore, and let it run out over the stern of the boat," said Roxana. "Let it run out loosely, and it will float on the water. When you want to come back you can turn around and wind it in as you come. *I* can read the Flats like a book, but they 're very blinding to most people; and you might keep going round in a circle. You will do better not to go far, anyway. I 'll wind the bugle on the roof an hour before sunset; you can start back when you hear it; for it 's awkward getting supper after dark." With this musical promise we took the clew of twine which Roxana rigged for us in the stern of our boat, and started away, first releasing Captain Kidd, who was pacing his islet in sullen majesty, like another Napoleon on St. Helena. We took a new channel and passed behind the house, where the imported cattle were feeding in their little pasture; but the winding stream soon bore us away, the house sank out of sight, and we were left alone.

We had fine sport that morning among the ducks,—wood, teal, and canvas-back,—shooting from behind our screens woven of rushes; later in the day we took to fishing. The sun shone down, but there was a cool

September breeze, and the freshness of the verdure was like early spring. At noon we took our lunch and a *siesta* among the water-lilies. When we awoke we found that a bittern had taken up his position near by, and was surveying us gravely:—

> "'The moping bittern, motionless and stiff,
> That on a stone so silently and stilly
> Stands, an apparent sentinel, as if
> To guard the water-lily,'"

quoted Raymond. The solemn bird, in his dark uniform, seemed quite undisturbed by our presence; yellow-throats and swamp-sparrows also came in numbers to have a look at us; and the fish swam up to the surface and eyed us curiously. Lying at ease in the boat, we in our turn looked down into the water. There is a singular fascination in looking down into a clear stream as the boat floats above; the mosses and twining water-plants seem to have arbors and grottos in their recesses, where delicate marine creatures might live, naiads and mermaids of miniature size; at least we are always looking for them. There is a fancy, too, that one may find something,—a ring dropped from fair fingers idly trailing in the water; a book which the fishes have read thoroughly; a scarf caught among the lilies; a spoon with unknown initials; a drenched ribbon, or an embroidered handkerchief. None of these things did we find, but we did discover an old brass breastpin, whose probable glass stone was gone. It was a paltry trinket at best, but I fished it out with superstitious care, — a treasure-trove of the Flats. "'Drowned,'" I said, pathetically, "'drowned in her white robes —'"

"And brass breastpin," added Raymond, who objected to sentiment, true or false.

"You Philistine! Is nothing sacred to you?"

"Not brass jewelry, certainly."

"Take some lilies and consider them," I said, plucking several of the queenly blossoms floating alongside.

"Cleopatra art thou, regal blossom,
Floating in thy galley down the Nile, —
All my soul does homage to thy splendor,
All my heart grows warmer in thy smile;
Yet thou smilest for thine own grand pleasure,
Caring not for all the world beside,
As in insolence of perfect beauty,
Sailest thou in silence down the tide.

"Loving, humble rivers all pursue thee,
Wasted are their kisses at thy feet;
Fiery sun himself cannot subdue thee,
Calm thou smilest through his raging heat;
Naught to thee the earth's great crowd of blossoms,
Naught to thee the rose-queen on her throne;
Haughty empress of the summer waters,
Livest thou, and diest, all alone."

This from Raymond.

"Where did you find that?" I asked.

"It is my own."

"Of course! I might have known it. There is a certain rawness of style and versification which—"

"That 's right," interrupted Raymond; "I know just what you are going to say. The whole matter of opinion is a game of 'follow-my-leader'; not one of you dares admire anything unless the critics say so. If I had told you the verses were by somebody instead of a nobody, you would have found wonderful beauties in them."

"Exactly. My motto is, 'Never read anything unless it is by a somebody.' For, don't you see, that a nobody, if he is worth anything, will soon grow into a somebody, and, if he is n't worth anything, you will have saved your time!"

"But it is not merely a question of growing," said Raymond; "it is a question of critics."

"No; there you are mistaken. All the critics in the world can neither make nor crush a true poet."

"What is poetry?" said Raymond, gloomily.

At this comprehensive question, the bittern gave a hollow croak, and flew away with his long legs trailing behind him. Probably he was not of an æsthetic turn of mind, and dreaded lest I should give a ramified answer.

Through the afternoon we fished when the fancy struck us, but most of the time we floated idly, enjoying the wild freedom of the watery waste. We watched the infinite varieties of the grasses, feathery, lance-leaved, tufted, drooping, banner-like, the deer's tongue, the wild-celery, and the so-called wild-rice, besides many unknown beauties delicately fringed, as difficult to catch and hold as thistle-down. There were plants journeying to and fro on the water like nomadic tribes of the desert; there were fleets of green leaves floating down the current; and now and then we saw a wonderful flower with scarlet bells, but could never approach near enough to touch it.

At length, the distant sound of the bugle came to us on the breeze, and I slowly wound in the clew, directing Raymond as he pushed the boat along, backing water with the oars. The sound seemed to come from every direction. There was nothing for it to echo against, but, in place of the echo, we heard a long, dying cadence, which sounded on over the Flats fainter and fainter in a sweet, slender note, until a new tone broke forth. The music floated around us, now on one side, now on the other; if it had been our only guide, we should have been completely bewildered. But I wound the cord steadily; and at last suddenly, there before us, appeared the house with Roxana on the roof, her figure outlined against the sky. Seeing us, she played a final salute, and then descended, carrying the imprisoned music with her.

That night we had our supper at sunset. Waiting Samuel had his meals by himself in the front room.

"So that in case the spirits come, I shall not be there to hinder them," explained Roxana. "I am not holy, like Samuel; they will not speak before me."

"Do you have your meals apart in the winter, also?" asked Raymond.

"Yes."

"That is not very sociable," I said.

"Samuel never was sociable," replied Roxana. "Only common folks are sociable; but he is different. He has great gifts, Samuel has."

The meal over, we went up on the roof to smoke our cigars in the open air; when the sun had disappeared and his glory had darkened into twilight, our host joined us. He was a tall man, wasted and gaunt, with piercing dark eyes and dark hair, tinged with gray, hanging down upon his shoulders. (Why is it that long hair on the outside is almost always the sign of something wrong in the inside of a man's head?) He wore a black robe like a priest's cassock, and on his head a black skull-cap like the *Faust* of the operatic stage.

"Why were the Flats called St. Clair?" I said; for there is something fascinating to me in the unknown history of the West. "There is n't any," do you say? you, I mean, who are strong in the Punic wars! you, too, who are so well up in Grecian mythology. But there is history, only we don't know it. The story of Lake Huron in the times of the Pharaohs, the story of the Mississippi during the reign of Belshazzar, would be worth hearing. But it is lost! All we can do is to gather together the details of our era, — the era when Columbus came to this New World, which was, nevertheless, as old as the world he left behind.

"It was in 1679," began Waiting Samuel, "that La Salle sailed up the Detroit River in his little vessel of sixty tons burden, called the Griffin. He was accompanied by thirty-four men, mostly fur-traders; but there were among them two holy monks, and Father Louis Hennepin, a friar of the Franciscan order. They passed up the river and entered the little lake just south of us, crossing it and these Flats on the 12th of August, which is Saint Clair's day. Struck with the gentle beauty of the scene, they named the waters after their saint, and at sunset sang a *Te Deum* in her honor."

"And who was Saint Clair?"

"Saint Clair, virgin and abbess, born in Italy, in 1193, made superior of a convent by the great Francis, and canonized for her distinguished virtues," said Samuel, as though reading from an encyclopædia.

"Are you a Roman Catholic?" asked Raymond.

"I am everything; all sincere faith is sacred to me," replied the man. "It is but a question of names."

"Tell us of your religion," said Raymond, thoughtfully; for in religions Raymond was something of a polyglot.

"You would hear of my faith? Well, so be it. Your question is the work of spirit influence. Listen, then. The great Creator has sowed immensity with innumerable systems of suns. In one of these systems a spirit forgot that he was a limited, subordinate being, and misused his freedom; how, we know not. He fell, and with him all his kind. A new race was then created for the vacant world, and, according to the fixed purpose of the Creator, each was left free to act for himself; he loves not mere machines. The fallen spirit, envying the new creature called man, tempted him to sin. What was his sin? Simply the giving up of his birthright, the divine soul-sparkle, for a promise of earthly pleasure. The triune divine deep, the mysterious fiery triangle, which, to our finite minds, best represents the Deity, now withdrew his personal presence; the elements, their balance broken, stormed upon man; his body, which was once ethereal, moving by mere volition, now grew heavy; and it was also appointed unto him to die. The race thus darkened, crippled, and degenerate, sank almost to the level of the brutes, the mind-fire alone remaining of all their spiritual gifts. They lived on blindly, and as blindly died. The sun, however, was left to them, a type of what they had lost.

"At length, in the fulness of time, the world-day of four thousand years, which was appointed by the council in heaven for the regiving of the divine and forfeited soul-sparkle, as on the fourth day of creation the great sun was given, there came to earth the earth's compassionate Saviour, who took upon himself our degenerate body, and revivified it with the divine soul-sparkle, who overcame all our temptations, and finally allowed the tinder of our sins to perish in his own painful death upon the cross. Through him our paradise body was restored, it waits for us on the other side of the grave. He showed us what it was like on Mount Tabor, with it he passed through closed doors, walked upon the water, and ruled the elements; so will it be with us. Paradise will come again; this world will, for a thousand years, see its first estate; it will be again the Garden of Eden. America is the great escaping-place; here will the change begin. As it is written, 'Those who escape to my utmost borders.' As the time draws near, the spirits who watch above are permitted to speak to those souls who listen. Of these listening, waiting souls am I; therefore have I withdrawn myself. The sun himself speaks to me, the greatest spirit of all; each morning I watch for his coming; each morning I ask, 'Is it to-day?' Thus do I wait."

"And how long have you been waiting?" I asked.

"I know not; time is nothing to me."

"Is the great day near at hand?" said Raymond.

"Almost at its dawning; the last days are passing."

"How do you know this?"

"The spirits tell me. Abide here, and perhaps they will speak to you also," replied Waiting Samuel.

We made no answer. Twilight had darkened into night, and the Flats had sunk into silence below us. After some moments I turned to speak to our host; but, noiselessly as one of his own spirits, he had departed.

"A strange mixture of Jacob Bœhmen, chiliastic dreams, Christianity, sun-worship, and modern spiritualism," I said. "Much learning hath made the Maine farmer mad."

"Is he mad?" said Raymond. "Sometimes I think we are all mad."

"We should certainly become so if we spent our time in speculations upon subjects clearly beyond our reach. The whole race of philosophers from Plato down are all the time going round in a circle. As long as we are in the world, I for one propose to keep my feet on solid ground; especially as we have no wings. 'Abide here, and perhaps the spirits will speak to you,' did he say? I think very likely they will, and to such good purpose that you won't have any mind left."

"After all, why should not spirits speak to us?" said Raymond, in a musing tone.

As he uttered these words the mocking laugh of a loon came across the dark waste.

"The very loons are laughing at you," I said, rising. "Come down; there is a chill in the air, composed in equal parts of the Flats, the night, and Waiting Samuel. Come down, man; come down to the warm kitchen and common-sense."

We found Roxana alone by the fire, whose glow was refreshingly real and warm; it was like the touch of a flesh-and-blood hand, after vague dreamings of spirit-companions, cold and intangible at best, with the added suspicion that, after all, they are but creations of our own fancy, and even their spirit-nature fictitious. Prime, the graceful *raconteur* who goes a-fishing, says, "firelight is as much of a polisher in-doors as moonlight outside." It is; but with a different result. The moonlight polishes everything into romance, the firelight into comfort. We brought up two remarkably easy old chairs in front of the hearth and sat down, Raymond still adrift with his wandering thoughts, I, as usual, making talk out of the present. Roxana sat opposite, knitting in hand, the cat purring at her feet. She was a slender woman, with faded light hair, insignificant features, small dull blue eyes, and a general aspect which, with every desire to state at its best, I can only call commonplace. Her gown was limp, her hands roughened with work, and there was no collar around her yellow throat. O magic rim of white, great is thy power! With thee, man is civilized; without thee, he becomes at once a savage.

"I am out of pork," remarked Roxana, casually; "I must go over to the mainland to-morrow and get some."

If it had been anything but pork! In truth, the word did not chime with the mystic conversation of Waiting Samuel. Yes; there was no doubt about it. Roxana's mind was sadly commonplace.

"See what I have found," I said, after a while, taking out the old breastpin. "The stone is gone; but who knows? It might have been a diamond dropped by some French duchess, exiled, and fleeing for life across these far Western waters; or perhaps that German Princess of Brunswick-Wolfen-something-or-other, who, about one hundred years ago, was dead and buried in Russia, and travelling in America at the same time, a sort of a female wandering Jew, who has been done up in stories ever since."

(The other day, in Bret Harte's "Melons," I saw the following: "The singular conflicting conditions of John Brown's body and soul were, at that time, beginning to attract the attention of American youth." That is good, is n't it? Well, at the time I visited the Flats, the singular conflicting conditions of the Princess of Brunswick-Wolfen-something-or-other had, for a long time, haunted me.)

Roxana's small eyes were near-sighted; she peered at the empty setting, but said nothing.

"It is water-logged," I continued, holding it up in the firelight, "and it hath a brassy odor; nevertheless, I feel convinced that it belonged to the princess."

Roxana leaned forward and took the trinket; I lifted up my arms and gave a mighty stretch, one of those enjoyable lengthenings-out which belong only to the healthy fatigue of country life. When I drew myself in again, I was surprised to see Roxana's features working, and her rough hands trembling, as she held the battered setting.

"It was mine," she said; "my dear old cameo breastpin that Abby gave me when I was married. I saved it and saved it, and would n't sell it, no matter how low we got, for someway it seemed to tie me to home and baby's grave. I used to wear it when I had baby — I had neck-ribbons then; we had things like other folks, and on Sundays we went to the old meeting-house on the green. Baby is buried there — O baby, baby!" and the voice broke into sobs.

"You lost a child?" I said, pitying the sorrow which was, which must be, so lonely, so unshared.

"Yes. O baby! baby!" cried the woman, in a wailing tone. "It was a little boy, gentlemen, and it had curly hair, and could just talk a word or two; its name was Ethan, after father, but we all called it Robin. Father was mighty proud of Robin, and mother, too. It died, gentlemen, my baby died, and I buried it in the old churchyard near the thorn-tree.

But still I thought to stay there always along with mother and the girls; I never supposed anything else, until Samuel began to see visions. Then, everything was different, and everybody against us; for, you see, I would marry Samuel, and when he left off working, and began to talk to the spirits, the folks all said, 'I told yer so, Maria Ann!' Samuel was n't of Maine stock exactly: his father was a sailor, and 't was suspected that his mother was some kind of an East-Injia woman, but no one knew. His father died and left the boy on the town, so he lived round from house to house until he got old enough to hire out. Then he came to our farm, and there he stayed. He had wonderful eyes, Samuel had, and he had a way with him — well, the long and short of it was, that I got to thinking about him, and could n't think of anything else. The folks did n't like it at all, for, you see, there was Adam Rand, who had a farm of his own over the hill; but I never could bear Adam Rand. The worst of it was, though, that Samuel never so much as looked at me, hardly. Well, it got to be the second year, and Susan, my younger sister, married Adam Rand. Adam, he thought he'd break up my nonsense, that's what they called it, and so he got a good place for Samuel away down in Connecticut, and Samuel said he'd go, for he was always restless, Samuel was. When I heard it, I was ready to lie down and die. I ran out into the pasture and threw myself down by the fence like a crazy woman. Samuel happened to come by along the lane, and saw me; he was always kind to all the dumb creatures, and stopped to see what was the matter, just as he would have stopped to help a calf. It all came out then, and he was awful sorry for me. He sat down on the top bar of the fence and looked at me, and I sat on the ground a-crying with my hair down, and my face all red and swollen.

"'I never thought to marry, Maria Ann,' says he.

"'O, please do, Samuel,' says I, 'I 'm a real good housekeeper, I am, and we can have a little land of our own, and everything nice —'

"'But I wanted to go away. My father was a sailor,' he began, a-looking away off toward the ocean.

"'O, I can't stand it, — I can't stand it,' says I, beginning to cry again. Well, after that he 'greed to stay at home and marry me, and the folks they had to give in to it when they saw how I felt. We were married on Thanksgiving day, and I wore a pink delaine, purple neck-ribbon, and this very breastpin that sister Abby gave me, — it cost four dollars, and came 'way from Boston. Mother kissed me, and said she hoped I 'd be happy.

"'Of course I shall, mother,' says I. 'Samuel has great gifts; he is n't like common folks.'

"'But common folks is a deal comfortabler,' says mother. The folks never understood Samuel.

"Well, we had a chirk little house and bit of

land, and baby came, and was so cunning and pretty. The visions had begun to appear then, and Samuel said he must go.

"'Where?' says I.

"'Anywhere the spirits lead me,' says he.

"But baby could n't travel, and so it hung along; Samuel left off work, and everything ran down to loose ends; I did the best I could, but it was n't much. Then baby died, and I buried him under the thorn-tree, and the visions came thicker and thicker, and Samuel told me as how this time he must go. The folks wanted me to stay behind without him; but they never understood me nor him. I could no more leave him than I could fly; I was just wrapped up in him. So we went away; I cried dreadfully when it came to leaving the folks and Robin's little grave, but I had so much to do after we got started, that there was n't time for anything but work. We thought to settle in ever so many places, but after a while there would always come a vision, and I 'd have to sell out and start on. The little money we had was soon gone, and then I went out for days' work, and picked up any work I could get. But many 's the time we were cold, and many 's the time we were hungry, gentlemen. The visions kept coming, and by and by I got to like 'em too. Samuel he told me all they said when I came home nights, and it was nice to hear all about the thousand years of joy, when there 'd be no more trouble, and when Robin would come back to us again. Only I told Samuel that I hoped the world would n't alter much, because I wanted to go back to Maine for a few days, and see all the old places. Father and mother are dead, I suppose," said Roxana, looking up at us with a pathetic expression in her small dull eyes. Beautiful eyes are doubly beautiful in sorrow; but there is something peculiarly pathetic in small dull eyes looking up at you, struggling to express the grief that lies within, like a prisoner behind the bars of his small dull window.

"And how did you lose your breastpin?" I said, coming back to the original subject.

"Samuel found I had it, and threw it away soon after we came to the Flats; he said it was vanity."

"Have you been here long?"

"O yes, years. I hope we shall stay here always now,—at least, I mean until the thousand years of joy begin,—for it 's quiet, and Samuel 's more easy here than in any other place. I 've got used to the lonely feeling, and don't mind it much now. There 's no one near us for miles, except Rosabel Lee and Liakim; they don't come here, for Samuel can't abide 'em, but sometimes I stop there on my way over from the mainland, and have a little chat about the children. Rosabel Lee has got lovely children, she has! They don't stay there in the winter, though; the winters *are* long, I don't deny it."

"What do you do then?"

"Well, I knit and cook, and Samuel reads to me, and has a great many visions."

"He has books, then?"

"Yes, all kinds; he 's a great reader, and he has boxes of books about the spirits, and such things."

"Nine of the night. Take thou thy rest. I will lay me down in peace and sleep; for it is thou, Lord, only, that makest me dwell in safety," chanted the voice in the hall; and our evening was over.

At dawn we attended the service on the roof; then, after breakfast, we released Captain Kidd, and started out for another day's sport. We had not rowed far when Roxana passed us, poling her flat-boat rapidly along; she had a load of fish and butter, and was bound for the mainland village. "Bring us back a Detroit paper," I said. She nodded and passed on, stolid and homely in the morning light. Yes, I was obliged to confess to myself that she *was* commonplace.

A glorious day we had on the moors in the rushing September wind. Everything rustled and waved and danced, and the grass undulated in long billows as far as the eye could see. The wind enjoyed himself like a mad creature; he had no forests to oppose him, no heavy water to roll up, — nothing but merry, swaying grasses. It was the west wind, — "of all the winds, the best wind." The east wind was given us for our sins; I have long suspected that the east wind was the angel that drove Adam out of Paradise. We did nothing that day, — nothing but enjoy the rushing breeze. We felt like Bedouins of the desert, with our boat for a steed. "He came flying upon the wings of the wind," is the grandest image of the Hebrew poet.

Late in the afternoon we heard the bugle and returned, following our clew as before. Roxana had brought a late paper, and, opening it, I saw the account of an accident, — a yacht run down on the Sound and five drowned; five, all near and dear to us. Hastily and sadly we gathered our possessions together; the hunting, the fishing, were nothing now; all we thought of was to get away, to go home to the sorrowing ones around the new-made graves. Roxana went with us in her boat to guide us back to the little lighthouse. Waiting Samuel bade us no farewell, but as we rowed away we saw him standing on the house-top gazing after us. We bowed; he waved his hand; and then turned away to look at the sunset. What were our little affairs to a man who held converse with the spirits!

We rowed in silence. How long, how weary seemed the way! The grasses, the lilies, the silver channels, — we no longer even saw them. At length the forward boat stopped. "There 's the lighthouse yonder," said Roxana. "I won't go over there to-night. Mayhap you'd rather not talk, and Rosabel Lee will be sure to talk to me. Good by." We shook hands, and I laid in the boat a sum of money to help the little household through the winter; then we rowed on toward the lighthouse. At the turn I looked back; Roxana was sitting motionless in her boat; the dark clouds were rolling up behind her; and the Flats looked wild and desolate. "God help her!" I said.

A steamer passed the lighthouse and took us off within the hour.

Years rolled away, and I often thought of the grassy sea, and intended to go there; but the intention never grew into reality. In 1870, however, I was travelling westward, and, finding myself at Detroit, a sudden impulse took me up to the Flats. The steamer sailed up the beautiful river and crossed the little lake, both unchanged. But, alas! the canal predicted by the captain fifteen years before had been cut, and, in all its unmitigated ugliness, stretched straight through the enchanted land. I got off at the new and prosaic brick lighthouse, half expecting to see Liakim and his Rosabel Lee; but they were not there, and no one knew anything about them. And Waiting Samuel? No one knew anything about him, either. I took a skiff, and, at the risk of losing myself, I rowed away into the wilderness, spending the day among the silvery channels, which were as beautiful as ever. There were fewer birds; I saw no grave herons, no sombre bitterns, and the fish had grown shy. But the water-lilies were beautiful as of old, and the grasses as delicate and luxuriant. I had scarcely a hope of finding the old house on the island, but late in the afternoon, by a mere chance, I rowed up unexpectedly to its little landing-place. The walls stood firm and the roof was unbroken; I landed and walked up the overgrown path. Opening the door, I found the few old chairs and tables in their places, weather-beaten and decayed, the storms had forced a way within, and the floor was insecure; but the gay crockery was on its shelf, the old tins against the wall, and all looked so natural that I almost feared to find the mortal remains of the husband and wife as I went from room to room. They were not there, however, and the place looked as if it had been uninhabited for years. I lingered in the doorway. What had become of them? Were they dead? Or had a new vision sent them farther toward the setting sun? I never knew, although I made many inquiries. If dead, they were probably lying somewhere under the shining waters; if alive, they must have "folded their tents, like the Arabs, and silently stolen away."

I rowed back in the glow of the evening across the grassy sea. "It is beautiful, beautiful," I thought, "but it is passing away. Already commerce has invaded its borders; a few more years and its loveliness will be but a legend of the past. The bittern has vanished; the loon has fled away. Waiting Samuel was the prophet of the waste; he has gone, and the barriers are broken down. Farewell, beautiful grass-water! No artist has painted, no poet has sung your wild, vanishing charm; but in one heart, at least, you have a place, O lovely land of St. Clair!"

THE

LADY OF LITTLE FISHING.

IT was an island in Lake Superior.

I beached my canoe there about four o'clock in the afternoon, for the wind was against me and a high sea running. The late summer of 1850, and I was coasting along the south shore of the great lake, hunting, fishing, and camping on the beach, under the delusion that in that way I was living "close to the great heart of nature," — whatever that may mean. Lord Bacon got up the phrase; I suppose he knew. Pulling the boat high and dry on the sand with the comfortable reflection that here were no tides to disturb her with their goings-out and comings-in, I strolled through the woods on a tour of exploration, expecting to find bluebells, Indian pipes, juniper rings, perhaps a few agates along-shore, possibly a bird or two for company. I found a town.

It was deserted; but none the less a town, with three streets, residences, a meeting-house, gardens, a little park, and an attempt at a fountain. Ruins are rare in the New World; I took off my hat. "Hail, homes of the past!" I said. (I cultivated the habit of thinking aloud when I was living close to the great heart of nature.) "A human voice resounds through your arches" (there were no arches, — logs won't arch; but never mind) "once more, a human hand touches your venerable walls, a human foot presses your deserted hearth-stones." I then selected the best half of the meeting-house for my camp, knocked down one of the homes for fuel, and kindled a glorious bonfire in the park. "Now that you are illuminated with joy, O Ruin," I remarked, "I will go down to the beach and bring up my supplies. It is long since I have had a roof over my head; I promise you to stay until your last residence is well burned; then I will make a final cup of coffee with the meeting-house itself, and depart in peace, leaving your poor old bones buried in decent ashes."

The ruin made no objection, and I took up my abode there; the roof of the meeting-house was still water-tight (which is an advantage when the great heart of nature grows wet). I kindled a fire on the sacerdotal hearth, cooked my supper, ate it in leisurely comfort, and then stretched myself on a blanket to enjoy an evening pipe of peace, listening meanwhile to the sounding of the wind through the great pine-trees. There was no door to my sanctuary, but I had the cosey far end; the island was uninhabited, there was not a boat in sight at sunset, nothing could disturb me unless it might be a ghost. Presently a ghost came in.

It did not wear the traditional gray tarlatan armor of Hamlet's father, the only ghost with whom I am well acquainted; this spectre was clad in substantial deer-skin garments, and carried a gun and loaded game-bag. It came forward to my hearth, hung up its gun, opened its game-bag, took out some birds, and inspected them gravely.

"Fat?" I inquired.

"They 'll do," replied the spectre, and forthwith set to work preparing them for the coals. I smoked on in silence. The spectre seemed to be a skilled cook, and after deftly broiling its supper, it offered me a share; I accepted. It swallowed a huge mouthful and crunched with its teeth; the spell was broken, and I knew it for a man of flesh and blood.

He gave his name as Reuben, and proved himself an excellent camping companion; in fact, he shot all the game, caught all the fish, made all the fires, and cooked all the food for us both. I proposed to him to stay and help me burn up the ruin, with the condition that when the last timber of the meeting-house was consumed, we should shake hands and depart, one to the east, one to the west, without a backward glance. "In that way we shall not infringe upon each other's personality," I said.

"Agreed," replied Reuben.

He was a man of between fifty and sixty years, while I was on the sunny side of thirty; he was reserved, I was always generously affable; he was an excellent cook, while I — well, I was n't; he was taciturn, and so, in payment for the work he did, I entertained him with conversation, or rather monologue, in my most brilliant style. It took only two weeks to burn up the town, burned we never so slowly; at last it came the turn of the meeting-house, which now stood by itself in the vacant clearing. It was a cool September day; we cooked breakfast with the roof, dinner with the sides, supper with the odds and ends, and then applied a torch to the framework. Our last camp-fire was a glorious one. We lay stretched on our blankets, smoking and watching the glow. "I wonder, now, who built the old shanty," I said in a musing tone.

"Well," replied Reuben, slowly, "if you really want to know, I will tell you. I did."

"You!"

"Yes."

"You did n't do it alone?"

"No; there were about forty of us."

"Here?"

"Yes; here at Little Fishing."

"Little Fishing?"

"Yes; Little Fishing Island. That is the name of the place."

"How long ago was this?"

"Thirty years."

"Hunting and trapping, I suppose?"

"Yes; for the Northwest and Hudson Bay Companies."

"Was n't a meeting-house an unusual accompaniment?"

"Most unusual."

"Accounted for in this case by—"

"A woman."

"Ah!" I said in a tone of relish; "then of course there is a story?"

"There is."

"Out with it, comrade. I scarcely expected to find the woman and her story up here; but since the irrepressible creature would come, out with her by all means. She shall grace our last pipe together, the last timber of our meeting-house, our last night on Little Fishing. The dawn will see us far from each other, to meet no more this side heaven. Speak then, O comrade mine! I am in one of my rare listening moods!"

I stretched myself at ease and waited. Reuben was a long time beginning, but I was too indolent to urge him. At length he spoke.

"They were a rough set here at Little Fishing, all the worse for being all white men; most of the other camps were full of half-breeds and Indians. The island had been a station away back in the early days of the

Hudson Bay Company; it was a station for the Northwest Company while that lasted; then it went back to the Hudson, and stayed there until the company moved its forces farther to the north. It was not at any time a regular post; only a camp for the hunters. The post was farther down the lake. O, but those were wild days! You think you know the wilderness, boy; but you know nothing, absolutely nothing. It makes me laugh to see the airs of you city gentlemen with your fine guns, improved fishing-tackle, elaborate paraphernalia, as though you were going to wed the whole forest, floating up and down the lake for a month or two in the summer! You should have seen the hunters of Little Fishing going out gayly when the mercury was down twenty degrees below zero, for a week in the woods. You should have seen the trappers wading through the hard snow, breast high, in the gray dawn, visiting the traps and hauling home the prey. There were all kinds of men here, Scotch, French, English, and American; all classes, the high and the low, the educated and the ignorant; all sorts, the lazy and the hard-working. One thing only they all had in common, — badness. Some had fled to the wilderness to escape the law, others to escape order; some had chosen the wild life because of its wildness, others had drifted into it from sheer lethargy. This far northern border did not attract the plodding emigrant, the respectable settler. Little Fishing held none of that trash; only a reckless set of fellows who carried their lives in their hands, and tossed them up, if need be, without a second thought."

"And other people's lives without a third," I suggested.

"Yes; if they deserved it. But nobody whined; there was n't any nonsense here. The men went hunting and trapping, got the furs ready for the bateaux, ate when they were hungry, drank when they were thirsty, slept when they were sleepy, played cards when they felt like it, and got angry and knocked each other down whenever they chose. As I said before, there was n't any nonsense at Little Fishing, — until *she* came."

"Ah! the she!"

"Yes, the Lady, — our Lady, as we called her. Thirty-one years ago; how long it seems!"

"And well it may," I said. "Why, comrade, I was n't born then!"

This stupendous fact seemed to strike me more than my companion; he went on with his story as though I had not spoken.

"One October evening, four of the boys had got into a row over the cards; the rest of us had come out of our wigwams to see the fun, and were sitting around on the stumps, chaffing them, and laughing; the camp-fire was burning in front, lighting up the woods with a red glow for a short distance, and making the rest doubly black all around. There we all were, as I said before, quite easy and comfortable, when suddenly there appeared among us, as though she had dropped from heaven, a woman!

"She was tall and slender, the firelight shone full on her pale face and dove-colored dress, her golden hair was folded back under a little white cap, and a white kerchief lay over her shoulders; she looked spotless. I stared; I could scarcely believe my eyes; none of us could. There was not a white woman west of the Sault Ste. Marie. The four fellows at the table sat as if transfixed; one had his partner by the throat, the other two were disputing over a point in the game. The lily lady glided up to their table, gathered the cards in her white hands, slowly, steadily, without pause or trepidation before their astonished eyes, and then, coming back, she threw the cards into the centre of the glowing fire. 'Ye shall not play away your souls,' she said in a clear, sweet voice. 'Is not the game sin? And its reward death?' And then, immediately, she gave us a sermon, the like of which was never heard before; no argument, no doctrine, just simple, pure entreaty. 'For the love of God,' she ended, stretching out her hands towards our silent, gazing group,—'for the love of God, my brothers, try to do better.'

"We did try; but it was not for the love of God. Neither did any of us feel like brothers.

"She did not give any name; we called her simply our Lady, and she accepted the title. A bundle carefully packed in birch-bark was found on the beach. 'Is this yours?' asked black Andy.

"'It is,' replied the Lady; and removing his hat, the black-haired giant carried the package reverently inside her lodge. For we had given her our best wigwam, and fenced it off with pine saplings so that it looked like a miniature fortress. The Lady did not suggest this stockade; it was our own idea, and with one accord we worked at it like beavers, and hung up a gate with a ponderous bolt inside.

"'Mais, ze can nevare farsen eet wiz her leetle fingares,' said Frenchy, a sallow little wretch with a turn for handicraft; so he contrived a small spring which shot the bolt into place with a touch. The Lady lived in her fortress; three times a day the men carried food to her door, and, after tapping gently, withdrew again, stumbling over each other in their haste. The Flying Dutchman, a stolid Holland-born sailor, was our best cook, and the pans and kettles were generally left to him; but now all wanted to try their skill, and the results were extraordinary.

"'She 's never touched that pudding, now,' said Nightingale Jack, discontentedly, as his concoction of berries and paste came back from the fortress door.

"'She will starve soon, I think,' remarked the

Doctor, calmly; 'to my certain knowledge she has not had an eatable meal for four days.' And he lighted a fresh pipe. This was an aside, and the men pretended not to hear it; but the pans were relinquished to the Dutchman from that time forth.

"The Lady wore always her dove-colored robe, and little white cap, through whose muslin we could see the glimmer of her golden hair. She came and went among us like a spirit; she knew no fear; she turned our life inside out, nor shrank from its vileness. It seemed as though she was not of earth, so utterly impersonal was her interest in us, so heavenly her pity. She took up our sins, one by one, as an angel might; she pleaded with us for our own lost souls, she spared us not, she held not back one grain of denunciation, one iota of future punishment. Sometimes, for days, we would not see her; then, at twilight, she would glide out among us, and, standing in the light of the camp-fire, she would preach to us as though inspired. We listened to her; I do not mean that we were one whit better at heart, but still we listened to her, always. It was a wonderful sight, that lily face under the pine-trees, that spotless woman standing alone in the glare of the fire, while around her lay forty evil-minded, lawless men, not one of whom but would have killed his neighbor for so much as a disrespectful thought of her.

"So strange was her coming, so almost supernatural her appearance in this far forest, that we never wondered over its cause, but simply accepted it as a sort of miracle; your thoroughly irreligious men are always superstitious. Not one of us would have asked a question, and we should never have known her story had she not herself told it to us; not immediately, not as though it was of any importance, but quietly, briefly, and candidly as a child. She came, she said, from Scotland, with a band of God's people. She had always been in one house, a religious institution of some kind, sewing for the poor when her strength allowed it, but generally ill, and suffering much from pain in her head; often kept under the influence of soothing medicines for days together. She had no father or mother, she was only one of this band; and when they decided to send out missionaries to America, she begged to go, although but a burden; the sea voyage restored her health; she grew, she said, in strength and in grace, and her heart was as the heart of a lion. Word came to her from on high that she should come up into the northern lake-country and preach the gospel there; the band were going to the verdant prairies. She left them in the night, taking nothing but her clothing; a friendly vessel carried her north; she had preached the gospel everywhere. At the Sault the priests had driven her out, but nothing fearing, she went on into the wilderness, and so, coming part of the way in canoes, part of the way along-shore, she had reached our far island. Marvellous kindness had she met with, she said; the Indians, the half-breeds, the hunters, and the trappers had all received her, and helped her on her way from camp to camp. They had listened to her words also. At Portage they had begged her to stay through the winter, and offered to build her a little church for Sunday services. Our men looked at each other. Portage was the worst camp on the lake, notorious for its fights; it was a mining settlement.

"'But I told them I must journey on towards the west,' continued our Lady. 'I am called to visit every camp on this shore before the winter sets in; I must soon leave you also.'

"The men looked at each other again; the Doctor was spokesman. 'But, my Lady,' he said, 'the next post is Fort William, two hundred and thirty-five miles away on the north shore.'

"'It is almost November; the snow will soon be six and ten feet deep. The Lady could never travel through it, — could she, now?' said Black Andy, who had begun eagerly, but in his embarrassment at the sound of his own voice, now turned to Frenchy and kicked him covertly into answering.

"'Nevare!' replied the Frenchman; he had intended to place his hand upon his heart to give emphasis to his word, but the Lady turned her calm eyes that way, and his grimy paw fell, its gallantry wilted.

"'I thought there was one more camp, — at Burnt-Wood River,' said our Lady in a musing tone. The men looked at each other a third time; there was a camp there, and they all knew it. But the Doctor was equal to the emergency.

"'That camp, my Lady,' he said gravely, — 'that camp no longer exists!' Then he whispered hurriedly to the rest of us, 'It will be an easy job to clean it out, boys. We 'll send over a party to-night; it 's only thirty-five miles.'

"We recognized superior genius; the Doctor was our oldest and deepest sinner. But what struck us most was his anxiety to make good his lie. Had it then come to this, — that the Doctor told the truth?

"The next day we all went to work to build our Lady a church; in a week it was completed. There goes its last cross-beam now into the fire; it was a solid piece of work, was n't it? It has stood this climate thirty years. I remember the first Sunday service: we all washed, and dressed ourselves in the best we had; we scarcely knew each other, we were so fine. The Lady was pleased with the church, but yet she had not said she would stay all winter; we were still anxious. How she preached to us that day! We had made a screen of young spruces set in boxes, and her figure stood out against the dark green background like a thing of light. Her silvery voice rang through the log-temple, her face seemed to us like a star. She had no color in her cheeks at any time; her dress, too, was colorless. Although gentle, there was an iron inflexibility about her slight, erect form. We felt, as we saw her standing there, that if need be she would walk up to the lion's jaws, the cannon's mouth, with a smile. She took a little book from her pocket and read to us a hymn,—'O come, all ye faithful,' the old 'Adeste Fideles.' Some of us knew it; she sang, and gradually, shamefacedly, voices joined in. It was a sight to see Nightingale Jack solemnly singing away about 'choirs of angels'; but it was a treat to hear him, too,—what a voice he had! Then our Lady prayed, kneeling down on the little platform in front of the evergreens, clasping her hands, and lifting her eyes to heaven. We did not know what to do at first, but the Doctor gave us a severe look and bent his head, and we all followed his lead.

"When service was over and the door opened, we found that it had been snowing; we could not see out through the windows because white cloth was nailed over them in place of glass.

"'Now, my Lady, you will have to stay with us,' said the Doctor. We all gathered around with eager faces.

"'Do you really believe that it will be for the good of your souls?' asked the sweet voice.

"The Doctor believed — for us all.

"'Do you really hope?'

"The Doctor hoped.

"'Will you try to do your best?'

"The Doctor was sure he would.

"'I will,' answered the Flying Dutchman, earnestly. 'I moost not fry de meat any more; I moost broil!'

"For we had begged him for months to broil, and he had obstinately refused; broil represented the good, and fry the evil, to his mind; he came out for the good according to his light; but none the less did we fall upon him behind the Lady's back, and cuff him into silence.

"She stayed with us all winter. You don't know what the winters are up here; steady, bitter cold for seven months, thermometer always below, the snow dry as dust, the air like a knife. We built a compact chimney for our Lady, and we cut cords of wood into small, light sticks, easy for her to lift, and stacked them in her shed; we lined her lodge with skins, and we made oil from bear's fat and rigged up a kind of lamp for her. We tried to make candles, I remember, but they would not run straight; they came out hump-backed and sidling, and burned themselves to wick in no time. Then we took to improving the town. We had lived in all kinds of huts and lean-to shanties; now nothing would do but regular log-houses. If it had been summer, I don't know what we might not have run to in the way of piazzas and fancy steps; but with the snow five feet deep, all we could accomplish was a plain, square log-house, and even that took our whole force. The only way to keep the peace was to have all the houses exactly alike; we laid out the three streets, and built the houses, all facing the meeting-house, just as you found them."

"And where was the Lady's lodge?" I asked, for I recalled no stockaded fortress, large or small.

My companion hesitated a moment. Then he said abruptly, "It was torn down."

"Torn down!" I repeated. "Why, what —"

Reuben waved his hand with a gesture that silenced me, and went on with his story. It came to me then for the first time, that he was pursuing the current of his own thoughts rather than entertaining me. I turned to look at him with a new interest. I had talked to him for two weeks, in rather a patronizing way; could it be that affairs were now, at this last moment, reversed?

"It took us almost all winter to build those houses," pursued Reuben. "At one time we neglected the hunting and trapping to such a degree, that the Doctor called a meeting and expressed his opinion. Ours was a voluntary camp, in a measure, but still we had formally agreed to get a certain amount of skins ready for the bateaux by early spring; this agreement was about the only real bond of union between us. Those whose houses were not completed scowled at the Doctor.

"'Do you suppose I'm going to live like an Injun when the other fellows has regular houses?' inquired Black Andy, with a menacing air.

"'By no means,' replied the Doctor, blandly. 'My plan is this: build at night.'

"'At night?'

"'Yes; by the light of pine fires.'

"We did. After that, we faithfully went out hunting and trapping as long as daylight lasted, and then, after supper, we built up huge fires of pine logs, and went to work on the next house. It was a strange picture: the forest deep in snow, black with night, the red glow of the great fires, and our moving figures working on as complacently as though daylight, balmy air, and the best of tools were ours.

"The Lady liked our industry. She said our new houses showed that the 'new cleanliness of our inner man required a cleaner tabernacle for the outer.' I don't know about our inner man, but our outer was certainly much cleaner.

"One day the Flying Dutchman made one of his unfortunate remarks. 'De boys t'inks you 'll like dem better in nize houses,' he announced when, happening to pass the fortress, he found the Lady standing at her gate gazing at the work of the preceding night. Several of the men were near enough to hear him, but too far off to kick him into silence as usual; but they glared at him instead. The Lady looked at the speaker with her dreamy, far-off eyes.

"'De boys t'inks you like dem,' began the Dutchman again, thinking she did not comprehend; but at that instant he caught the combined glare of the six eyes, and stopped abruptly, not at all knowing what was wrong, but sure there was something.

"'Like them,' repeated the Lady, dreamily; 'yea, I do like them. Nay, more, I love them. Their souls are as dear to me as the souls of brothers.'

"'Say, Frenchy, have you got a sister?' said Nightingale Jack, confidentially, that evening.

"'Mais oui,' said Frenchy.

"'You think all creation of her, I suppose?'

"'We fight like four cats and one dog; *she* is the cats,' said the Frenchman concisely.

"'You don't say so!' replied Jack. 'Now, I never had a sister, — but I thought perhaps —' He paused, and the sentence remained unfinished.

"The Nightingale and I were house-mates. We sat late over our fire not long after that; I gave a gigantic yawn. 'This lifting logs half the night is enough to kill one,' I said, getting out my jug. 'Sing something, Jack. It's a long time since I've heard anything but hymns.'

"Jack always went off as easily as a music-box:

you had only to wind him up; the jug was the key. I soon had him in full blast. He was giving out

'The minute gun at sea, — the minute gun at sea,'

with all the pathos of his tenor voice, when the door burst open and the whole population rushed in upon us.

"'What do you mean by shouting this way, in the middle of the night?'

"'Shut up your howling, Jack.'

"'How do you suppose any one can sleep?'

"'It 's a disgrace to the camp!'

"'Now then, gentlemen,' I replied, for my blood was up (whiskey, perhaps), 'is this my house, or is n't it? If I want music, I'll have it. Time was when you were not so particular.'

"It was the first word of rebellion. The men looked at each other, then at me.

"'I'll go and ask her if she objects,' I continued, boldly.

"'No, no. You shall not.'

"'Let him go,' said the Doctor, who stood smoking his pipe on the outskirts of the crowd. 'It is just as well to have that point settled now. The Minute Gun at Sea is a good moral song in its way, — a sort of marine missionary affair.'

"So I started, the others followed; we all knew that the Lady watched late; we often saw the glimmer of her lamp far on towards morning. It was burning now. The gate was fastened, I knocked; no answer. I knocked again, and yet a third time; still, silence. The men stood off at a little distance and waited. 'She shall answer,' I said angrily, and going around to the side where the stockade came nearer to the wall of the lodge, I knocked loudly on the close-set saplings. For answer I thought I heard a low moan; I listened, it came again. My anger vanished, and with a mighty bound I swung myself up to the top of the stockade, sprung down inside, ran around, and tried the door. It was fastened; I burst it open and entered. There, by the light of the hanging lamp, I saw the Lady on the floor, apparently dead. I raised her in my arms; her heart was beating faintly, but she was unconscious. I had seen many fainting fits; this was something different; the limbs were rigid. I laid her on the low couch, loosened her dress, bathed her head and face in cold water, and wrenched up one of the warm hearth-stones to apply to her feet. I did not hesitate; I saw that it was a dangerous case, something like a trance or an 'ecstasis.' Somebody must attend to her, and there were only men to choose from. Then why not I?

"I heard the others talking outside; they could not understand the delay; but I never heeded, and kept on my work. To tell the truth, I had studied medicine, and felt a genuine enthusiasm over a rare case. Once my patient opened her eyes and looked at me, then she lapsed away again into unconsciousness in spite of all my efforts. At last the men outside came in, angry and suspicious; they had broken down the gate. There we all stood, the whole forty of us, around the deathlike form of our Lady.

"What a night it was! To give her air, the men camped outside in the snow with a line of pickets in whispering distance from each other from the bed to their anxious group. Two were detailed to help me, — the Doctor (whose title was a sarcastic D. D.) and Jimmy, a gentle little man, excellent at bandaging broken limbs. Every vial in the camp was brought in, — astonishing lotions, drops, and balms; each man produced something; they did their best, poor fellows, and wore out the night with their anxiety. At dawn our Lady revived suddenly, thanked us all, and assured us that she felt quite well again; the trance was over. 'It was my old enemy,' she said, 'the old illness of Scotland, which I hoped had left me forever. But I am thankful that it is no worse; I have come out of it with a clear brain. Sing a hymn of thankfulness for me, dear friends, before you go.'

"Now, we sang on Sunday in the church; but then she led us, and we had a kind of an idea that after all she did not hear us. But now, who was to lead us? We stood awkwardly around the bed, and shuffled our hats in our uneasy fingers. The Doctor fixed his eyes upon the Nightingale; Jack saw it and cowered. 'Begin,' said the Doctor in a soft voice; but gripping him in the back at the same time with an ominous clutch.

"'I don't know the words,' faltered the unhappy Nightingale.

> "'Now thank we all our God,
> With hearts and hands and voices,'

began the Doctor, and repeated Luther's hymn with perfect accuracy from beginning to end. 'What will happen next? The Doctor knows hymns!' we thought in profound astonishment. But the Nightingale had begun, and gradually our singers joined in; I doubt whether the grand old choral was ever sung by such a company before or since. There was never any further question, by the way, about that minute gun at sea; it stayed at sea as far as we were concerned.

"Spring came, the faltering spring of Lake Superior. I won't go into my own story, but such as it was, the spring brought it back to me with new force. I wanted to go,—and yet I did n't. 'Where,' do you ask? To see her, of course,—a woman, the most beautiful,—well, never mind all that. To be brief, I loved her; she scorned me; I thought I had learned to hate her—but—I was n't sure about it now. I kept myself aloof from the others and gave up my heart to the old sweet, bitter memories; I did not even go to church on Sundays. But all the rest went; our Lady's influence was as great as ever. I could hear them singing; they sang better now that they could have the door open; the pent-up feeling used to stifle them. The time for the bateaux drew near, and I noticed that several of the men were hard at work packing the furs in bales, a job usually left to the *voyageurs* who came with the boats. 'What 's that for?' I asked.

"'You don't suppose we 're going to have those bateaux rascals camping on Little Fishing, do you?' said Black Andy, scornfully. 'Where are your wits, Reub?'

"And they packed every skin, rafted them all over to the mainland, and waited there patiently for days, until the train of slow boats came along and took off the bales; then they came back in triumph. 'Now we 're secure for another six months,' they said, and began to lay out a park, and gardens for every house. The Lady was fond of flowers; the whole town burst into blossom. The Lady liked green grass; all the clearing was soon turfed over like a lawn. The men tried the ice-cold lake every day, waiting anxiously for the time when they could bathe. There was no end to their cleanliness; Black Andy had grown almost white again, and Frenchy's hair shone like oiled silk.

"The Lady stayed on, and all went well. But,

gradually, there came a discovery. The Lady was changing, — had changed! Gradually, slowly, but none the less distinctly to the eyes that knew her every eyelash. A little more hair was visible over the white brow, there was a faint color in the cheeks, a quicker step; the clear eyes were sometimes downcast now, the steady voice softer, the words at times faltering. In the early summer the white cap vanished, and she stood among us crowned only with her golden hair; one day she was seen through her open door sewing on a white robe! The men noted all these things silently; they were even a little troubled as at something they did not understand, something beyond their reach. Was she planning to leave them?

"'It 's my belief she 's getting ready to ascend right up into heaven,' said Salem.

"Salem was a little 'wanting,' as it is called, and the men knew it; still, his words made an impression. They watched the Lady with an awe which was almost superstitious; they were troubled, and knew not why. But the Lady bloomed on. I did not pay much attention to all this; but I could not help hearing it. My heart was moody, full of its own sorrows; I secluded myself more and more. Gradually I took to going off into the mainland forests for days on solitary hunting expeditions. The camp went on its way rejoicing; the men succeeded, after a world of trouble, in making a fountain which actually played, and they glorified themselves exceedingly. The life grew quite pastoral. There was talk of importing a cow from the East, and a messenger was sent to the Sault for certain choice supplies against the coming winter. But, in the late summer, the whisper went round again that the Lady had changed, this time for the worse. She looked ill, she drooped from day to day; the new life that had come to her vanished, but her former life was not restored. She grew silent and sad, she strayed away by herself through the woods, she scarcely noticed the men who followed her with anxious eyes. Time passed, and brought with it an undercurrent of trouble, suspicion, and anger. Everything went on as before; not one habit, not one custom was altered; both sides seemed to shrink from the first change, however slight. The daily life of the camp was outwardly the same, but brooding trouble filled every heart. There was no open discussion, men talked apart in twos and threes; a gloom rested over everything, but no one said, 'What is the matter?'

"There was a man among us, — I have not said much of the individual characters of our party, but this man was one of the least esteemed, or rather liked; there was not much esteem of any kind at Little Fishing. Little was known about him; although the youngest man in the camp, he was a mooning, brooding creature, with brown hair and eyes and a melancholy face. He was n't hearty and whole-souled, and yet he was n't an out-and-out rascal; he was n't a leader, and yet he was n't follower either. He would n't be; he was like a third horse, always. There was no goodness about him; don't go to fancying that that was the reason the men did not like him, he was as bad as they were, every inch! He never shirked his work, and they could n't get a handle on him anywhere; but he was just — unpopular. The why and the wherefore are of no consequence now. Well, do you know what was the suspicion that hovered over the camp? It was this: our Lady loved that man!

"It took three months for all to see it, and yet never a word was spoken. All saw, all heard; but they might have been blind and deaf for any sign they gave. And the Lady drooped more and more.

"September came, the fifteenth; the Lady lay on her couch, pale and thin; the door was open and a bell stood beside her, but there was no line of pickets whispering tidings of her state to an anxious group outside. The turf in the three streets had grown yellow for want of water, the flowers in the little gardens had drooped and died, the fountain was choked with weeds, and the interiors of the houses were all untidy. It was Sunday, and near the hour for service; but the men lounged about, dingy and unwashed.

"'A'n't you going to church?' said Salem, stopping at the door of one of the houses; he was dressed in his best, with a flower in his button-hole.

"'See him now! See the fool,' said Black Andy. 'He's going to church, he is! And where's the minister, Salem? Answer me that!'

"Why, — in the church, I suppose,' replied Salem, vacantly.

"'No, she a'n't; not she! She's at home, a-weeping, and a-wailing, and a-ger-nashing of her teeth,' replied Andy with bitter scorn.

"'What for?' said Salem.

"'What for? Why, that's the joke! Hear him, boys; he wants to know what for!'

"The loungers laughed, — a loud, reckless laugh.

"'Well, I'm going any way,' said Salem, looking wonderingly from one to the other; he passed on and entered the church.

"'I say, boys, let's have a high old time,' cried Andy, savagely. 'Let's go back to the old way and have a jolly Sunday. Let's have out the jugs and the cards and be free again!'

"The men hesitated; ten months and more of law and order held them back.

"'What are you afraid of?' said Andy. 'Not of a canting hypocrite, I hope. She's fooled us long enough, I say. Come on!' He brought out a table and stools, and produced the long-unused cards and a jug of whiskey. 'Strike up, Jack,' he cried; 'give us old Fiery-Eyes.'

"The Nightingale hesitated. Fiery-Eyes was a rollicking drinking song; but Andy put the glass to his lips and his scruples vanished in the tempting aroma. He began at the top of his voice, partners were chosen, and, trembling with excitement and impatience, like prisoners unexpectedly set free, the men gathered around, and made their bets.

"'What born fools we've been,' said Black Andy, laying down a card.

"'Yes,' replied the Flying Dutchman, 'porn fools!' And he followed suit.

"But a thin white hand came down on the bits of colored pasteboard. It was our Lady. With her hair disordered, and the spots of fever in her cheeks, she stood among us again; but not as of old. Angry eyes confronted her, and Andy wrenched the cards from her grasp. 'No, my Lady,' he said, sternly; 'never again!'

"The Lady gazed from one face to the next, and so all around the circle; all were dark and sullen. Then she bowed her head upon her hands and wept aloud.

"There was a sudden shrinking away on all sides, the players rose, the cards were dropped. But the Lady glided away, weeping as she went; she entered the church door and the men could see her taking her accustomed place on the platform. One by one they followed; Black Andy lingered till the last, but he came. The service began, and went on falteringly, without spirit, with palpable fears of a total breaking down which never quite came; the Nightingale sang almost alone, and made sad work with the words; Salem joined in confidently, but did not improve the sense of the hymn. The Lady was silent. But when the time for the sermon came she rose and her voice burst forth.

"'Men, brothers, what have I done? A change has come over the town, a change has come over your hearts. You shun me! What have I done?'

"There was a grim silence; then the Doctor rose in his place and answered,—

"'Only this, madam. You have shown yourself to be a woman.'

"'And what did you think me?'

"'A saint.'

"'God forbid!' said the Lady, earnestly. 'I never thought myself one.'

"'I know that well. But you were a saint to us; hence your influence. It is gone.'

"'Is it all gone?' asked the Lady, sadly.

"'Yes. Do not deceive yourself; we have never been one whit better save through our love for you. We held you as something high above ourselves; we were content to worship you.'

"'O no, not me!' said the Lady, shuddering.

"'Yes, you, you alone! But—our idol came down among us and showed herself to be but common flesh and blood! What wonder that we stand aghast?

What wonder that our hearts are bitter? What wonder (worse than all!) that when the awe has quite vanished, there is strife for the beautiful image fallen from its niche?'

"The Doctor ceased, and turned away. The Lady stretched out her hands towards the others; her face was deadly pale, and there was a bewildered expression in her eyes.

"'O, ye for whom I have prayed, for whom I have struggled to obtain a blessing,—ye whom I have loved so,—do *ye* desert me thus?' she cried.

"'*You* have deserted us,' answered a voice.

"'I have not.'

"'You have,' cried Black Andy, pushing to the front. 'You love that Mitchell! Deny it if you dare!'

"There was an irrepressible murmur, then a sudden hush. The angry suspicion, the numbing certainty had found voice at last; the secret was out. All eyes, which had at first closed with the shock, were now fixed upon the solitary woman before them; they burned like coals.

"'Do I?' murmured the Lady, with a strange questioning look that turned from face to face,—'do I?—Great God! I do.' She sank upon her knees and buried her face in her trembling hands. 'The truth has come to me at last,—I do!'

"Her voice was a mere whisper, but every ear

heard it, and every eye saw the crimson rise to the forehead and redden the white throat.

"For a moment there was silence, broken only by the hard breathing of the men. Then the Doctor spoke.

"'Go out and bring him in,' he cried. 'Bring in this Mitchell! It seems he has other things to do, — the blockhead!'

"Two of the men hurried out.

"'He shall not have her,' shouted Black Andy. 'My knife shall see to that!' And he pressed close to the platform. A great tumult arose, men talked angrily and clinched their fists, voices rose and fell together. 'He shall not have her, — Mitchell! Mitchell!'

"'The truth is, each one of you wants her himself,' said the Doctor.

"There was a sudden silence, but every man eyed his neighbor jealously. Black Andy stood in front, knife in hand, and kept guard. The Lady had not moved; she was kneeling, with her face buried in her hands.

"'I wish to speak to her,' said the Doctor, advancing.

"'You shall not,' cried Andy, fiercely interposing.

"'You fool! I love her this moment ten thousand times more than you do. But do you suppose I would so much as touch a woman who loved another man?'

"The knife dropped; the Doctor passed on and took his place on the platform by the Lady's side. The tumult began again, for Mitchell was seen coming in the door between his two keepers.

"'Mitchell! Mitchell!' rang angrily through the church.

"'Look, woman!' said the Doctor, bending over the kneeling figure at his side. She raised her head and saw the wolfish faces below.

"'They have had ten months of your religion,' he said.

"It was his revenge. Bitter, indeed; but he loved her.

"In the mean time the man Mitchell was hauled and pushed and tossed forward to the platform by rough hands that longed to throttle him on the way. At last, angry himself, but full of wonder, he confronted them, this crowd of comrades suddenly turned madmen! 'What does this mean?' he asked.

"'Mean! mean!' shouted the men; 'a likely story! He asks what this means!' And they laughed boisterously.

"The Doctor advanced. 'You see this woman,' he said.

"'I see our Lady.'

"'Our Lady no longer; only a woman like any other,—weak and fickle. Take her,—but begone.'

"'Take her!' repeated Mitchell, bewildered, — 'take our Lady! And where?'

"'Fool! Liar! Blockhead!' shouted the crowd below.

"'The truth is simply this, Mitchell,' continued the Doctor, quietly. 'We herewith give you up our Lady, — ours no longer; for she has just confessed, openly confessed, that she loves you.'

"Mitchell started back. 'Loves me!'

"'Yes.'

"Black Andy felt the blade of his knife. 'He 'll never have her alive,' he muttered.

"'But,' said Mitchell, bluntly confronting the Doctor, 'I don't want her.'

"'You don't want her?'

"'I don't love her.'

"'You don't love her?'

"'Not in the least,' he replied, growing angry, perhaps at himself. 'What is she to me? Nothing. A very good missionary, no doubt; but *I* don't fancy woman-preachers. You may remember that *I* never gave in to her influence; *I* was never under her thumb. *I* was the only man in Little Fishing who cared nothing for her!'

"And that is the secret of *her* liking,' murmured the Doctor. 'O woman! woman! the same the world over!'

"In the mean time the crowd had stood stupefied.

"'He does not love her!' they said to each other; 'he does not want her!'

"Andy's black eyes gleamed with joy; he swung himself up on to the platform. Mitchell stood there with face dark and disturbed, but he did not flinch. Whatever his faults, he was no hypocrite. 'I must leave this to-night,' he said to himself, and turned to go. But quick as a flash our Lady sprang from her knees and threw herself at his feet. 'You are going,' she cried. 'I heard what you said, — you do not love me! But take me with you, — oh, take me with you! Let me be your servant — your slave — anything — anything, so that I am not parted from you, my lord and master, my only, only love!'

"She clasped his ankles with her thin, white hands, and laid her face on his dusty shoes.

"The whole audience stood dumb before this manifestation of a great love. Enraged, bitter, jealous as was each heart, there was not a man but would at that moment have sacrificed his own love that she might be blessed. Even Mitchell, in one of those rare spirit-flashes when the soul is shown bare in the lightning, asked himself, 'Can I not love her?' But the soul answered, 'No.' He stooped, unclasped the clinging hands, and turned resolutely away.

"'You are a fool,' said the Doctor. 'No other woman will ever love you as she does.'

"'I know it,' replied Mitchell.

"He stepped down from the platform and crossed the church, the silent crowd making a way for him as he passed along; he went out into the sunshine, through the village, down towards the beach, — they saw him no more.

"The Lady had fainted. The men bore her back to the lodge and tended her with gentle care one week, — two weeks, — three weeks. Then she died.

"They were all around her; she smiled upon them all, and called them all by name, bidding them farewell. 'Forgive me,' she whispered to the Doctor. The Nightingale sang a hymn, sang as he had never sung before. Black Andy knelt at her feet. For some minutes she lay scarcely breathing; then suddenly she opened her fading eyes. 'Friends,' she murmured, 'I am well punished. I thought myself holy, — I held myself above my kind, — but God has shown me I am the weakest of them all.'

"The next moment she was gone.

"The men buried her with tender hands. Then, in a kind of blind fury against Fate, they tore down her empty lodge and destroyed its every fragment; in their grim determination they even smoothed over the ground and planted shrubs and bushes, so that the very location might be lost. But they did not stay to see the change. In a month the camp broke up of itself, the town was abandoned, and the island deserted for good and all; I doubt whether any of the men ever came back or even stopped when passing by. Probably I am the only one. Thirty years ago, — thirty years ago!"

"That Mitchell was a great fool," I said, after a long pause. "The Doctor was worth twenty of him; for that matter, so was Black Andy. I only hope the fellow was well punished for his stupidity."

"He was."

"O, you kept track of him, did you?"

"Yes. He went back into the world, and the woman he loved repulsed him a second time, and with even more scorn than before."

"Served him right."

"Perhaps so; but after all, what could he do? Love is not made to order. He loved one, not the other; that was his crime. Yet, — so strange a creature is man, — he came back after thirty years, just to see our Lady's grave."

"What! Are you — "

"I am Mitchell, — Reuben Mitchell."

THE END.